MW00584307

Still Life

A Novel

Katherine
Packert Burke

W. W. NORTON & COMPANY

Independent Publishers Since 1923

For Andy, Erik, Erin, and Rae

For information about permission to reproduce selections from this book,
write to Permissions, W. W. Norton & Company, Inc.,
500 Fifth Avenue, New York, NY 10110

For information about special discounts for bulk purchases, please contact
W. W. Norton Special Sales at specialsales@wwnorton.com or 800-233-4830

Manufacturing by Lakeside Book Company
Book design by Brian Mulligan
Production manager: Louise Mattarelliano

ISBN 978-1-324-07636-0

W. W. Norton & Company, Inc., 500 Fifth Avenue, New York, N.Y. 10110
www.wwnorton.com

W. W. Norton & Company Ltd., 15 Carlisle Street, London W1D 3BS

1 2 3 4 5 6 7 8 9 0

And you think of all of the things you've seen
And you wish that you could live in between
And you're back again
Only different than before

—*Into the Woods*

Second week of this poor deluded bluebird pecking
at his own reflection. He will never mate, or nest,
or propel his DNA into the next generation nor even
have time for an auto fiction about his atrophied life.

—*@joycecaroloates*

E DITH'S TOOTH HURT ALL THE WAY TO BOSTON. THIS was the price for four years of avoiding dentists—fingers in her mouth, a drill hacking away rot, and a sickly yellow cap that she could not stop tonguing. What if it fell off in Boston and she was unable to eat? Were there dental emergency rooms? Her undergraduate advisor had been forced to get emergency dental work in England once and suffered consequences years later; she'd missed several thesis meetings. Edith settled, aching, against the shuttered window of the plane, waiting to be soothed by the engines' tumble and roar.

Despite the pain, there was something satisfying in having rot cut away. There'd been a burning smell that reminded her of laser hair removal. A kind of magic that you could permanently remove a piece of your body that no longer served you. If only it were so easy to cut anything from your life.

What she hated was the fingers in her mouth. Unable to ask questions, or communicate at all except in grunts and cries of pain. Dentists never felt the need to explain themselves.

WHEN ADAM had invited her to read at the college where he taught, she'd been dubious. *C'mon*, he said, *don't you miss it up here?*

Boston in February. October Texas sun bore down on her. *How romantic.*

Adam was one of the only people she'd kept in touch with from undergrad. They'd worked at the writing center together and both come out as trans afterward. *We should have coordinated*, she told him once. *We could have swapped names.*

In the eight years since college, she found she'd never really been friends with most of her classmates. Like prisoners of war, they'd been brought close by circumstances: the same stresses, same exams, same blue punch served from industrial gray trash cans. Edith had assumed these things were the bonds of real friendship. But even during her two postgrad years in Boston, she'd barely kept in touch with the people she'd once seen daily. Adam had been in grad school in New York. Mostly there'd been Tessa and Valerie. Edith's contact with Tessa had been sporadic since they'd broken up. And even before Valerie died, she was the one who'd find you—who set the tone for every conversation.

I'd love to see you, Adam said. *I know Tess would too.*

If that were true, why wasn't Tessa the one telling her?

Can the university pay me? Edith asked. A woman in a flesh-toned bathing suit swam laps in the courtyard pool.

We can pay for your flight.

Six nights, Wednesday to Tuesday. She'd been meaning to go back since she left. What was she afraid of?

H ER LAST MEMORY OF BOSTON WAS THE LAST TIME
she'd seen Tessa. Edith abandoned everything but her books
and clothes and a desk that her college roommate, Charlie, had
given her. These things she packed into a friend's old minivan,
which she'd drive to Alabama. It seemed significant that her two
largest possessions were hand-me-downs, given up when they'd
outlived their use.

Tessa held her for a long time. Wet spots on both their shirts
when Edith pulled away.

You sure you want to do this, Joni?

Why would you ask me that. The old nickname annoyed Edith.
A signifier of intimacy that had been emptied out. After months of
worrying what would happen if she didn't get into grad school, the
decision was settled by geography. After two years of dating and
years more of love, they'd go their separate ways.

Because I'm afraid, dumbass.

Sorry. She wrapped Tessa in her arms again. If only she could hold
on. If she could squeeze their bodies closer. She didn't want to fight.

*You know that when you sleep in a bed, you leave some of your
cells behind and take some of the bed's cells with you? The longer
you stay in the same bed, the more you and the bed become a part
of each other.*

Yeah.

They'd share their beds with new people—strangers, probably,
and friends.

Did she want to leave? It didn't matter. She was leaving.

Look, I saved you from grad school once.

I'll be okay this time.

You better be. You know my number.

The Boston sun was too much. How bad would it be in Alabama?

We can't stand here forever, Tessa said.

Well. Not with that attitude. They laughed. The distance between them unbearably small. A line that could never be broken into smaller lines.

I'll be back, Edith said.

Of course. I'll look forward to it.

The line was thickening. A no-man's-land that could be crossed at some enormous cost.

I love you.

I love you so much.

Already the world was projecting Edith away—to grad school, to the writer she'd become. When she returned, she'd return in triumph.

Well. See you around.

EDITH ARRIVED AT ADAM'S SOMERVILLE APARTMENT red-cheeked and numb. The first thing she said was, *It's not going to snow, is it? I don't own boots anymore.* The first thing Adam said was, *Holy shit look at you!* His shirt read REJECT THE ORDER OF CREATION. DISFIGURE THE FACE OF MAN AND WOMAN. A quote from the pope. He held Edith's shoulders, studying her in the doorway, mindless of the wind whipping in until his boyfriend called from the couch: *Adam, door.*

Edith found herself slightly embarrassed to have transitioned since she'd last seen Adam. How she looked now and how she used to, every piece of her loudly out of proportion. Six years ago, she wouldn't have been caught dead with her nails painted. Here she was now with ketchup stains on her dress from an airport hot dog.

Edith, Michael. Adam's boyfriend held a throw pillow on his lap and stared at the TV.

I didn't know they still ran I Love the 80s.

They don't.

Michael owns the largest private archive of 2000s reality shows. Caught between irony and admiration.

Second largest. I'm still trying to track down a few seasons of Room Raiders.

Edith sat on the kitchen counter while Adam prepared the kettle. Hands in her armpits, coat draped across her. Adam's shoulders were bare in his tank top. There was his tattoo of the moon, the dark hair sweeping from his arms. He didn't have the beard of most trans dudes she knew, instead affecting neat stubble. It shaped his face the way shadows shape a room.

You look really great, Adam.

So do you, girl. And his voice—still his, but honey-thick and beautiful where hers was scratchy and hopeless and ungirlish. They texted each other almost every day. Why was she self-conscious? Edith leaned back and unsettled a basket of bananas.

Adam did not stop moving when the tea was done. He mixed some sort of powder in a Pyrex measuring cup. He poured a bag of vegetables into a pan of cold oil.

Your apartment is so beautiful.

It's all Michael. His taste, his money. Had Adam always been this energetic, or was it the hormones? Would Edith's hands still be so cold, wrapped around the scalding mug, if not for the sluggishness of her blood? *I'm fucking him for the furniture.*

Michael from the living room: *I heard that.*

Love you, Mouse.

She turned the mug through her hands, letting different parts of her palms get burned.

Mouse?

Oh, 'cause you've never had a stupid pet name.

Not for a long time.

Adam asked if she was dating anyone.

You'd be the first to know if I were.

I hope I'd be, at best, third. The smell of sizzling onions and spices. The memory of college meals cobbled together from dining hall dishes. Edith was only good at following instructions; Adam, like Valerie, experimented with the recombinant qualities of food until he made either masterpiece or disaster. *Tessa does know you're in town, right?*

Yeah of course. The thought of coming here without seeing Tessa made Edith sad on the scale of having her cat, Treats, die. She took out her phone to check in with Seb, who was cat-sitting back in Texas, but Adam said, *You having second thoughts?*

About Tess? No, why?

You know why.

We've been talking. Maybe ten phone calls in the last six years, maybe half those after Valerie died. *Things have been good between us. Normal, even.* Surely by saying this she could learn to believe it.

That's good. Adam looked at her across his moon tattoo. She thought he'd say something about Valerie then, but all he said was, *You seem really good.*

At the dining room table, Edith coaxed pilaf onto her fork—a mixture of rice, pine nuts, raisins, other small things. They talked about Michael's podcast, *I Love "I Love the 80s,"* and his job as a software engineer. Adam and Edith commiserated over their job searches. *So many people want what I have,* he said, *and it makes me fucking miserable.* Being an assistant professor of English literature was not the gateway to happiness he'd dreamed it'd be. *The only thing that keeps me going is the kids. There's like one other tranny on faculty, and these poor students.* A small shake of his head.

Edith wrote SEO articles for websites of doubtful legitimacy. "*Whether or not you believe you need a crocodile-skin wallet,*" she quoted, "*it's hard to deny that they are versatile and fashionable for all occasions.*"

Not a fund-raiser for crocodile conservation, Adam said.

Meeting your boyfriend's vegan parents.

Or if you're wearing a shirt that says, "No, I Don't Like Crocodile-Skin Wallets, Please Stop Asking."

Edith said she'd amend it to *nearly any occasion.*

From their texts and calls, each knew the shape of the other's days but not the texture. Edith loved seeing Adam and Michael together. Their gentle coaxing through the border between passion and hyperfixation. Michael's project to dissect people's nostalgia for earlier nostalgias intrigued her, though it seemed exhausting in practice.

But still that discomfort. *The last time you were in Boston,* she thought, *you were a dude. Whereas Adam became a dude here. A discontinuity that six days couldn't solve.*

How's your new book going, Edith? Adam sounded coy.

Oh, what's it about?

She won't tell, babe.

Edith was not superstitious about sharing her work. It only sounded so dull and hollow when summarized. Her first novel, *Someday We Won't Remember This*, was half about the persecution of Christians in the Roman Empire, half about two trans astronauts in a space station circling a dying star. Usually, if she shared this with a stranger, they'd bring up *Interstellar* or ask what church she went to. If she'd been able to do it justice in her summary, maybe she'd have had an easier time getting it published. Maybe it would have made some sort of impact—in her life, in others.

I'm not sure anyone but me would care about it.

It's not autofiction, is it?

Edith snorted. *No,* she said, which was not exactly a lie. It didn't seem to her she had enough in common with the people who wrote those sorts of books—middle-aged cis people with tenure, unspooling their barely fictionalized lives—to ally her work with theirs. She was saved from saying more: a pine nut cracked between her tooth and plastic crown. She cried out, and Adam and Michael jolted from their seats, hoping to fix whatever hidden thing was broken.

THE BOOK Edith had been failing to write for a year now was sometimes called *The Grasshopper Lies Heavy* and sometimes called *Black Pear Tree* and sometimes *Evening All Afternoon*. It refused to stay contained to a narrow period of her life. It would grow until it became a Borgesian map the same size as its territory.

Many of the books she loved were about people trying and failing to write books. Sometimes it was the book you were reading, sometimes an unrealized project—a shadow text haunting the thing you held. People appreciated this illusory failure. Holding proof the writer had succeeded eventually. It let everyone hold their survivorship bias a little closer.

She was on her fourth attempt at the new book. She'd been sending scraps to the editor who'd bought her first; the editor said, *Cool! Let me know when you have a whole thing.* Edith had promised she would by September. The same time—in a move that Seb called *fucking stupid*—that her lease would end.

She'd been trying to write about Valerie. Two trans girls circling a dead love neither could live without. But she couldn't talk about Val without talking about Tessa, and college, and all their years of love, and all their years of silence. Couldn't tell stories about her life when she understood it so poorly.

*

THERE WAS a time when each lovely day was marked by the knowledge that Edith could not repeat it. She didn't miss being young—those alien years of boydom—but missed wanting so little. The fake ghost-hunting documentaries she made with high school friends. The hungover college days with no obligations but instant ramen and *Gossip Girl* with Tess and Val. She knew: we won't get this again; we might get something else good, but it won't be this.

She'd thought transition would mitigate the worst of her nostalgia. That you could not feel homesick for a time before you were yourself.

In the morning, she walked the familiar path toward Harvard

Square. There was the laundromat packed with used books. There was a bakery that she'd never gone into. The bar she and Tessa had seen women sobbing outside of on election night. She'd forgotten how nostalgia was geographically produced.

(Ancient memories of wind shredding her clothes as carefree undergrads passed her; the promise of bed, and warmth, and Tessa at the other end of this street. A summer day, not long before she left, eating small, expensive cups of frozen yogurt on a bench. The early mornings she'd slipped from bed before Tessa woke, writing in Peet's Coffee—stories, unfinished novels, grad school applications.)

Adam had work. He asked her the night before what she'd do with her day. *Any old haunts you want to check out?*

I feel like all I ever did was go to coffee shops and bookstores.

That's good. You can commune with Boston's true heart at Dunkin' Donuts.

She stopped when she hit a fork in the sidewalk. Dizzy, her path tangled, unsure which way was fastest to the Square. The benches were too cold and so she crouched, hovering above the pavement to keep her black jeans clean. Impossible that so much was the same. Adam and Tessa had been living there all that time, but she had to come back a stranger.

She'd felt this way when she'd gone home to see her dad in the hospital. Not yet a girl, or not in any way she'd claim. And yet that same sense of unfairness. Things staying the same and things changing. At least then Val had been with her.

There'd been a scene like that in her first book, a moment of the astronauts returning home before their final voyage. The Earth seemed both more and less solid. Every place so open, so crowded. One last look before fleeing from a broken life to a dying star.

But that hadn't quite captured it. She'd wanted something like Vasily Grossman's *Everything Flows*. The hero returns to Leningrad after years in the gulag, and wonders at the Hermitage: "How could all those paintings have remained as beautiful as ever while he was being transformed into an old man? Why had they not changed? Maybe their immutability—their eternity—was not a strength but a weakness? Perhaps this was how art betrays the human beings that have engendered it?" Edith would like to think her mutability was a strength, but it had left her there, crouched inches above the frigid pavement.

Edith stood, brushed her clean knees cleaner. Seb had sent a picture of Treats cuddling with a stuffed IKEA shark twice her size. *Perfect angel*, Seb wrote. And then: *She bit me like three seconds after this.*

EACH WRITING session began the same way: she put on the 1994 cast recording of *Merrily We Roll Along* and stared at one of Francis Bacon's paintings until she began to cry. Today it was *Painting 1946*. It was usually *Painting 1946*. Something about the meat and rent bodies.

The music didn't quite obscure the crowded bakery-café around her. Edith had claimed one corner of a table with her latte, her laptop, her copy of Sophie Calle's *Address Book*. She'd eyed the seven-dollar pastries downstairs but deprived herself of their pleasure. On some deep level, she believed good work came from Protestant abstinence. All those mornings she could have stayed in bed beside Tessa and instead heaved herself through the cold.

In her headphones, a seduction unfolded: "Life is knowing what you want, darling. That's the thing you have to know."

Edith had only been to this bakery once, with Tessa and one of her dyke friends. They'd sat maybe ten feet away. You could see brick university buildings through the window, the leafless trees scratching the gray sky. They had probably talked about some protest, and Edith probably questioned their efficacy, and the friend probably rolled her eyes at Tessa like, *Ugh, men.* If she could remember what happened, Edith would run into that friend here again; she'd have married her girlfriend, maybe they'd have a kid. And Edith would say, *We've met before.* A familiar confusion across the woman's face, the trick of matching past to present. The puzzle piece—*oh shit he's a girl now?*—that allowed them to make sense of it.

Maybe she wouldn't deal with that hitch of uncertainty if she passed better. Bigger tits, higher voice, flattering clothes. Her old self illegible to people—here's this tall and striking girl in a coat no match for Boston wind. The undercutted barista would flirt with her. All her dreams would be beautiful black-and-white pastiches of classic Hollywood.

She was getting away with something, being here. Hiding the person she used to be. The mistakes that person made.

The music moved on to the painfully hopeful closing number and she stopped crying. She shut her computer without writing and read for a while. Sophie Calle was calling every name in an address book she'd found, interviewing people about its owner. Probably as good a way of arriving at knowledge as any other.

AS SHE left the café, a ringing cut through her headphones, interrupting *Merrily We Roll Along.* Her mother's name, first and last, flashing on her phone. She thumbed it away.

Cambridge's bookstores were large, warm, almost memoryless places. She'd always gone to them alone. She'd finished Sophie Calle; she'd brought a handful of others, but none of them felt right.

Merrily We Roll Along was perhaps too on the nose. The musical proceeds backward in time, chronicling the dissolution of three friends' relationships. "How did you get to be here?" the musical asks. "What was the moment? How can you get so far off the track? Why don't you turn around and go back?"

(A memory: Tessa sticking her finger to the place Edith's book would one day live. *You'll write so many they'll have to give you your own shelf.* An endless string of Edith McAllisters. But here the books were packed tight, and no spine bore Edith's name.)

In two days she'd see Tessa. Tomorrow was the reading, but she insisted Tessa not come. *Readings are terrible. I'm terrible. It won't be fun.*

It would absolutely be fun, Tessa said, *but I do have plans, unfortunately.*

At the breakfast table that morning, Edith had admitted she half-expected Tessa to bail.

She would never. Adam scraped more yogurt and granola out of his Portmeirion bowl. Floral patterns smeared with white like a new kind of snow.

Yeah, but why should she see me? What's it going to do for her?

You think everyone but you is so mercenary.

No, I'm mercenary too. Edith popped a dried cherry in her mouth. *I'm only here to steal your fancy granola.*

When she'd called to tell Tessa she'd be in Boston, had there been hesitation before Tessa said, *That's amazing, it'll be so good to see you?* A memory of the street, the hill. Unasked questions, unstated prayers. Or were these Edith's alone to bear?

In her headphones: "We're not the three of us anymore, Mary. Now we're one and one and one."

Edith toyed with buying a dozen different books but wound up with only two: Emily Wilson's translation of *The Odyssey* and the journals of Katherine Mansfield. There was comfort in being taken away from yourself. There was comfort in being brought back.

MICHAEL WAS recording a podcast episode that evening, so Edith and Adam went out for dinner. Veggie Galaxy was decked out in the same Diner Chic as six years before: Formica tables, red vinyl stools.

New undergrads the inheritors of old habits: in the booths blowing straw wrappers at friends' faces; on the sidewalk sucking smoke from ember-eyed cigarettes.

Oh my god. Edith studied both sides of the laminated menu. *They got rid of the falafel burger?*

Plus ça change.

Everything was shockingly expensive. Sixteen dollars for a bean burger, six more for fries. No wonder she never ate out when she lived here.

Rent only keeps going up, Adam said between bites of portobello. *How much did you and Tessa pay for your place?*

Like a thousand each.

He shook his head. *You'd never manage that now.* It was inexplicable. *No one's moving here and it keeps getting worse.*

Every conversation Edith had in Texas eventually turned to the cost of living, too. New people moved there all the time. Was this simply part of getting older—the endless financial climb? Were there people who didn't think about these things, who weren't tech bros or Deloitte consultants?

It used to be easier, Edith said. You could forgo comforts when you were twenty-three. You could shiver through heatless nights or let yourself grow waifish on steamed vegetables and brown rice. She nibbled her bean patty accusatorily; it was no falafel. *And with Val*—Valerie had a way of freeing Edith from her financial anxiety. What was sixteen dollars? What was a hundred? You'd get it back somehow. But this moment—this bright and perfect flame—would be extinguished with the dawn.

Hey, Adam said, resting a hand on Edith's knee. She tried to fix her face. *I'm really sorry—*

Nothing to be sorry for.

You seem fine, though.

Yeah, I'm good.

It's barely been a year, it doesn't have to be fine.

But it is.

He'd given his condolences over the phone. She'd forgotten most of the month after Tessa's call. The car crash. There'd been no funeral, only a gravestone somewhere in west Texas that she'd never seen. Adam had offered to come see Edith, but she couldn't have borne feeling pitied like that. At least she and Tessa had already been speaking; at least it hadn't taken a death to bring them back to each other.

You still haven't talked to Tessa about it. You and Val.

Good—something to dry her eyes.

I'm sure she knows.

That wasn't the question, Edie. He bit his lip and flinched. *You'd be surprised what people miss.*

It's not a real question if you already know the answer. Her first proper bite of the burger was delicious. Warm and hearty and texturally dense. *Y'all still hang out, right?*

Of course.

How does she seem to you?

She's the same.

Another bite. Had she eaten lunch? Or had trekking up and down Cambridge left her so starving?

What about me?

Adam laughed. *You're the same, too.*

FRIDAY MORNING. Alone, again, in Cambridge, until the evening's reading. She'd missed Boston's grayness. The short buildings pressed against the paved sky. A place where, should you stand still long enough, the past's light might come back to you. Bounced all across the universe only to return to your eyes, showing you who you used to be on a day no different from today.

His voice seeped up to her from the back of the bagel line, saying, *Okay so tomato cream cheese if they do have everything bagels, but plain for a salt bagel?* She turned back to scope out Charlie from the crowd. Hunched, as she knew he would be, in a black wool peacoat. A finger in one ear, his phone to his other. No different than in college.

What if they're out of both? A pause. *I mean they could.* A pause. *I like salt bagels. You like salt bagels. There are dozens of us.*

Edith fought to make her voice soft and fem while ordering her plain butter bagel and large black coffee. Faced the windows while she waited. When she'd been home with Valerie, someone from high school had stopped beside them at a traffic light. He hadn't hesitated a moment before calling out her old name. Never mind the years, her long hair, her smooth face.

Living with Charlie sophomore year left her with plenty of fondness for him. He used to get crossfaded beyond reason and start swing dancing. It had become so irrepressible he believed he had a strain of the sixteenth-century dancing plague. He'd gone to counseling.

But their lives had diverged. He'd stayed straight, gotten married. Edith had become a girl—a great excuse to lose touch with people. To most old friends it would come as a shock. The whiplash breaking whatever they'd built together.

Or so she assumed.

C'mon bitch, she thought. Be a fucking adult for once in your life.

Steeled for the inevitable (*Haha yeah I'm a girl now isn't that weird*), she tapped his shoulder. Hand still cold with outside air. *Hey*, she said. *Charlie.*

He turned, probably expecting any number of more likely actors. He had a whole history here, a sprawling web of acquaintances and friends and coworkers and exes. The consequences of a still life. Any of them more plausibly behind him than Edith—this woman who used to be a boy he knew.

Oh my god, Edith?

Outside, their bagged bagels in hand, breath clouded the space between them.

I can't believe you're here! What are the odds. He nodded at her grease-spattered bag. *You should eat that before it gets cold.*

What about you?

He hoisted his slightly fatter bag. *Gotta get these back to Polly.* The glut of food for two, the paleolithic intimacy of bringing back what you foraged. (A cold night outside the campus bar, their fake IDs denied. Charlie asking, *Why are there so many pretty girls. Am I ever going to be happy.* Edith said, *Cheer up, Chuck, I'll dance with you,* and he said, *It's not the same.*)

How long are you here for? I'd love for you to meet her. What are you doing in town? Visiting Teresa? She didn't tell him she was reading that night, only that she'd visit Adam's class Monday. *You're like a big deal writer now, huh?*

Something like that. Butter leaked onto her hands as she bit into the bagel. There were no good bagels in Texas; she'd lost the knack for them.

Triumphant homecoming and all. And all what? Neither *triumph* nor *home* nor *coming* seemed appropriate. She'd been dragged here. Before she could swallow her mouthful of gluten and salt, Charlie said, *My wife read your book. Polly did. I haven't had a chance to myself.*

The bagel nearly fell from her hands. No one had read her book except a hodgepodge of very kind booksellers, editors of niche literary journals, and dorks on Twitter. *Really?*

Laughter from Charlie. Good old Charlie. *What, you think I'd lie? What did she think?*

Ask her yourself. Come over for lunch Monday, before your class. He and Polly worked from home. *We'll make you something.*

Edith tried to picture Charlie in domesticity. In college, he'd never so much as hung a poster. All she could see were stark plaster walls, a futon on its aluminum skeleton. A case of sugar-free energy drinks.

But Polly would have put up needlepoints and art prints, curated from Cambridge's thrift stores. There'd be a rocking chair, probably. A scratchy yellow afghan big enough for two. The shock of this distance might kill her. That her own life might have looked like this.

Sure, she said.

Amazing! She'll be thrilled.

Another remark on the coincidence. A quick hug, a phone number conversation. Neither had changed. Edith watched Charlie go, confident steps down the brick sidewalk. A path so familiar he probably dreamed about it.

(If he really wanted you to come over, he'd have asked you to now.)

But then, she hadn't even let him know she was in town.

IT FELT like a kind of magic when the bouldering gym took Edith's membership card. She'd felt betrayed, back in Texas, when Seb told her the gym was a national chain. *Seattle Bouldering Project, Chicago Bouldering Project, Boulder Bouldering Project. Interchangeable.* The illusion of locality. Now she was thankful: too wound up to work, ruminating on Charlie, trying not to think about that evening's reading. She'd almost texted Tessa. Instead she borrowed a pair of Adam's shorts, rented shoes for four dollars. She would not betray her impatience.

Somerville Bouldering Project was enormous, a cave-shaped cathedral. Color-coded knobs and rough beige walls to hide you from the horrors of surface life. A dance of gravity, and friction, and body.

At the back wall, people climbed higher than Edith dared. It was her fear of heights that made climbing useful for managing other anxieties. Nothing to think about when you were up ten, fifteen feet except not falling. It was a victory every time she got on the wall.

Headphones hooked to her ears. Sporty Somervilleans with chalky palms. She climbed, and tried not to think.

It wasn't a lie when she told Tessa the reading would be bad. The idea appealed to her—all those nights she'd gone to bookstores in Cambridge and Brookline to hear real writers' voices. The authority of it. The intimate history of geography, and class, and love that a voice carried. The patterns they'd burnished out and those left rough enough to show at certain angles: the slight twang of a Mississippi writer saying *radio*; an unplaceable vocabulary suddenly sensible in the accent of an Australian–South African writer. And the minor ways writers altered their sentences, proving you cannot return to the past—even fixed in black marks on the page—without wishing it a little changed.

Edith hated reading, though. She didn't like her voice, didn't know how fast to read, couldn't act out dialogue. Characters became flat, mirthless shadows that left the audience wishing they could see the brilliant light that cast them.

She lay on the floor to catch her breath.

The trouble with her new book was that she didn't have any idea why someone would read it. It used to be that the showiness of her imagination stood in for substance; you read to find out what on earth could happen next. But her life with Valerie had been predictable from the start. Val came, and she went; they loved each other, and they didn't. She was there through the thickest, thorniest moments, she was gone the second things got tough. Predictable was perhaps not the word for it. Tedious, maybe.

When she'd wanted to be a sci-fi writer, it had seemed so manageable. Now she'd be happiest writing books about lonely women living in New York City and thinking about dead German men and/or David Wojnarowicz. But she'd never lived in New York and didn't care for Walser or Kafka. She didn't have a single interesting thought.

Halfway up the wall, she had no idea if she was stable enough to grab the next handhold. The walls of her Texas gym only gave up their secrets to her over the course of weeks. She knew when to push herself and when to let go. Being good at climbing is not about failing to fall; it's about knowing that if you do, you'll be fine.

She dropped down, tried the wall again, and got stuck in the same spot.

In her headphones: "How does it start to go? Does it slip away slow, so you never really notice it's happening?"

Edith loved *Merrily We Roll Along*. She loved all of Sondheim's musicals, those rainy-day records in Tessa's dorm room. The man wrote about obsession driving people to destroy their lives. Fairy tales taken past their moment of perfection until they succumbed to grim reality.

In *Merrily*'s reversed chronology, everyone grows more optimistic and in love with each other as they grow younger. Friendships and career dreams slip backward from despairing reality into bright hope. Characters lose the knowledge the audience is cursed with: there will be no redemption here. In the final, endlessly optimistic song "Our Time," the three friends, hardly more than children, watch Sputnik move across the night sky. "After this moment, this moment that the three of us are sharing," one reflects, "nothing is ever going to be the way it was ever again." There's no ambivalence in their hearts. The audience has to bear the pain alone.

Edith wished she could talk about this instead of reading anything she'd written. She could lecture there, halfway up the wall where her arms were shaking: unable to hold herself up, unwilling to let herself fall. Barely, she jumped, the shock of impact palpable in her knees. That was enough of that.

There were tables along the gym's sidelines. Her mother called the moment she sat down.

Hey, Mom, this isn't the best time. She got her computer from her bag, opened a PNG of *Painting 1946* from her desktop.

Where are you? Are you at a club? "Hyperballad" was playing on the gym speakers.

Yes, Mother, I'm at a club at eleven o'clock on a Friday morning, and they're playing Björk because the year is 1997.

What? Edith, I can't hear you.

At least her mother was getting her name right. *I'm in Boston.*

Boston? You'll go to Boston but not Virginia? Who's in Boston?

Tessa. Adam. Half a million Red Sox fans.

Dear, I was watching Singin' in the Rain *the other day—do you remember that movie? We watched it when you were, oh, seven, eight years old.*

Sure. It didn't matter what she said. Across the gym the few Friday stragglers, safe from winter chill, climbed on. There were men in short yellow shorts, there was a woman with Kool Aid–blue hair. A pair of enbies who might be lovers and might be twins. The locker room would probably be safe without her wearing a full face of makeup. They climbed like Valerie used to dance. The fluid motion of a whole body.

She'd barely thought of Valerie in Boston. Everywhere Val went had been hers, all American roads and cities. Anywhere Edith smelled gasoline and spearmint gum. A net cast wide, a life inescapable.

—and I got to thinking, her mother said, *how beautifully Debbie Reynolds's voice matched up with Jean Hagen's mouth, and I thought that maybe you—*

Mother, it's not a good time.

A sigh from the other side. She wondered if her father was listening on. *I thought you and Tessa stopped speaking,* her mother said.

Only temporarily. Something their relationship could use.

Another sigh. Before her mother could admonish her further, she goodbyed and set her phone on silent. Edith googled, *is mer-*

cury in retrograde. No, the internet reported. Something else must be wrong with you.

With this in mind, she tried to pick something to read that evening.

At the table across from me, two people divvy up old photographs. They must have belonged to some lost family member, part of a long-established birthright. The photos, none larger than a palm, are of yellowed, far-off places. One of the people lists the documented subjects aloud, deals the pictures like cards in an inscrutable game.

I can make out the same three or four figures in each. What a world it would be if every piece of self was carried in photos too—not only their images but their desires, hates, embarrassments. The memories that an onion cooking with green pepper and garlic brought to mind. The drum of blood, a beating heart, separated from your ear by only a few layers of tendon and skin.

Then again, perhaps these images' keepers *can* conjure a whole world, a whole person, from these flat, glossy stills. Perhaps what I'm really wishing is that I, too, could access it—could dive into their lives and come up, cupped hands dripping with pearls of lives so different from my own.

Or else I'm thinking of how few photos of V. I have. All from college, when even she looked less like herself, and I look like a stranger.

It was unlikely to make her cry, or less likely than some sections. There were few worse ways she could imagine the evening going—sobbing at the podium over a story that carried no emotional freight for anyone else. Like crying over the crumpled weight of a Taco Bell bag.

Experimentally, she studied one of the sex scenes. Something

she'd never read, that probably wouldn't make it into the book—
for its falseness, for its truth. Her narrator-analog, her nameless I,
pulled a knife over her girlfriend's skin:

> The horrible truth is that I liked this. Not because of the
> pleasure it gave her, or not solely. I wanted to punish her.
> Wanted to betray her, cut my heart into her back. I wanted
> to taste her blood so that there'd forever be a part of her,
> a microscopic iron core, that I carried in my own heart.
>
> When she said, That's enough. When she said, Babe,
> stop. I wanted to point the knife tip at every time she left
> me. At the scars on her legs and stomach. I wanted to re-
> mind her that you can only know what's enough by know-
> ing what's more than enough.
>
> Instead, I took the towel, the peroxide squares she used
> for hormone shots. I dabbed the blood from her back, kissed
> each vertebra. I coaxed her long body into my arms, know-
> ing we'd both learn new limits in time.

Seb sent another picture of Treats. The cat curled in a window,
green towel cushioning her orange head. *Always already angelic,*
Seb texted. *What's up in Boston, you see your ex.*

*She's a friend, and no. I'm at Somerville Bouldering Project if you
can believe it.*

That's not a real place.

One of the guys in yellow shorts settled at a table across from
Edith. He pulled a book from his bag, one she couldn't identify at
a distance.

Edith called Seb.

What's up?

It wasn't worth unpacking the malaise her mother's call had left.
Seb had heard it all before.

What do you think about autofiction?

I love it.

I do too.

Books about cars, right? Christine, *et cetera.*

Yeah exactly. Noted autofiction pioneer, Stephen King. Edith looked in time to catch the man smirking.

Are you thinking about writing it?

Not exactly. She Ctrl+F'd through her draft, deleting every instance of the word "just." *Why do you say it like that?*

I think writing too directly from your life would fuck you up, you specifically. You'd lose track of where you end and the book begins.

Yeah probably. The solution, she thought, was to make it all true. Five years' full emotions set down like a name in wet cement. But then there were ethical issues. *I told you how mad Val got when Tessa tried to write that play about us, right?*

More than once. Could you justify leaving a "just" if you meant it in the sense of "justice"? This was the problem with rules—following them only led to more questions. *So you're like terrified of seeing her tomorrow, huh.*

What makes you say that?

You're, like, quaking in your fucking gym shoes. I can hear from here.

You keep in touch with your exes, right? It's never weird?

I get hotter every day, what's there to be weird about. Why are you worried?

Edith didn't know. It was the same inexplicable embarrassment to have left here a man and come back a girl. It was fear that Tessa would be mad about her and Valerie. Or worse—that everything would feel exactly the same. That she would be unable to escape the past's pull.

She had no regrets about tapping Charlie's shoulder, calling out his name. But to step into his apartment on Monday. To sit down to lunch with Tessa in a café where they might've once held each other close, traded bites of dessert, talked about a future together. All the eventualities she'd removed herself from. All the leaving she'd done.

A rustling in the background, a scampering.

Is that Treats? Put her on.

She's climbing the shower curtains, I'll put you on speaker.

Edith remembered too late that the cooing endearments one gives a pet are not suited to public spaces. The man was still eyeing her as she baby-talked into her phone. As seriously as she could, she said, *I love you, kitten.* Plausibly directed at a human love, though that was an embarrassing thought. *Mother will see you soon. I miss you so much.* This was getting worse.

Seb laughed. *You make it sound like you've sent her into the country to escape the Blitz.*

After they hung up, she took a final look at the guy's book. It bothered her when she couldn't identify something by sight. The guy held her gaze a little too long. Some shift of lid and brow. He set the book down and walked toward the men's locker room.

Goddammit. She never got cruised like this when she was a dude. The polite thing would be to go suck this guy off. But she didn't want to be the kind of girl who sucked dick out of obligation, only out of passion for the art of it.

This would never happen in Texas, she muttered, sloppily packing her things and putting on her thin coat. At least she'd never have to come back here.

EDITH READ slowly and tried not to think about the pitch of her voice. She tried not to think about her dress, her boots, her hands on the podium. Tomorrow she'd see Tessa. Tess would look no different—she'd be wearing the same banana-yellow coat she'd had since sophomore year. There'd be that chime in her laughter, that glow in her eyes. *Hey there, Joni,* she'd say. *Been a while.*

The section she read was from her first book. One of the astronauts told the other about her mother's prophetic visions. "*A path toward the end of the world,*" Edith read, "*and the exact steps to avert it. Every word to say, every move to make to ensure that future became fact. Stage-managing everyone into the correct positions. A kind of hell, a kind of prison. No life at all, only a character in someone else's story.*"

Maybe she wouldn't publish the new book at all. Maybe it would only be for her, a digital gravestone to all her memories. But then she wouldn't get paid for it.

Only one person asked a question. *Were you thinking,* the blue-haired girl asked from her seat, *of the split between Old and New Testaments? The way that one is meant to be a prefiguration of the next?* In the sort of books Edith wrote, she'd be the same blue-haired girl from the climbing gym. Coincidences stacking up until characters became unignorable.

Edith said, *I saw Jenny Offill read once. Someone began a question: "Is it intentional that—" and before they could finish, Jenny Offill said, "Yes."* Scattered laughter from the students. Edith found Adam smiling in the front row, encouraging. *It's a testament to how finely worked Offill's novels are. She knows every detail, every fragment, is in its right place. Were I so clever, I wouldn't have written a book that's twice as long as any of hers.* More laughter. *Anyway, the short answer is no, it's not intentional. The longer answer is that I noticed it, too, at some point in rewriting, and left it that way. Like any of the few things in life we can actually control.*

Don't listen to me, Edith thought. Do the opposite of everything I say. I left this place to become someone and now I'm back and it's clear I failed. It is better to do things by intent. It is better you make the world your puzzle box. Edith's tooth ached as she clenched her jaw.

I don't want to sound too woo-woo, but I believe in the novel as a living thing. They take so long to write, you're inevitably several different people before they're done. The novel becomes a shadow of your life. You step into the world and the world steps into you.

That was something Val had said to her. She'd never disentangle who she was from all the people she'd loved. She might as well have read part of the new novel. She might as well have broken down in front of all these twenty-year-olds, it would all come out the same.

This was good, though. She was right about writing. This was the only thing she'd dedicated a decade of her life to.

Some people can tame all the pieces. They know which belong. Some people—she gestured with her book—*don't.* The girl seemed happy with this answer, as though she'd won an argument. Edith felt pleased. Felt like a writer.

The dinner after was a small production in the Alumni House. There were two married women, one a scholar of Romantic poetry and one in Hispanic Studies. There was a lanky man with long gray hair, damaged from being straightened; he'd given up on writing poetry to be department chair. There were three other professors, whose positions and names Edith forgot. There was a basket of rolls, pillow-soft and golden, which she did not touch.

God, Adam said to her quietly, *remember going to these as students?* They'd gone to every reading together senior year. Whether or not the visiting writers were good, producing a book was enough to charm Edith. To have part of yourself crystallize in the real world—a lingering thing. By now she'd learned you had to be comfortable with everything disappearing. The death of the last person who knew your name would come on a day like any other. The world a little lighter for your loss.

We were such babies.

You all should have seen Edith in college, Adam said to the table. *Always first in line to get her books signed.*

I was justified! Anne Carson only signed like five books before she went back to her room.

"*I won't be doing any more of that,*" Adam said. Everyone laughed at his impression of the austere poet.

Were you so charming back then? the poetry professor asked. Edith eyed her, her wife beside her. Was she being flirted with? This was the reason to meet strangers: to make you alien to yourself. All your carefully rehearsed stories and tired interests, suddenly amusing again. She was charming. She was easy to love.

I was a math major. People laughed at her tone. *I decided I needed to be more insufferable and that seemed the easiest way.* More laughter. Edith took a sip of wine, took a roll.

The English chair was really indignant whenever she'd show up at these dinners, Adam said. "*Shouldn't you be doing calculus or something?*"

And I pointed out that David Foster Wallace, Dostoevsky, Lewis Carroll—all started in mathematics.

He was such a dick about it! Adam flushed, smacking the table. They were a two-person comedy for academics. They could do a national tour. "*Look what happened to Foster Wallace! And Lewis Carroll, why, he was diddling that Liddle girl!*"

I should thank him, really. For years I wrote to spite him.

Well, the chair said, raising his glass of wine to her. *Math major or not, we're thrilled to have you here with us tonight.*

Hear, hear! Adam said. He, and the chair, and Edith drained their glasses. It didn't matter how much they drank. There was the pleasure of the moment. There was the warmth of the lights and salmon, cooked perfectly, served with lemon.

Conversation flowed. They talked about her work, about Philip K. Dick and Roberto Bolaño. Adam got into a good-natured argument with the Romantic poetry professor about Kathy Acker. *However you feel about her, students always have something to say.*

Wish I could say the same for Keats. The professor rolled her eyes and refilled her glass.

Keats never wrote about talking dogs, to be fair.

The Hispanic Studies professor was researching the memorialization of atrocities in Argentina and Chile. America's comparative failure to reckon with genocide.

I feel like Germany only confronted their past because they had to, Edith said. *No one's made America do the work.*

There's something to that. But often these memorials are thought to be enough. The appearance of reckoning without the work.

Edith was drunk and tired and happy enough that when the chair asked what she was working on next, and Adam began to answer for her—*She won't talk about*—she cut him off.

It's about this friend of mine. Another sip of wine, another roll. Dessert was brought out on a silver cart. *Reckoning with*— With what? Her life, her death. The spaces they bridged and the bridges they burned. Maybe there was no need to close the prepositional phrase. Reckoning with. Full stop.

I didn't know that, Adam said.

There's nothing to know.

The chair—oblivious or eager to move past this quiet—said, *Friendship is a tremendous topic in literature. From* Don Quixote *onward. Onegin. Crusoe and Friday.* People went around adding examples: *Brideshead Revisited, Frog and Toad.* Edith was tempted to write these down, as though they might offer her tools to work through. To reckon with. Adam's eyes stayed on her.

The moment passed. People wanted to know what it was like living in Texas. By the end of the night, everyone was effusively thanking her for joining them. She thought about asking if they wanted to give her a job. But no—let this be enough. To feel like a real writer, a real person. To feel warm. Not her endless days of love and hope and life with Tessa—but warmth all the same. Let the night end here, with nothing more complicated in the days to follow.

AN ANTICLIMAX: THE NIGHT BEFORE COLLEGE GRADU-
ation, they burned all their old notebooks and marked-up
exams. Someone threw a fire-retardant couch in the bonfire and people cheered when it caught flame. Everyone's hair carried the smell
of woodsmoke come morning. The commencement speaker made a
joke about the campus's so-called "sex tree." It rained off and on and
the sun's heat, when it came, was unbearable in their black robes.
Edith found Valerie far behind her, Tessa ahead, and cursed the
alphabet's invented order for making them sit separately through
this. That night, they all got very drunk and fell asleep on the floor
of Valerie's off-campus apartment, furnished by its landlord with
grandma-chic floral chairs and spindly end tables. The next day her
friends left. Edith was staying in the Hudson Valley for a fifth year
to get a master's in math. She wasn't interested in math anymore,
hadn't been since sophomore year. But it was free, and she'd only be
in a couple of classes. Lots of time to write.

There was no housing for master's students, and not enough
funding to afford somewhere off-campus. She lived in the dorms on
a hall of freshmen. They pinballed down the halls in party dresses
and skinny jeans, shouting with the joy of youth's first intoxication.
She cooked most of what she ate crouched over a hotplate.

College with Tessa and Valerie had been the kind of life Edith
figured no one got outside of books and TV. It had been late-night
Chopped competitions using Sour Patch Kids and tofu dogs. It had
been library scavenger hunts to distract from finals. Reading *Oedi-*

pus aloud on the quad. (*There's a lot of sexual tension between this shepherd and messenger, huh?*) When fall filled the air with smells of cold cement and dying oak leaves, it came with the promise of movie marathons, warm cider with honey whiskey, nights crashing on each other's floors. Edith and Val ran shirtless through the snow to prove they could. Edith and Tess cooked a perfect soufflé to prove they could. Everything was everything.

It was shocking how quickly a place could lose its hearth-warmth.

Are you okay? Tessa asked on the phone. *What are you doing with your time?*

You know. Passing it. Edith had been cutting class. She'd been wandering campus, smoking too many cigarettes. She skipped meals and grew resentful of children who didn't know how good their lives were.

Remind me why you're doing this again?

School was all she'd ever known. She wasn't like Tessa, already entrenched in Boston's world of nonprofit housing. Valerie, who'd been desperate all her life to break free, to zigzag the country and have devastating love affairs and see every good piece of land art.

Valerie didn't bother with pleasantries. *That place is killing you. I like being here.*

Oh babe. Not anymore, you don't.

Valerie was staying in a motel in the southwestern desert. The craggy, copper earth. *It's very heartening how much of this country is empty*, she said. *It makes you think there's a limit to how bad we can fuck it up.* She'd stopped to borrow a soldering iron to fix up her old coffeemaker. It was one of the only things she owned, carted from Texas to school and now around the vastness of America

They sell those in stores now, I hear, Edith said.

Don't act like you're so unsentimental, babe. This old pot has kept me watchful and safe on every endless road.

Edith's floor held an electric kettle, a French press of oily, gummy grounds. Every cup tasted like cigarette ash.

What if this was the rest of Edith's life? She'd never thought about killing herself before. Like sucking dick or going to church, suicide was something other people did. But there'd always been something next, something better to look forward to.

It was only nine months. You can survive anything for nine months.

The Tuesday before Thanksgiving, there was a knock at her door. Tessa strode in, dressed in tight black clothes like she was robbing the place. *Look at this.* She toed a pile of shirts. *Were you this messy when you were eighteen and alone?*

No, I had tuberculosis. Edith attributed this—her inability to drink her first year of college while on antibiotics—to not meeting Tessa earlier. A whole year of life together, lost.

Tessa grabbed a duffel from the closet and tossed it on the pile of clothes. *Pack those up.*

I don't need you to do my laundry.

What are you reading right now? Edith gestured with a fistful of socks at the Jenny Offill book, splayed on the bed like a slain bird. *Oh, that won't last you past dinnertime.* She scanned Edith's shelves, seeking something untouched. Some weight great enough to pin Edith in place.

Tessa. What are we doing here.

We're getting you out. She plucked out a copy of *Frisk*. So thin it left no observable space. *Dennis Cooper is good for you. Your intellectual development.*

As happy as I am to go to yours for Thanksgiving—

No, Joni, you're coming to live with me.

A pause. Balled-up black jeans halfway to the bag. *I'm what.*

You're leaving this misery behind.

You have a housemate.

Had. They live at an ashram now.

I have class.

You're not going. Edith struggled for other excuses against spontaneity. *Less talking, more packing.*

They were on the Taconic State Parkway before she could say, *I would have thought of a reason not to come.* Her duffel in the backseat was proof against this counterfactual. *If you'd given me long enough, I would have come up with something.*

I know you would have. Tessa's knuckles tightened on the steering wheel. Her hands were chapped and cracked from the hours smoking in the cold. She did not look from the road as she said, *I love you, Joni.*

Those silly nicknames. Old as their friendship and feeling somehow older. Edith settled her head against the cool window and closed her eyes. She never got tired of hearing it. *I love you, Joan.*

HOW'S DOMESTICITY treating you, babe? Valerie's voice crackled, swelled and faded. Her car had died, then her cell. She was waiting for a tow at a payphone outside Missoula.

It's good. Edith was folding clothes. *Did you know Tessa keeps exotic fish now? I'd hoped we could get a cat.*

She and Tessa shared a two-bedroom in the top right corner of a fourplex. Somerville's gray December was no colder than where they'd gone to college in upstate New York. Edith had inherited a bed and dresser from Tessa's ex-roommate. She'd go back for her summer clothes, the rest of her books. Tessa had promised a trip to Savers soon.

A cat would only tie you down.

Well we can't all do the wild and wooly Kerouac life.

You haven't tried. I'm serious, Valerie said. *Come on the road with me. We'll scream into the Grand Canyon. We'll blow up Mount Rushmore.*

That sounds like a lot of work. One T-shirt after another into the particleboard drawers. All gray and blue and black. *Why are my clothes so boring?*

Valerie snorted. *You'll fit right in in Beantown.*

Aren't road trips supposed to be fun? You know, stopping at holes in the wall for burgers that might kill you. Sleeping under the stars, playing the license plate game.

What the hell is the license plate game?

I don't know. Something people do on road trips.

Isn't the trip itself exciting enough? Valerie's voice had taken on a new energy since graduation. A pleasure, a rightness, that Edith imagined must parallel that of transition. *You spend your whole life trapped, and then*—a click of Val's tongue—*none of the stuff that held you still matters. Not the wasted days or the days of getting wasted.*

I think I can count the number of times you've been drunk on one hand.

The times you've seen *me drunk, babe. You have no idea how free it is out here.*

Edith added the next line: *"The peacefulness is so big it dazes you."* Unclear whether Valerie meant to quote Plath or not, whom she'd always called *hopelessly recherché.* They were older; anything could change.

Hell yes it is. Valerie had been working at a farm in exchange for board. *They had a whole gaggle of baby goats. The heater in the barn broke, so they'd sleep in the living room. I'll send a pic when my phone's not dead.*

The baby goats were tempting. Their small fuzzy faces, their nascent horns. But there was safety in having a home to go back to. A door your key would always fit inside. There were times that Edith worried Valerie's travels were more than manic-pixie flightiness. That she was consciously inviting harm. A woman traveling alone through unknown territory seemed a bad idea. A trans woman, far worse. *Don't you worry someone is gonna, you know?*

Hate-crime me? You get a good sense of these things. Plus I have the Punisher. The Punisher was a four-inch switchblade with the vigilante superhero's skull emblem on the handle.

So what, instead they'll think you're a cop?

Very funny, babe. Val coughed into the phone. *Anything happen between you and Tess yet?*

She's gay, Valerie.

Doesn't mean you don't want to.

And I don't want to. Valerie had long been convinced the two of them would hook up. Midway through their sophomore year, she'd taken Edith aside at a party and said, *I see how you look at her, but don't. She's not going to be your* Chasing Amy. And it was true, then, that Edith wondered how firm Tessa's sexuality was. Now that Edith had grown a beard, her chances were likely nil.

Meanwhile Edith had always figured Valerie and Tessa would have a fling. It'd be the thing that tore apart the circle of love and trust they'd built—or else the thing that excised her from it. A deeper knowledge of each other than she'd ever find herself. But Valerie insisted she didn't fuck her friends. *That's why I transferred colleges,* she said. Abandoning her midwestern liberal arts school after her first year. Edith always thought she'd left because of her transition.

If you hurt her, Val said, *I will hurt you twice as bad.*

Thanks for your faith in me.

Same goes for if she hurts you.

You should come visit, Edith said. *Maybe Boston will be the city that tames your wanderlust. You'll meet a beautiful butch with screws in her ears and a heart of gold.*

There are beautiful butches everywhere, babe.

———

IT TOOK Edith and Charlie an hour to get the desk up the four-plex's narrow stairs. *What if we flip it. Table it, so it's easier to hold,* Edith said.

The problem isn't holding it. Charlie's face red with exertion. *Can we set it down?*

They got their wind back over a thermos of soup. *Welcome to the big city, bud.* Charlie clapped her on the back. *Better get used to making do. Big things in small spaces.*

Finally they maneuvered it into the apartment. Two doors, taken off their hinges, lay like forgotten pieces in some architectural domino game. Charlie patted the desk's flat flank. *Good desk.* Whatever creep owned it before him had painted it baby blue. He'd stripped it, varnished it himself. When the weather was hot the desk smelled like airplane glue. *I'm glad it's here.*

The hour we've had, it's never leaving.

The end of days will come, oceans will rise and the city will fall, and still above it all will sit the desk. Another pat. *So, don't get me wrong. I'm happy you're here. But I still don't understand how you left school.*

Tessa extracted me.

You said. I can't believe you bought a twin bed.

The last person left it. A pause. *What do you mean by that?*

What?

Any of it.

Did you want to come here?

Edith laughed. *I wouldn't have come if I didn't.*

So Teresa asked you, "Hey do you want to come live with me," and you evaluated the options, and pictured your life without an M.A., and—

Not all of us have the future mapped out on a spreadsheet, Chuck. A low blow; Charlie did have a spreadsheet, a five-year plan. The spreadsheet had brought him to a science-writing degree at MIT.

Right, okay. His patting became a tic. The desk resounding in steady rhythm. Where did he find a coat that fit him so well? Why did his legs look so much less weird than hers? *'Cause see what it sounds like is you went from one path of least resistance to a different path of equally little resistance.*

That's me, bitch. Back and forth like the Chicago River.

Don't say "bitch." You're not exactly filling me with confidence here.

Charlie, what do you want me to say?

I want to make sure you're okay. In the silence after his tapping: the skate of tires on wet asphalt, trash clamoring in dumpsters, the hydraulic whir of a tow truck. A man yelled, *Hey that's my car!* and another yelled back, *Too fuckin' bad!*

Charlie picked his words carefully. *Did you and Teresa ever talk about last Christmas?*

Edith never should have told him. Even Valerie didn't know, and she'd been with them at Tessa's parents'. *Sure we did*, Edith lied.

Everything good there?

Oh yeah. She strode across the room, rapped her knuckles on the desk. A hollower sound than at Charlie's touch. *Everything's great.*

THE SHOW was a last-minute thing. An old-school emo band back together for a few nights only. There was no shortage of things to do, living with Tessa: bar trivia, skeeball, art markets. Things that, in college, would have felt kitschy—playing at adulthood—now felt real. No longer life postponed, but life itself.

Edith and Tessa walked through the Cambridge night. College students huddled outside bars with their hands in each other's coat pockets. Their breath hung in the streetlights' gold. A nebula spun from all their lungs, brilliant beneath the starless sky.

Tessa lit two cigarettes and handed Edith one. Her parents mailed her cartons from North Carolina so she wouldn't waste all her money paying Massachusetts prices. The sweet smell of unburned tobacco never matched their sweaty smoke.

Is that girl you told me about going to be there? Edith asked. *Meghan?*

May-gan, not Meg-an.

Right. Edith looked up and down the waiting line. *What's she look like?*

She's inside already. She does reviews and things.

And yet you're outside with me.

A soft grin. Wind pressed through the narrow streets and Tessa leaned against Edith, cigarette bobbing freely. *Oh, Joni.*

A group called Sapphic Somerville organized events every two weeks. Tessa went to each while Edith stayed home and wrote. The events were the same sort of things they might do together, but for lesbians: coffee, with lesbians; skeeball, with lesbians; a screening of *Carol*, bring your own tissues. Two weeks earlier, Tessa had come home hoarsely gushing about Meghan. They'd spent all three hours of lesbian karaoke talking, shouting in the corner to be heard above the music. Tessa lost her voice but got Meghan's number.

How'd your job interview go? she asked.

I dunno. It was for a temporary office position at one of the universities. *They asked how I organized my personal email. What am I, a psycho?*

Hope you led with that, they'd love that energy.

Maybe I'll mooch off you forever. I could be your pool boy.

You'll get there. Again she put her shoulder to Edith's. Edith was haunted by Charlie's question about Christmas. There was nothing to talk about. What was one kiss, compared to the thousands of moments they'd spent not kissing?

The band was phenomenal. Symbolist lyrics natural in the singers' mouths as they'd been twenty years ago. One of them had transitioned during the band's hiatus. Edith tried not to watch her for signs of discomfort. It must be odd to sing a song from your teenage years, return to those old words, when you had so wholly changed your life. You'd have to learn new resonances, new valences to fit them to who you were now. Edith once asked Valerie to explain the affective experience of being trans—the certainty of change and uncertainty of destination. Val had wrinkled her nose. *Kind of the whole deal is that it defies language.*

"*No one can tell you what the Matrix is.*"

Edith meant it jokingly but Val nodded. *That's it exactly.*

After the show, they found Meghan outside. Everyone was slicked with sweat, shivering into Ubers and bars. Meghan was short. A pixie cut and hand tattoos of ivy leaves. Edith could see why Tess liked her. They made their introductions and wandered deeper into Cambridge, looking for a bar not overflowing with sloppy drunken children.

Meghan blew into her hands and talked about other shows. She'd gone to school here, been here forever.

I didn't expect to get so sweaty in January, Edith said. *My fingers are pruned.*

This is nothing, Meghan said. *I saw the Cap'n Jazz reunion tour in the middle of summer, no A/C in the building. The dress I was wearing still smells like other people's sweat.*

Tessa laughed. Too hard.

At the bar, Tessa sat between them. She and Meghan talked about other Somerville Sapphics. Two women who'd been together for years split when one left the other for her student, a college sophomore.

The worst part is, the ex teaches in the same department. The girl's going to have to take a class with her to meet a requirement.

How delicious.

Edith thought stereotypes were sometimes used to justify behavior that ought to be more carefully considered. There probably wasn't anything inherently wrong with a middle-aged woman dating a teenager, but that didn't make it a good idea. Tessa spent half their senior year living with a girl she'd only known a few months; in the course of their breakup, she and Edith sat on the roof of the science building drinking forties of Olde English. *Fucking lesbians*, Tessa lamented, *and their fucking U-Hauls.*

When Edith made a comment to this effect, Meghan rolled her eyes at Tessa. *I wouldn't expect a man to understand*, she said. *There's a political solidarity in women who love women. It subverts the entire relationship paradigm that you know.* Another eye roll. *I mean a heterosexual relationship is built on so much exploited emotional labor, you know?*

Yeah, said Tessa, *totally.*

Edith pulled at her beard, drank her beer, and shut the hell up. She and Tessa split a cigarette on the walk home. Three beers weren't enough to fight off the Boston cold. Tessa took Edith's hand in hers and it was like marble holding marble.

Dear Joni, you were not very nice to her.

Me? She treated me like I didn't exist.

You called her Morgan.

It was true; she'd accentuated it, so there could be no mistaking the slight.

She didn't ask me a single question about myself.

A sharp squeeze of her hand, and release. A more biting cold in its place. *You can't blame her for being skeptical of men.*

She didn't ask you anything either.

I know you're one of the good ones, but other people take time.

I guess. Edith took the cigarette from her, took a lungful of smoke, and held it for as long as she could. *I only want the best for you, is all.*

Tessa snuggled into her shoulder. *Love you, Joni. No one's gonna threaten that.*

Love you, Joan.

———

THE WINTER was ending but not yet over when Valerie came to stay with them. Her car had broken down twice on the way there. *I've seen you build a bed frame from scratch*, Edith said when Val called from a second repair shop lobby. *You can't replace a belt or whatever?*

I like the mystery, babe. Letting the world take me.

Christened by her arrival, after almost four months of living together, Tessa and Edith's place was finally a home. They stayed up too late the first night, drank too much. When Edith found the couch empty in the morning, her first thought was that Val had left already. In college, when the clocks neared midnight, she'd sometimes say, *Time to stop being a pumpkin*, and start plucking her eyebrows, making-up, slipping out to party-seek.

When Valerie came out of Tessa's room, Edith was left stammering. *Oh, babe*, Valerie said. *It's cold on the couch is all. I wouldn't do that to you.* She made pancakes with a puree of berries, Nutella, and chia seeds. It was the best breakfast Edith had in months.

Mostly they did nothing. They ate, they played records on Tess's turntable. They talked ceaselessly and went through a case of wine.

Valerie had been working at a record store in Nashville. *I know more about country music than I ever wanted to.* She played four bars of a Townes Van Zandt song on Tessa's guitar. *I was googling Stetson hats and cowboy boots, so I knew it was time to move on.*

Tessa rested her head on Val's left shoulder and Edith claimed the right. A pincer move; they'd hold her fiercely until the sun came up.

Why don't you stay here?

She took each of them under an arm. *And deprive you the pleasure of my visiting?*

Edith worked at a college that didn't care how she organized her email. Every day, bound by the admin office walls, she felt real life

was on hold. Trapped in the opening of *The Wizard of Oz* until
the world went Technicolor at five o'clock. At home, Valerie was
cooking something, Tessa chatting amiably, wine already open. The
apartment filled with a champagne light.

We ought to get you a maid outfit, Edith said.

What makes you think I don't have one?

There was so much to reminisce about. The morass of college
memories untangled the longer they spoke. *God, who was that girl
you slept with at the end of sophomore year?* Valerie asked. *With
the rabbits?*

They were taxidermied for a project! Tessa said. *It was art!*

They were on the bed. You said they were watching you.

At least I never fucked anyone in a cappella, Joni.

They didn't actually fuck, Valerie said. *Only talked a lot.*

Oh that's so much worse.

Only later, when Valerie had left, would Edith think about things
unsaid. The girl who'd assaulted Valerie; for a full day, Tessa had
begged her to not make a big deal of it (*It'd really hurt the queer
community*) until Tessa realized what she was asking and they
reported the girl. Smaller fights, too: when all three had a crush on
the bass player in a punk band; when Edith insisted Tessa's ex not
come to her apartment during a brief period of reunion. Was this
what it took to stay friends? Did you have to forget the bad things,
brighten the dark corners of your history with new memories? Or
did you learn not to think about it? Was the brain incapable of holding grudges against the people you loved?

Tessa was too responsible to fake sick, but Edith called out of
work on Val's last day. Their walk to Central Square was inter-
rupted by wobbly avian noises.

Uh-oh, we're going to want to cross.

What is that, a pigeon?

They rounded the bend. The stretch of Mass Ave. was dead at

that hour. The street was cold and straight. In the middle of the side-walk was the largest turkey either had ever seen.

How did that get there?

They wander out of the mouth of hell. Don't get any closer. Valerie did not listen. She held out a hand as though approaching a jungle cat. *I'm serious, Val, one put a child in the hospital.*

It'd be justified. Turkeys have probably been here since before the Puritans.

Justified nothing. You're not trying to make it into a sandwich.

The bird's head flipped left and right. More gobbling. Edith was in the middle of the street.

Hello, lovely. Valerie took a step. *We're all calm, aren't we?* Another step.

The turkey lunged. Val scarpered into the street, into Edith's arms. *I tried to tell you,* Edith laughed.

I recognize the turkey's right to this domain.

Coming back from hours of charity shops and record stores, they opted to take side streets.

Did one really put a child in the hospital?

Well, people say it happened.

Records shifted in their plastic bag. They'd gotten a Townes Van Zandt album for Tessa. Valerie had insisted on buying Edith a red-and-black checked flannel. Parting gifts.

I can't believe you're leaving already.

You know I'll be back. Val put a hand on Edith's back. *There's nothing I wouldn't do for you, babe.*

Stay, then.

That wouldn't be good for either of us. Edith knew that Valerie was right. Already Edith's life with Tessa had narrowed. And Val stiffened at the mere suggestion, the memory of her static Texas childhood. Tiny details: locks on the windows, fucking boys for rides away from home, a cross-shaped scar on her stomach. Never more than hints. As far as Edith knew, Valerie's life began at eighteen in a Planned Parenthood. *I can't want the same things as you two.*

But Edith wasn't used to missing her. Never knowing what hurts the country's vastness might invite. They'd almost had to stage an intervention junior year when Val stopped eating.

How do you do it, Val? Only a few months and it's like you've been away half my life.

I don't think about it, much. I don't expect anything. I open myself to the world and the world opens to me.

It's less lonely here with us.

Oh, sweetheart. You know I love you and Tessa. Love was never enough to keep her in place. She threaded her arm through Edith's and pulled her close. *Don't look, but there's a man following us.*

Sorry, are we playing spies now?

No. Edith did as she was told. *We're going to turn at the next intersection and see if we can get some distance, all right?*

They didn't run. To run would have been to admit fear, to make serious and scary what they might convince themselves was everyday. Edith tensed, shivered, and Valerie held her tighter.

Hey! the man yelled. Following Valerie's lead, Edith did not speed up. *Hey faggots! You wanna suck my cock?* They turned down another street, and another. The man followed like a teen scream slasher. *Hey man, you let your tranny boyfriend fuck you? Tell him to call me.*

Later they'd both laugh through the telling of it. *He barely knew what words to use,* Val would say. *He practically choked on the slur. Tr-anny! Tr-anny!*

Edith thought Valerie might pull her knife on the man. Bring him down to the level of her Doc Martens and not let him up till he sobbed for his mother. They only walked on. Tighter, now, the link of their arms. He could red-rover his way into them and they would not budge.

His voice faded. There were enough people now that they could call themselves safe. The first thing Valerie said was, *It's so silly. No one hurts white trans girls anyway.*

THE MONDAY after Valerie left there was a late winter storm. The roads were frosted with snow eighteen inches thick, pillowy swells and gentle dips hiding all the stuff of daily life. Edith and Tessa were glad for the day off. *Nothing to do but lounge*, Tessa said, stretched across the couch. *Please don't write today, dear Joni. Let's drink hot chocolate and smoke out open windows and watch every film of some wretched franchise.* Both were in recovery from Valerie's absence. Tessa texted her a photo of the smothered street and got, in return, an abandoned mental hospital in the wilds of the deep south.

It was a beautiful day. Hot chocolate sloshed sickly in their stomachs and smoke disappeared into gray heaven. The fish burbled in their tank. Blankets were pulled from new and unseen places to build a world of hermetic coziness. Not one important thing was said. No one formulated a new interpretation of the world. Too fatigued to go on after *A Nightmare on Elm Street 4: The Dream Master*, they listened to a Bing Crosby Christmas record. Each accused the other of putting it on. It was March after all. A Monday in March was about as far from Christmas as one could get.

Side by side but not touching. It was the not touching, Edith thought, that really did it. They were warm and full of Christmas feeling. *Our heads are really close together*, Tessa said. And she turned to Edith, and Edith turned to her, and their hearts were so loud, as they kissed, that each was certain the other would feel it in her lips.

F LAKES OF SNOW VANISHED WHERE THEY HIT THE
street, leaving only the shadow mark of a letter erased. Here
came Tessa in her banana-yellow coat, jeans tucked into her boots,
arms outstretched from halfway down the block. *Edith!* she said.
Oh my god, Edith. Edith did not let herself run. They collided mid-
sidewalk, a spot of warmth in the middle of the city. *Let me get a
look at you. This baby-fresh face.* The scratch of gloves over skin
once covered by beard.

Hey Joan. Been a minute.

An hour, at least. Tessa took her in. Edith felt like her old self in
these cold-weather clothes. Skinny jeans and a baggy sweater. Tits
reduced to vague lumps and hips nonexistent. *God you look great. I
can't believe you're here.*

So do you. She'd been right: Tessa looked no different. She'd
always be the girl Edith loved at nineteen. Twenty years might
pass, fifty.

My car's right down here.

You have a car again?

Plus ça change. Are you going to be warm enough?

Edith shivered. *But you loved the T.*

Don't worry, dear Edith, the T and I are still well acquainted.

Inside the car, Edith held her hands before the vents' blasted heat.
Here she was. Beside Tessa. Snow slushing off the windshield.

I also can't believe it, she said.

That's what I'm saying! What the fuck, girl. Tessa looked at her seriously. *You're not allowed to stay away this long again.*

What a warm way to live.

I promise.

Edith had not seen Boston from the front seat of many cars. It was easy to lose track of where they were, the city alien from the middle of intersections.

I feel so silly, coming back here as a girl.

What do you mean?

I don't spend a lot of time in places where I used to be a dude, she hazarded. *It feels so obviously wrong.* Getting away with something, or failing to.

Is it a feeling of risk? Like you used to have an easier time moving through these streets and now . . .

Maybe. That wasn't it at all. You return as a new person, a whole person, all the messy parts of the journey hidden away inside you. It's your responsibility to explain. Like being thrust into the second act of a play. Fifteen minutes and half a dozen years pass. Now the children are played by adults. Now the boy is played by a girl. In tonight's performance, the role of Edith will be played by an understudy.

But Valerie had been there, had known without words. That life was their life.

Each table at the sandwich shop was filled by a young couple or family. What did people see in her and Tessa? Did they have the draw, the intimacy crackling over short distances, that people in love carried? Edith felt like a heel of bread gone hard and dry in the freezer.

Her chicken salad was sweet with halved grapes. The coffee hot and rich. Before Tessa touched her chicken Caesar wrap, she drew the book out of her purse. *I don't want to forget*, she said. A felt-tip pen in her other hand. *Would you?*

Edith's name stared up at her. The gold wash of Helen Franken-thaler's *Persian Garden*. Title like a false promise: *Someday We Won't Remember This.*

Yeah, for sure. This embarrassed her too. *I didn't know you'd read it.*

Who do you think I am?

Tessa watched her. Years of signing *Edith* and still her pen stumbled.

Don't read the inscription until I'm not around.

That scathing, huh?

I won't have you seeing me sentimental.

Those nights, those weekend mornings. Slipped into the heart of the city to write some silly story. Tessa always asked to read them before they were ready.

As soon as she handed the book back, Tessa flipped to the title page.

Hey! For Tessa, my Joan, it read. You were there from the start. *Still incorrigible after all these years.*

Tessa grinned, picked up her wrap. *I have to tell you,* she said. *I read it practically peeking between my fingers. I was terrified I'd show up in there.*

Tessa was all over the book. Every person she'd loved was. She didn't know how to write an honest book—a book about love and friendship and uncertainty and loss—without bringing them in.

Why terrified?

Terrified it would be inaccurate. Terrified it would be exactly right. No one should be written about, I think. You get all caught up in the gaps of things. Are you all right? Edith coughed. An unchewed grape scraped her throat going down. *That book's going to be worth a lot if you choke to death, but I still won't forgive you.* Little by lit-tle sips of coffee cleared the cough away.

God, you know who I ran into yesterday? Charlie.

Oh yeah, we see each other now and then.

Do you hang out?

Not really. Her nose wrinkled. *You think some people get more hetero as time goes on?*

I for sure think Charlie has. All those Facebook posts of him and Polly. Posing in an apple orchard, posing on the beach, posing with Charlie's mother on Mother's Day. Visions of a life that so sickened Edith she'd deactivated all her social media. All those old posts, those internet memorials to boyhood, banished into the ether. *I'm getting lunch with them.*

Tell me what you think of Polly.

From their phone calls, each had a basic sketch of the other's life, now to be inked, shaded, colored.

Where are you living these days?

Literally across the street from our old place, if you can believe it. At night I can see the light in your old bedroom.

Tess still worked in the city's homelessness response systems. All the friends she mentioned had familiar names. She'd always been the one with friends. She and Valerie both—they knew how to make a world around them. Impossible not to love them.

Did you tell them about me?

What, that you're a girl now? Yeah, obviously, everyone's happy as shit for you.

Gotta be worth some clout in Somerville. Having a trans girl ex.

They're throwing me a parade. I'm going to be mayor for a day. Arca and Charli XCX are singing the national anthem.

Do you still talk to Meghan?

May-gen. And no, I don't.

The snow had stopped by the time they finished lunch. Nothing stuck. There was only the gray wash of sidewalk, street, and sky.

How're you doing with the cold? Want to walk down the bike path?

I can deal.

(On a midwinter night, they had waited for a bus that did not come. They'd gotten dinner in a far-flung part of Boston, gone to a bookstore they didn't usually visit. It had been nice up until the point they stopped moving. To stand freezing in the city you called home and recognize none of it. Edith wanted to give up and call a Lyft; Tessa had refused. *We're not going to contribute to the degradation of civic infrastructure.*)

Tessa scrounged in her pockets. *You have a quarter?* Edith passed one over. Tessa flipped it, scowled, flipped it again. *I've started doing this thing to cut down on smoking. I only have one if I flip heads.* Another flip. *Ideally it means I smoke half as much.* Another.

That's some kind of statistical anomaly you've got going.

It happens more often than you'd think.

Smoke the cig, Joan. I'll have one with you.

There we go! Washington's face silver in her palm. Edith made her keep it.

How're your parents? Edith had to resist asking the same question again and again: Who knows? Does everyone know? Had it come as a shock?

They don't still mail me cigarettes, if that's what you're asking. Come here. She lit both cigarettes behind a cupped hand. *Anyway my folks are good. They've been going on every cruise they can find.*

I'm sorry, they what?

They went on a Disney Cruise. They went on the Weezer Cruise.

Do they know who Weezer are?

They sure do now. Edith liked how their cigarette ash disappeared into the wet sidewalk. A small part of the pantomime. *I think they like boats is all. What about you? Your dad okay?*

That unimaginable Virginia summer. Valerie stretched across her parents' guest room bed. Immaterial days. Endless, uncertain days. This was the thing. That feeling hovering around her since that first gray morning. Boston was a home that no longer belonged to her. Exiled not from place, but from time.

He's holding up. They're the same as ever, I guess. Playground memories, pretending to smoke rolled-up pieces of paper as breath clouded cold air. *I dunno, Tess, the more time passes the less I feel like I know them. I always thought adulthood was when we'd have a real relationship.*

And then you realize that all there is is all there ever was.

Yeah.

Tessa lit a second cigarette with the end of her first. *They do love you, though.*

They do. But that wasn't enough. Love without substance was just language, just a game.

Edith's parents had visited her at college once a year. They took her and Tess and Val to the expensive seafood restaurant across the street, cajoled stories from Edith's friends, loved them. There were clear roles for everyone but her.

I thought maybe it would be different after my dad got sick. Might as well dive in. *Did Val tell you about that trip?*

We weren't talking in those days.

Edith had assumed Tessa also got calls from the road. Days Val would disappear into her relentless need for space—not only from people. She needed the openness of America between cities. *All those roads connect,* she said. *You won't believe where they'll lead.* Maybe Edith had been the only one she called. Her distorted voice, carried down those endless highways. Too much and never enough.

Edith stopped and Tessa kept going. *Look, Tess.*

Edith. Tessa turned toward her. There she was, that nineteen-year-old girl with choppy bangs and too much eyeshadow. There was Edith, the scruffy, gangly boy, awkward in his body with no hint of why. They could have been at a party. Jason Derulo pounding out the walls, and Edith bumming a cigarette, asking, *Does anyone actually like this music?* And Tessa firing back, *What, you'd rather they play Joni Mitchell?*

We don't need to talk about it, Tessa said.

I wish we didn't. She didn't want the loss. Didn't want to risk the fragile love, the spiderweb of smoke, that hung between them.

What if there were no past. What if there was only the bike path, the cold air, the fire that burned down to their fingertips. The two of them in motion. *I think—*

What. Tessa didn't sound angry. She didn't sound tired, or frustrated, or confused. *You want absolution? Fine, I absolve you.*

That isn't it.

What, then. Three men in red spandex biked by. What did they see—friends, family, strangers? *How long did it take for you guys to get together? A month? Six weeks?* It was longer, but not long enough. *You wanna know if that hurt? Of course it did.*

It had nothing to do with you.

I'm sure you think that's true. She threw down her second cigarette and fished the quarter back out. It came up tails.

Tessa, don't—

Hold on, would you?

Edith's cigarette had a column of ash jutting from it. She didn't move; if her fingers burned, let them.

Washington's face. The brief flame, the smoke that came after.

I'm sure you found yourself depressed, Tessa said, *discouraged, far from home. I'm sure you were only looking for some hand to hold, to pull you from the mire. But you had to know it would hurt me. Both of you.* She gestured, her cigarette toward Edith's. *Put that out before you hurt yourself.* Edith did. *Can we keep walking?*

The path was dotted with young couples swaddled in wool coats, bootied black dogs on retractable leashes. This could be worse. They weren't really talking about Valerie at all.

I know some of this is unfair, Tessa said. *I know that you get all my anger because you're here and she's not.* Had Tessa said Valerie's name all day? *You know I asked her once? Before you left.*

Asked her what?

If she was interested in you.

And she said no.

She said, I wouldn't do that to you.

Of course she did. The trouble with Valerie was that everything she said was true and everything was a kind of game she played against herself.

It was snowing again and going to snow. *Let's go back,* Tessa said. *You need a real coat.* Edith couldn't fathom a response that would fit this conversation's needs. *Tell you the truth, I'm not upset anymore. Or, I don't think about it enough to be upset. But at the time? It sucked.* Tessa handed her another cigarette and left her to light it herself. *The three of us loved one another so much.* ("We're not the three of us anymore, Mary.") *There was a unity to it. A kind of family.* ("It's just one and one and one.") *And when I found out that you two had gotten together—it was like we were all interchangeable. It was worse—like I'd been a placeholder for you. Magical, sparkling Valerie off in America's far reaches, manifesting her destiny et cetera and so forth. And so you settled for the nearest thing.*

Edith could have pointed out it was Tessa who suggested they split up. Tessa who decided they would never work. Edith had only followed suit because she always did. But Tess hadn't forgotten these things.

How did you find out?

She told me! She said she felt responsible, but I don't think that's why. She always needed us to know how okay she was.

Yeah. Edith fought the urge to brush accumulated snow from Tessa's hair and shoulders. *I'm sorry. Whatever that's worth.*

I don't need you to be sorry. It's a thing that happened. A million other things have happened since. Were happening even then.

She stopped, squeezed Edith's arm. *This is the thing about us being friends. And I wouldn't trade that. Complicated history and all.*

Edith wanted to tell Tess she loved her. When they'd begun dating, those words had taken on a permanent power, a wariness they'd never held before.

The wind picked up. Their cigarettes sizzled out in the snow. *Can we go somewhere?* Tessa said. *I'm freezing.*

THEY'D ALL met still bearing the last vestiges of their separate youths. With Valerie there was arm-wrestling and hand-slapping games. Each time she lost to Edith there'd come a little smile: *That's the most gender-affirming outcome for us both.* She spoke of depression as if she'd diagnosed it using Robert Burton. She never had trouble getting out of bed, only coming back to her own. Tessa had been borne on her own abandon—sleeping with every member of the women's ultimate frisbee team and smoking cigarettes. But the thing that Edith marveled at, that she found permanently, implacably wondrous, was the balance. They pulled each other back from their most self-destructive moments—*Joni, please bring your legs off the windowsill*—or leaned into them together, staying up all night before their art history final drinking Fireball whiskey and watching for the sunrise. (As they'd discover around the time the sky went eggshell, they were facing west.) There was no trial they would not take on together. But Edith never stopped worrying. Val springing the Punisher open and closed. *What do you need a knife for?* And Val said, *What does anyone need a knife for?* Tessa did coke off an ex-girlfriend's finger, ran it across her gums. Temptation and torture. They starved, craved, caroused. Paths crossed, eyes closed, hand in hand. Exes dogged by soft *oh*s.

They were children.

——

THEY STOPPED at CVS, ibuprofen for Edith's aching tooth. It
was risky to dull the pain—she might chew the wrong way, clench
her jaw—but she couldn't stand it. She'd seen pictures of the stump
of her rotless tooth. It looked like a bombed-out building. *People
don't usually bleed this much*, the dentist said.

Tessa stood past the checkout with Edith's book, flipping between
inscription and dedication. *For Valerie Green.*

Did she get to read it?

Some of it. Edith chewed one pill, a second. Her throat silted by
bitter powder.

Tessa winced. *Still doing that with pills, huh.*

It makes me believe in them.

The sky was gunmetal. They stepped into the first café they passed.

I forgot how fast it gets dark here.

God knew Boston would be too powerful if we had more light.

The café floor was spattered with snowmelt. Students read or
solved differential equations. There was a calmness to them all. The
early part of the semester, when you know your finals will never come.
Edith and Tessa claimed a table. Two coffees and a plate of biscotti.

Do you still write ever?

No. Tessa looked at all the hardworking children in the room.
*No, you know, I used to feel bad about that. Like, it felt so impor-
tant when we were in college—writing those little one-acts and getting people to perform them. You remember, I tore out half my hair
getting that girl to star.*

Their senior year, she'd adapted the biography of a Sixties It
Girl. She'd cast the most popular girl on campus to play the lead.
Imogen-someone had sown discord by sleeping with half the cast,
showing up at rehearsal drunk. She'd taken a year off, after, to go to
a recovery program.

As I recall, you were mostly stressed she wasn't sleeping with you.

Stressed that she wanted *to. It'd be an abuse of power. Anyway,*

Tessa said, *I still get ideas now and then. Little scenes in my head. Two people talking about someone they used to know who's gone missing, or a woman taking care of her dying mother. But eventually I realized that I'm never going to put them together.*

You still could.

I don't want to. I used to think writing would, like, change people's lives. But it turns out there are much, much easier ways to do that. The biscotto cracked in her hands. *We're getting affordable units set aside in luxury complexes. We're getting real childcare reforms. You know, I talk to people every day that don't know who Arthur Miller is, let alone Annie Baker, let alone whoever I would be.*

You're Tessa goddamn Pacheco.

Who is that, though? No one much in the grand scheme of it. But I don't care anymore. Who cares if life is small? It's still life. She broke the cookie into smaller pieces. Neither she nor Edith moved to eat one. *I think it was only ever being around you and Valerie that made me think I needed more. I was writing for you two as much as for me.*

Let's blame Val, since she's not here to defend herself.

No one's getting blamed. God, she could make the world seem so . . .

Interesting?

Ridiculous. Do you remember that Italian student she hired to read her letters?

What kind of monster would forget Carlo? "Beeg keeses."

The summer between junior and senior years, Valerie had gotten a scholarship for an intensive language program in Vermont. The program stipulated she couldn't write or speak in any language but Italian, and so she'd found Carlo, a rising sophomore, and paid him twenty dollars a letter to translate. All her letters were signed, *Big kisses, Val.* There was a palpable air of relief as Carlo reached the end: *Beeg keeses.* Sigh. *Val.*

Poor guy, we should've bought him a fruit basket or something, Tessa said.

He got paid.

This is what I mean. She'd corral whoever was nearby into her absurd vision of the world. They'd become a part of the performance with her.

We all had stuff we had to work through.

Yeah. One finger, pushing around the bituminous chunks of biscuit. *Look, Edie, can I ask? Do you think the accident was—*

It was like looking down from a very high place. It was like she had tried to drink an entire gallon of milk.

No. Edith had her doubts about Valerie's death. The foggy mountain road, the twisted guardrail. The mind reached for a story, and there were only so many ways trans stories ended. But, no, she didn't think Val had killed herself. *I don't want to talk about this, actually.*

Sorry. Each took long sips of their coffee. *What are you working on now?*

I don't want to talk about that either.

It wasn't fear of showing emotion. It wasn't that talking about Val's death would make it seem more real.

Okay well what do you want to talk about.

I'm sorry Tessa, it's not—

I forgot that you could be like this.

I'm not, not anymore, not usually.

The hour grew late. People packed their things, walked into the cold. There were well-lit dining halls with Sodexo feasts. There were homes with their partners, slouching into each other, a few hours of bad TV, and then sleep.

In every draft of her book about Valerie, Edith had been trying to write about home. Her first book was all about leaving—leaving Rome, leaving Earth. It was time to write about staying put. But she had never learned, not really, how to stop.

She didn't want to learn anything. She wanted to fold back time to those years when she loved Tessa so much, and Valerie, and knew that there would always be another day when the three of them came together again.

I don't know how much longer I can stay in Texas, she said.

Wow, this is a much cheerier topic, you're right. Edith couldn't help laughing. *Because of the politics?*

Because of money. If I don't finish another book soon, I dunno how I'm going to stay in my apartment. Edith hadn't said this aloud before.

Oh, but you can find another place. Or a roommate. Or a job you don't hate.

Right, sure. What lengths would she go to to stay in Texas? At what point did you cut and run? And how many more times could she upend her life?

Tessa monologued for a bit about various friends' housing situations. Women who'd gone on living with exes and their new girlfriends. People who'd moved to tiny houses in Maine. Serial house sitters who leapfrogged between furnished apartments every few months. *They keep finding academics who have exotic pets with special needs.* There was a parrot that would count down from a hundred when the lights went out. A rabbit that ate veggie broth through an infant's bottle. Colleen, Hila, Diana. Faces she'd still know on sight. If you stayed in place, the names stayed the same. You knew how to write about home and you weren't tempted to leave, because you never had.

Anyway, people work it out. Be glad it's cheaper to live down there.

Later, when she learned about Tessa's living situation, Edith would be glad she had not said *I never should have left.* Did she understand already that Tess was living with someone she loved? Were there subtle cues? Or was she sufficiently clear-eyed to know that coming back would never be the right thing?

AFTER BULGOGI and a bottle of wine, the night converged on Adam and Michael's. Edith lost track of how many cigarettes she'd had, her chest faintly tight with sky-colored smoke. *We really shoulda known you were a girl,* Tessa said. *I mean how many dykes did you hook up with in college?*

Present company excluded? Only two. Ellie came out after.

She counts. A fairy-tale number of queer girls, baffled by your charming face. Tessa cupped Edith's jaw. There was a wild moment where she thought Tess might kiss her. They kept walking.

It's nice to think that, whatever—

Girls could tell you were one of us? Tessa lit another cigarette. She'd given up her coin flips. *Your "female soul"?*

Okay, well, when you say it like that it sounds stupid. She wanted to ask, What was it? What drew them together, a girl and a girl in disguise? She wasn't sure she could bear an answer.

Tessa threw the door open. *Hello, dear ones!* She stomped ash and rock salt from her boots. *After many years at sea, I've returned.*

Cigarette, Teresa. Adam and Michael on the couch with a bowl of popcorn between them, *Vertigo* on the paused TV. Tessa tossed her cigarette back through the door. They shed their coats, they smelled of cold. Adam lifted the bowl and Tessa fell into its place. Edith didn't know where to sit.

We're still a little loopy from dinner.

This is pretty standard for her, Michael said.

What did you guys get up to today? Adam offered popcorn and Tessa took a fistful. The TV could wait. Kim Novak marking the tree ring where she was born, the tree ring where she died. The character her character plays, the trick of it all.

What didn't we get up to. Tessa told it in a way that exceeded the day's plainness. All they'd really done was get food and coffee and smoke and talk and talk and talk. It was a miracle to be around people you'd known for so long. The well of experience and interrelation, the sheer fact of years. A smaller piece in the shared narrative of their lives.

Don't let me forget to show you, Michael said, *I did a new sketch of Tamara for Killer Car Lesbians.*

Killer Car Lesbians is their tabletop game, Adam said.

The three stats are "kills" and "lesbian" and "car."

Edith nodded like she understood. She could have watched for hours from her wingback chair—all they had, all they knew. There was more chat. There was a show at the Museum of Fine Arts they decided to go to, a series of fakes and reproductions. Michael popped more popcorn on the stove.

How's your piece on Sondheim coming? Tessa asked Adam.

Oh, slow.

You're also writing about Sondheim?

And Lee Edelman. Into the Woods, *reproductive futurity. Wait, are you?*

Sort of.

My influence, Tessa said, *is boundless.* She tossed a puff of popcorn into her mouth.

Isn't it maddening how little she'll tell us about her book?

You forget, I had two years of living with her to get used to it. Michael returned, a second bowl piled high. *Aw, look at our beautiful little gay circle.*

Come sit on the couch, Edith, Michael said. *We can squeeze.*

We won't have to. Estrogen hasn't made your ass any less skinny.

You can't say that! Boys, Tessa's hate-criming me.

Now girls, Adam said in his most paternal voice. *Don't fight.*

Buzzed and exhausted, Edith only half-watched *Vertigo*. Her parents had shown it to her as a child. They'd tried to inculcate a love of classic Hollywood that mostly meant she got *Gossip Girl*'s references to Audrey Hepburn movies. She'd rewatched it with Valerie in Alabama. They'd lain awake, inventing a modern retelling:

a man becomes obsessed with buying a trans woman surgeries until she looks like his dead wife. It ends with her killing him, escaping with her hot lesbian lover. *To be played by Gina Gershon*, Valerie insisted, *circa 1995*.

The central threads eluded her. Kim Novak came back from the dead with a different name—a twin? a doppelgänger? She was a living doll for Jimmy Stewart's obsession. He dyed her hair and gave her clothes to make her again into the woman he loved. Retreading all the ugly steps of the past, up the steps of the bell tower. Her scream as she tumbled to the earth.

*

EDITH WOKE before her alarm, groggy but not hungover. A scrap of lyrics she couldn't quite identify circling in her head. There was popcorn salt beneath her nails and rheum in her eyes. The living room and sleeper sofa swept by passing headlights. People who went to church, or had small children, or brunch plans. She'd been nodding off by the end of the movie last night. In and out of the red-hued nightmare. She didn't normally do so much in a week as she had in one day.

Into sweatpants, into the kitchen. Eggs, flour, baking soda, milk. Nothing extravagant—not a blueberry or a chocolate chip. Only pancakes: bog-standard and fluffy. When was the last time she'd made breakfast?

Still that scrap of lyrics: "Oh, if life were made of moments, even now and then a bad one . . . but if life were only moments, then you'd never know you had one." Sondheim, but not *Merrily*. Google pinned it as *Into the Woods*. She felt guilty to have not named it unassisted.

There was the post-drunken sense that she'd done something to embarrass herself. Had she said something to Tessa? Made a joke that didn't land? Was it the slumber-party shame of passing out first? Tess and Adam lifted her from the couch by the arms and legs, jerking her awake. Edith had told her to stay, and there'd been some kind of sadness, some kind of smile. Tessa had said they were getting too old for sleeping on couches, or she'd said nothing.

Ridiculous. Pancakes could be an apology. Not for that in particular, but a blanket statement of sorriness.

She read a plot summary of *Vertigo* while she cooked. Jimmy Stewart's friend hired Kim Novak to pretend to be his wife, pretend to be crazy or possessed or both. He hired Jimmy Stewart to follow her, to testify to her craziness, so that when the man killed his real wife—tossed her from the bell tower—no one would guess it was murder. Naturally Stewart and Novak fall in love. Kim Novak shows back up, bad things happen. The girl dies at the end. Et cetera.

Dragged back into a part you'd given up playing, that woman you'd been hired to die as—how did you live with being someone else's ghost?

Had she said something about Val? Was that the source of this shame? She knew that she should talk to her friends about it, but what was left to say? Yes, it was a shame their friend had died. Yes, she missed Val every time she woke. But she'd missed Val plenty of times while she was still alive; you couldn't go on nursing the hole someone had left in your life. You had to forget about them, a little more each day. This was why you wrote: exorcise the past in private. Spit it out into the world fully processed. No longer hers to deal with; hers to deal with forever.

Edith stopped cooking long enough to eat two pancakes, then two more, skimming her copy of *The Odyssey* while she ate. She'd been starving.

THE MORNING AFTER THEY KISSED FOR THE SECOND time, Edith made breakfast. The night of the snowstorm had been languorous and warm; the sheer pleasure of being together under so many blankets instead of alone under too few. No words were needed to end up in Tessa's bed. They didn't have sex, only kissed more. They stared at one another, darkness bright with snow's reflection. Edith slipped from the dawn-soaked bed to make coffee, decant orange juice, fry bacon until brittle. Quiche with a crust from scratch. A bowl of sliced apricot, blueberries, apple. Tessa woke and watched from the doorway. *If I knew you'd cook like this,* she laughed, *I'd've kissed you a long time ago. Kissed you again, I mean.*

Christmas of their senior year, all three of them had gone to Tessa's home in North Carolina. Edith's family never made much of the holidays; Val usually stayed at school. *C'mon,* Tessa insisted. *We should do one Christmas together.*

North Carolina was unmagic—gray and wet and all the leafless trees scrabbled anxiously in the howling wind. Tessa didn't care to give them a tour. *There's a reason I got as far from here as I could,* she said.

You could've managed farther.

But we'd never have met, darling Val, and then where would I be?

As they drove to the town's one coffee shop or bar (the same place, different times of day), the record shop with dusty windows, the pizza place, Tessa might point through the car window and say, *There's where I took trumpet lessons in sixth grade,* or, *That's the field where they'd build a bonfire for Halloween. There's the library, I had my first gay kiss pressed up against the Michael Crichton shelf.* The past could not help coming in.

Edith always tried to picture people's homes—the cracked floral linoleum, the paving stone walkway leading to the back door—and her imagined spaces were never right. They were always an amalgam of her own childhood home, the books she'd read, the TV shows she watched. Usually, when she saw the thing itself, this old ideal faded. The real crowded it out. With Tessa's home and hometown, this fading never happened. Every image a double image, ghosted with Edith's version. Coeval like a song and its cover.

Their last night, they stayed up late, drinking wine in the basement and watching *Gossip Girl*.

I can't believe this show ended, Valerie said. *This show kept me from killing myself when I was a teenager.*

That's not funny, Tessa said.

It's not meant to be. I'd think about it, listening to the trains at night. And I'd think, "Oh but then you'd never know who Gossip Girl is."

It's better knowing, Edith said.

Of course you think so.

Dan Humphrey, the sensitive writer slash Brooklynite outsider, created the Gossip Girl blog to write himself into the story of the beautiful, popular kids.

No one in this basement is allowed to die, Tessa said.

On the TV, mentally ill teens bullied each other. Burned their dresses, poured yogurt on their shoes.

Why does the episode where Serena's brother comes out always make me cry? Edith said.

Same.

It's melodrama, Valerie said, *but it's effective melodrama. It's like*

*if someone starts playing "Good Riddance (Time of Your Life)."
We're programmed to have a feeling.*

Not a real feeling, though.

Tell us, dear Joni, what a fake feeling is.

Valerie turned in first. She had an early train. Tessa opened a second bottle of wine.

What do you think? Edith asked. *Good Christmas?*

The best. Tessa settled deeper into the couch, sliding closer to Edith. When Edith breathed in, their arms brushed. *Our own little family of freaks.*

Good of your parents to put up with us.

This was not what she meant to say.

Do you ever think about next year? Tessa's eyes slipped closed. Edith's head heavy with wine. Breathe in, the softest touch, breathe out. *You'll be writing the Great American Novel.*

If I ever so much as whisper "Great American Novel," please beat me to death with a rake.

And Valerie will be off on her Valerie adventures. Dancing with the Moscow Ballet or being a spy.

Or both. And you'll be writing your plays, saving the world.

Like a little La Bohème, *but slightly gayer.*

You mean like—

If the next word out of your mouth is "Rent" I swear to god.

Breathe in, breathe in. The warmth of a body beside you. In a pitch-dark room, Edith would know how close they were. Breathe out.

It's all—did you ever think your life would look like this?

Edith shook her head. *You?*

Yes. But I never believed it. Tessa's head on her shoulder.

Love you, Joan. Tessa made a small, sleepy sound. *You need to go to bed?*

Not yet.

Limbo. If they sat long enough, Edith would get used to the waiting. She could get used to pretty much anything.

Joni.

Yeah?

Edith looked at Tessa, or Tessa looked at Edith. Tessa moved to kiss her first.

You know you love me, the TV said. XOXO.

Back on campus, Edith tried to talk around it. *Don't overthink it, Joni,* Tessa said. Well, mistakes happen.

They were barely a year wiser in Boston. A week passed without talking it over. Only that reliable warmth, reliable joy each evening.

Okay, Tessa said over her Styrofoam clamshell of pasta. *We need to process this. What we're doing.*

Doing? Present progressive?

Don't try to grammar me through this. Seven nights of sharing a bed. Seven nights of softness. The brawl in her chest as Tessa's mouth matched her own.

Edith began, *If you want—*

Shut up for a second. The scuffed kitchen table between them. A forkful of chicken cacciatore. This was the end of something. *There's a lot I don't want to think about.*

Okay.

But if we do this, we have to accept that it might destroy our friendship. Not only ours.

More vague terms. Shouldn't they talk about what "do" and "this" meant? Edith didn't press her luck. She shoved as much garlic bread as would fit into her mouth. They'd figure out the rest later.

I believe in us, she said once she'd swallowed. *I can't imagine either of us living without the other.*

Okay, well, it might be worth stretching your precious writer's imagination, because I need you to tell me: is it worth that chance?

What a question. What impossibility. A fat stack of alternate universes to pick over in her idle hours, all facts forking from opposite possibilities. A coin flipped, a cigarette unsmoked. If it had played out another way—if they'd never spoken again after she left—it would not have been worth it. That's the absolute truth of it.

What about—I don't know how to ask this.

Tessa was gay. Tessa had dated one guy when she was fourteen and it was miserable. It didn't matter that Edith was a good and sensitive man. She was the *slightly* in their gayer *La Bohème*. She was, irreparably, a man. More forks, more coins flipped.

That's one of the things I don't want to think about.

They finished eating. Nina Simone on the stereo. The apartment decked in twilight's blue organza. Hand in hand they retreated. Shut Tessa's bedroom door as though there were something to keep out. Edith never slept in the twin bed again.

("HOW DID you get to be here? What was the moment?")

*

EDITH HAD been in love before. There'd been her high school girl-friend, the one who'd assaulted her. There'd been Ellie, the quiet chem major freshman year. There'd been books at Christmas and brunch on weekends and trips to the city for museums and shows. Inevitably, her feelings reached a limit. There were only so many mornings she could wake next to Ellie before wishing she were alone. Nights they'd made plans when she'd rather be somewhere with Val and Tess. Later in college, she'd hook up with lesser friends, and there came a moment before sleep where she'd catch herself thinking, *What if I did this for a long, long time?* That tenderness was banished by the sun. She stumbled to the bathroom to scrape the night from her tongue and wash her face before finding her real friends and a hot bagel.

What if part of me is broken, she wondered. She knew that period of early love—where every song is your song, where fires all burn twice as hot and the donut shop never runs out of your favorites on Saturday morning. Where did it go?

Did you know you talk in your sleep? Edith asked one morning. She'd spent the past hour watching Tessa's face in the velvet sun, each hair drawn in gold across the pillow. The weather was getting warmer; Tessa promised Boston would be unrecognizable after winter.

I know I used to. Her face scrunched, puffy with sleep. *What did I say?*

"*I have hands with which I, in theory, see Jeff.*"

Hard to argue with that.

Tessa picked up exotic fruits from the health food store. Plantains they'd fry and eat with vanilla ice cream. Spiny dragonfruit with insides like a poppyseed muffin. Lychee, rambutan, durian.

People say it's an acquired taste.

Oh yeah? What do they say about the smell?

They were lost in the other's gaze. Recycling piled up. Clouds of dust clotted the corners. Soup-caked dishes. What did these things matter when they could be together on the couch, reading and napping and watching Kirsten Dunst movies.

Edith's old room looked so small, so fragile. This life brought north in Tessa's car and abandoned. Sick of traffic, Tessa sold the car that winter. Easier to stay home.

The refrain of those early months: *Did you ever think your life would look like this?*

Never. Edith still didn't believe. *How long have you known?*

Not forever. But long enough. Fingertips tracing the length of Edith's hand. *I should have gotten here sooner.*

We almost did.

The softness of Tessa's skin erased any memory before this. Lying here with their legs forked together.

That was stupid, she said. *To kiss you without thinking.*

What changed?

I'm not sure. I don't care. Her eyes full of dying afternoon light. *You're so beautiful.*

Edith thought she really might be.

CHARLIE WAS the first person Edith told. On a rainy Sunday afternoon they browsed CDs at Newbury Comics. Charlie grinned at her across the shelves. *That's great, dude.*

Thanks, Chuck. Jewel cases snapped by, glimpses of cover art. *You don't think we're making a mistake, do you?*

You've both had like a million years to think about how you feel. It's what you want, right?

It is. Edith studied the back of a Fleetwood Mac album. Charlie ignored her shaking hands. *It's only that, um, I really love her.*

Aw, dude. Charlie came around the wide bins and wrapped Edith in a hug. *I'm so happy for you. And not just because Valerie's going to owe me fifty dollars.*

You guys made a bet?

No actual money's trading hands, don't worry.

Val bet against us?

Charlie waved her off. *It's a stupid standing bet from college. I doubt she remembers.* He went back to browsing; Edith misshelved the copy of *Tusk*. *It was SpringFest, everyone was wasted. We went to get food and came back and you guys were napping on the picnic blanket, curled up together. Mostly we were happy we didn't have to share our fries.* There was nothing wrong with betting on your friends' relationships; she'd made a half dozen similar

claims over the years. A shot called out of a desire for her happiness, and Tessa's. Every bet required that people divide into *for*
and *against*.

Still the nagging thought: Valerie didn't believe in them.

Look, dude, it's great. Don't sweat it. Charlie held her by the
shoulder, put *Tusk* in its proper place with his free hand. *You guys
are getting the ending everyone wants.* Only three years out from
those bar nights, asking: Why are there so many pretty girls. What is
wrong with me. *A perfect love story.*

Edith knew within five minutes when Tessa had told Valerie. Val
called her work phone.

Comp Lit department.

Oh my god you little scamp. Val's voice cut apart by wind's static.
Who knew you had it in you!

Love the confidence my friends have in me.

None of that, I'm thrilled for you both.

Thanks, Val.

Just—Her voice cut out.—*know when you'll have this happiness.*

What was that?

Enjoy it, babe. Enjoy all of it!

The six months that followed might well have been perfect, might
well have been paradise. What did the small flaws, the early seeds of
doubt matter? They had each other; that was all.

PART OF THE GENIUS OF *MERRILY WE ROLL ALONG* IS its reuse of melody. Lyrics change as the story moves backward in time, indexing the shifts in relationships. A cheesy showstopper becomes an intimate moment between friends. "Not a day goes by" moves from a cry of despair to a statement of love. The characters are not on a linear slide into hate. It's a cyclical, recursive shift. The stories that once provoked laughter now bring everyone to tears. "How does it happen? How did you get so far off the track? Why can't you turn around and go back?" The present is a consequence of all the moments that came before. No single choice, no single failure. You know what you want, you go out and get it; it's not the thing you want anymore. Not what you thought it'd be. This is the only true story wanting tells.

EDITH EXPECTED the exhibit to be a small number of forgeries tucked into some well-lit corner. Photos of the originals for comparison. A Walter Benjamin quote on the wall about the unforgeability of a work's presence in time and space. She wasn't all wrong: there was the Benjamin quote, there was a fake Rothko from the Knoedler Gallery scandal. But here was Damien Hirst's shark in a tank, recreated after the original shark rotted in its poorly mixed embalming fluid. Here were all eighteen versions of *The Disquieting Muses* that De Chirico painted over two decades. The stones Vija

Celmins made out of brass and paint, each set beside its real-world referent. Any made thing could be made again.

Tessa caught her eye as they circled the gallery, almost smirking. She was right to; how had Edith not known about this show? In her first book, men with white tents move from city to city displaying expert forgeries. There was no market for new artists, and so if one produced original work, it had to come with an invented history. The details of a new life, a new oeuvre, codified through endless repetition. Maybe there never was a Picasso, a Rembrandt, a Cézanne. They're all stories everyone has been telling for so long they forget that no such person existed.

People dismiss forgeries because they come with the wrong story. Next to the Rothko, there was an account from the rich person who'd been tricked into buying it. *Overnight, it went from being worth millions to worthless.* Edith saw the same things in it she saw in other Rothkos: the violence of day's end, the tension between explosive light and muted dark. She saw a clip of Alfred Molina playing Rothko on Broadway, platitudes given authority by the skill of his acting. If it's really worthless, she thought, give it to me. I'll give it a good home.

In the museum café after, Tessa asked everyone what their favorite reproduction was.

Well, I know what yours was. Adam forked a bit of chocolate cake into his mouth. *You looked at that shark for close to an hour.*

It's so much realer than in photos. Tessa was eating her biscotti. Edith had coffee and ibuprofen and a red velvet cupcake. *You're like, so what, it's a shark. But it looks like it could leap through the glass and thrash on the floor. Plus, I realized I'd misunderstood the title.*

What, The Impossibility of Death in the Mind of the Living?

The Physical *Impossibility of Death,* Michael corrected. *In the Mind of Someone Living.*

I'd always taken it to mean that the living can't really die. The shark stays preserved as long as society cares to keep it.

Unless you're a jackass who does a bad job of preserving your shark, Edith said. But if Hirst had done a better job, the shark wouldn't have been in the exhibit. Accident and incident conspired to make a world.

Really, though, it's saying that we can't conceive of death while alive. Pick your metaphor—it's a black box, an impenetrable veil. I was guilty of the exact thing the work names. Thinking that nothing really vanishes.

Valerie would be so mad if she could see it, Adam said. No one looked at Edith. She put down her cupcake, half-eaten.

Oh I know, Tessa said. *"If you're going to have that Goldsmiths cunt you better fucking well have Tracey Emin too. Gillian Wearing. Sarah Lucas."*

She probably would've grabbed a museum guard and demanded the curator come explain himself. "We're here to celebrate art, not marine biology."

She could be so maddening.

Never knew when to stop.

She knew, Edith said. Staring down at the tiny café plate. The smears of snowy frosting, cake crumbs like petals of a blood-red rose. None of the others really knew her, was the thing. They'd barely seen her in the years between college and her death. Edith had barely seen her. *She didn't care.*

No one said anything. No one knew if Edith wanted to say more.

Here they were, Valerie-less. What was life on a planet minus someone you'd loved? Was it life at all, or only a sham? Worthless overnight.

Do you guys ever forget? Edith said. *I do.* Such a fucking cliché. Writing a text, getting ready to call her. Any girl at a gas station swinging a plastic sack of sugar-free Monsters might be her. Sometimes she sent the texts anyway. *I wish I didn't.*

I wish I did. Tessa's voice was soft. *Every tall girl in a black coat. Every song she danced to. There's never a gap between memory and fact. Just her absence.*

We should have a toast, Adam said. *In her memory.*

This kept Edith from crying. A toast wouldn't honor her any more than a fistful of plastic flowers on a West Texas grave. They should burn down a building. They should host a demolition derby. There should be a catastrophe so large it's visible from space.

Four cups, mostly empty, came together at table's center.

To Valerie, Adam said.

To Val, Tessa said. *You jerk.*

Still leaving us behind.

VALERIE HAD been the only person Edith knew in college who wasn't rich but had a car. Her first breakup came after she disappeared for their two-week spring break, her girlfriend's ever-more frantic phone calls unanswered. She'd been working as a boat guide at Niagara Falls; *It's a break*, she insisted to her imminent ex, who was still too busy sobbing to be as angry as she would later. *What else is a break for?* The summer Edith and Tessa worked on campus, Valerie didn't visit once. You had to go to her, with her, wherever the car took her. To jazz concerts in mapless places; to amateur taxidermy museums and film festivals and fly-fishing trade shows. Val could walk into any place without paying; god forbid you stumble.

It wasn't fair that she should be buried in a single place, stuck in the parched Texan earth. It wasn't fair they'd never visited her grave. One day, Edith promised herself, she'd find the graveyard, find the stone—whatever name was on it—and take some of the grave dirt with her. Only a symbol, no matter which part of someone you took.

She'd fashion a reliquary, a silver vial hanging between her breasts. That earth going everywhere she did.

*

IT WAS raining when Michael and Adam drove them to Mount Auburn Cemetery. It seemed the only place to go. A dry run at a new kind of mourning.

I feel like we're your gay dads, dropping you off at soccer practice, Adam said.

Edith laughed. *It might help if you played something other than Peter Gabriel.*

The CD is stuck!

Why would we want to help it, Michael said. *Let's lean in.*

Rustle up some apple slices and juice boxes for you.

Now remember, kids, it's not about winning or losing.

Don't listen to Dad Two, children, Daddy One doesn't love a loser.

Daddy One only says that because of his own childhood failures on the field hockey team.

Mouse! I told you that in confidence! The car juddered toward the line as Adam shoved his partner. None of them could stop laughing.

This is really normal, you guys, Tessa said, half-breathless. *I'm definitely not gonna talk about this in therapy.*

There were more juice box jokes as the boys dropped them off. Tessa and Edith walked from the car arm in arm beneath a wide black umbrella. The laughter had subsided, leaving a tombstone void, a monument to silence.

Edith didn't want to think about what Valerie's death might mean to Tessa, to Adam. Other people's grief, like their dreams, is not very interesting unless you're its object. It was for the best there'd been no funeral; Edith would have spent the whole thing looking around for Val, Tom Sawyering in the balcony.

The rain made a gauzy curtain between them and the graves. It was easy to forget the earth was studded with bodies. Whenever Edith thought about killing herself, she thought of her body mixing with minerals and insects. All her water returning to the sky. An image peaceful enough that it brought her back to herself.

Tell me something nice, Tessa said. *Something else to pin to the moment.*

Well, why not. *I really love you, Tessa.*

Of course you do, Edie. Something else. Tell me about Texas.

Edith was still full of the past. The Orange Line out to Jamaica Plain, the lushness of the arboretum. Fire escape, cigarette in the dark, Tessa's hand on her wrist when she tripped over the railing. All those mornings she'd come home, the day's writing done, and slid into bed beside a still sleeping Tessa. Bodies trading heat beneath the sheets. In Texas there were power outages and protests. There were Seb and Treats and a twenty-four-hour coffee shop when she couldn't sleep.

I was the one who picked Texas. Val would've been happy to never go back. Don't talk about Val. *There was a part of me that did it to punish her.* Don't. The moment has passed.

Good on you, making choices. Tessa didn't need to ask: punish her for what? *You know part of me thought you'd come back here.*

I thought about it. But I'd have been chasing an old life. One we'd both left behind. Edith's elbow was getting peppered with drizzle and Tessa pulled her closer. Edith's voice edgy and small as she said, *How would you feel? If I did move back?*

I don't know. There was no surprise in it. *We're both older, Edith.*

You're older; I'm a child again. A stupid little girl with stupid little girl problems.

Yeah. I guess.

There had to be some redemption in this graveyard. She'd come back to Boston; she'd seen Tessa, and Adam, and even fucking Charlie. There was a circle that was closing. No way could it end without Val. No way could it finish without death. A body is only a few trace minerals once it's lost its numinous flare.

Is it hard? Being there without her?

I was there without her all the time.

And when she was there?

You don't want to hear about this.

What you mean is, you don't want to talk about it.

Both those things could be true. Edith had always hated how easily she cried. Standing in her doorway, watching Valerie's dark green Subaru vanish down the drive; walking in the cemetery, looking as far from Tessa as her head would turn.

Sometimes things were good, sometimes they were bad. She had a habit of vanishing when I needed her. But up until that point, she'd do anything.

I could never picture you guys together. I knew that each of you had to have changed so much for a thing like that to happen.

Edith didn't know why this was what broke her. If it had been any other place on any other day, she would have kept walking, would have found something to say to disarm Tessa like Tessa had disarmed her.

She knelt. Graveyard mud stained her tights, her too-thin black dress. There had to be a way to get this sob under control. This viscous, soppy hiccoughing that she'd dragged down into the earth. The umbrella fell from Tessa's hands as she held Edith, and they were bathed together in rain.

I'm so fucking angry, she managed.

I know, Edith, I know.

At herself. At Valerie—not for dying, but all the things before. All the things after.

Tessa pulled a handkerchief from a jacket pocket. Edith laughed snottily, made a joke about Tessa being a country dandy. *Since when do you carry a handkerchief?* But Tessa didn't rise to the bait. She didn't offer the cloth to Edith, didn't wipe the snot from her face. Only the rainwater and tears. Both soon replaced, both soon wiped away again.

Edith didn't know how to express her love for Tessa in this moment. It could have been six years ago, or ten. It could have been a hundred years in the future.

There were graves strewn with plastic flowers and piled with stones. Neither of them stood. Tessa wiped the rain from Edith's face.

The last time I saw her, Tessa said, *was at this queer lady picnic. I had no idea she was in town, but she must've known I'd be there.* Valerie went back once a year to get her hormone levels taken at a free clinic. Sometimes she stuck around. *It was the oddest thing. Everyone I was sitting with had met her before, but when she called out my name and walked over, everyone looked at me like, who's this? New lady in your life?* The rain was petering out. *I knew you guys had been dating or whatever. And I just—didn't care anymore. I'd been so frustrated with you both, more than makes sense. I really loved you, Edith, but that kind of love was a long time ago.* It took a superhuman effort for Edith to not press on this, to not ask, Did it really fade so much for you? What would've happened if I had come back? If I'd been a girl then the way I am now? *I realized that while the two of you had been living it up down south, I'd been right here with the same girls, on the same ratty picnic blanket Colleen always brought. I knew that was all correct. That nothing needed to be any other way.*

The rain paused. Edith's face was dry, or close enough.

People were going around introducing themselves—Hila, Vex, Meghan. And Val was humoring them, acting like they'd never met before. Later she'd pull out the little details she remembered like a magic trick—where their brothers lived or which stone fruits they were allergic to. But when the circle got to me, I did it too. I said, "Hi, I'm Teresa." Even though she'd called out my name. Even though we all knew she knew. The others sort of laughed it off. Val, though—I could tell it hurt her. "Hi, Teresa." That moment of ice between us. Waiting for the thaw.

She never said.

It was only a moment. She sat with us, doing the charming Valerie thing where she talks like a Katharine Hepburn movie. Valerie would have owned the moment—but only a moment. At day's end, she would have gone back to whatever floor she was crashing on, and the next morning she would leave. Tessa would still be here, and no one would ever forget they'd met her before. *It probably didn't matter to her. We might've laughed about it later. If there'd been a later.* Grief was narcissistic that way: it all ended up about you. *You ready to keep walking?*

Edith was. Her dress and tights were probably ruined. It was worth the embarrassment to feel the soft pass of the handkerchief, again and again, across her face. Tessa retrieved the muddy umbrella. They didn't need to shelter under it anymore. They still walked arm in arm.

They paused on their way to the bus stop so Tessa could catch her breath.

Sorry. Too many cigarettes.

Edith felt better than she had in a long time.

Flip your coin, Joan.

Spent it on gum.

Chew your gum, then.

Don't tell me what to do, Joni. She pulled out a green pack of Orbit, offered Edith a piece.

The bus stop was translucent with raindrops. A million little gems, distorting the world.

What should we do now? In two days, Edith would be gone. The flat spread of Texas was waiting. The strip malls, the big sky, the river.

I probably need to go home, Tessa said. *Get dry, warm up.*

Tessa's home would be plastered with silk-screened posters and photos cut from magazines. There'd be ten different plants hanging in the windows. There'd be a beautiful assortment of mugs—all the same ones she'd had six years earlier chipped with the excesses of use. She'd have the bed, the same bed, still holding little particles of Edith.

I'd love to see your place. If you'd have me.

Look at you, asserting your desires. A tiny squeeze at her biceps. *I'm proud of who you've become, Joni. I really am.*

You can just say "no," you know.

Edith. She paused—not thinking better of the question, only holding the moment before she asked it. *Are you seeing anyone back in Texas?*

There was a time Edith would've been idiot enough to interpret this as flirting. Her throat was sharp edges and sour pennies. *Not since Val.* If that counted as dating. If that counted as life. *What's her name, Tess?*

Devin.

Pretty name. Had she really thought Tessa might be as loveless as her? That they could come back together and—what? Not fall in love again. But share in something. Prove that their lives were not so far apart. She must have missed a thousand hints, a hundred tiny pauses marking elisions. *So, what, you live with her, bicycles hanging side by side on the wall, homebrew kombucha fermenting on the kitchen counter. You take cross-stitching classes and read Audre Lorde to each other in bed.*

Not exactly. Tessa did not flinch. *Devin's a guy.*

A cis guy?? Tessa looked at her. *Okay, so you sit in bed reading, what, Chuck Palahniuk.*

You're really white-knuckling that umbrella.

I hope you and Dave are real happy together, Teresa.

This isn't about you.

You were so fucking self-righteous yesterday about me and Val and for what?

Tessa fumbled her pack of cigarettes from her jacket, lighter clicking without fire. *We were both going through shit back then.*

What, yesterday? Tessa didn't humor her. The lighter sparked: click, click. *You really wanna compare? Not knowing you're a trans girl to being slightly less gay than you thought?*

Goddammit. The lighter clattered to the wet pavement and sat there like a stray bit of light. White lighters, Valerie would scold, were unlucky. *Edith, things between us were good, they were really good. It's tempting to act like they got out of control. That we passed a point of complication that we didn't know how to deal with. But they were always complicated.*

We could have worked through them.

Maybe we could have, but there was shit you needed to take care of. Edith made a sweeping gesture at her lately feminized body. *Shit you still haven't taken care of, if I'm being honest. I don't know if you remember this but we were friends—friends for a long time before we ever dated. We were better then.*

You said we were "fundamentally incompatible in a core way."

You also thought we should break up! We weren't happy, Edith.

Well at least one of us is now. In a nice, happy relationship with a guy who probably has never sucked a dick in his life.

I don't know how to spell out more clearly that you do not have a monopoly on crises of identity— And in her frustration, in returning to the symptom of that complication, she did not call her Edith, or

Joni, but by the name she'd been given at birth. A name that no one in Texas knew.

This didn't especially bother Edith. How often had she mentally referred to Adam by the wrong name? The brain was plastic, but the tectonic furrows of the past ran deep. Even Val had fucked up from time to time. The melodramatic language of "deadnaming" did nothing for her.

It was, however, extremely easy to exploit.

Fuck, Edith, I'm sorry, I didn't mean.

All right. She held out the umbrella in false sacrifice.

I'm really sorry.

A mistake. The name slip. The argument itself. Spending so many hours together and thinking some essential closeness had surpassed time, and distance, and all else the years brought.

Tessa held the umbrella in one hand, unlit cigarette in the other. Edith walked down the road without looking back. *Look, I said I was sorry.* Tessa's voice rising to keep up with the distance. *You can be mad but don't walk away.* The sky was the sort of dark that might promise more rain and might only promise sunset. Edith kept walking.

S EX HAD ALWAYS GIVEN EDITH TROUBLE. SHE NEVER
lost herself to the obliterating black box of desire. Only ever: Is
this enough? Is this too much? Sometimes she'd end up crying. Sometimes she'd tell her partner about the girlfriend who'd assaulted her,
who teased her for crying after.

In the early months, it was enough to want and be wanted. Tessa
was gorgeous and confident and hungry. There were hours in bed,
the press of body against body, meals cobbled together in the thin
hours of morning.

It was when the newness wore off that Edith began to worry. At a
party, she overheard Meghan saying, *You were practically gold-star,
what are you doing.* Heard Tessa responding, *Who fucking cares?*
And Edith wondered: don't you?

In bed, Edith drifted from the place where Tess's body and hers
met. She couldn't compete with gay girls' natural intimacy. Her amateur skill would be weighed against the countless ranks of women
who knew how to fist someone.

Joni? You with me?

Tessa above her, glistening in the lamplight. Cupping Edith's chin.

Can we change the music?

Sorry. She did. *Sondheim's not exactly mood music.*

Neither was Silver Jews, to be fair, but Edith wasn't going to
ask again.

Better?

Yeah. Tessa coaxed Edith back inside her, and both shuddered. *Only—*

Yeah?

You want this, right?

Of course I do. Warmth. Body, hand, hip, kiss. Edith was still and it was all pleasure. A shift like refocusing her eyes: it was easy to picture Tessa topping her.

Say it again, Tess.

I want this. I want you.

Keep going.

I want this.

A week later, Tessa proposed something new.

What is it?

One second. Nimble movements in the bedroom's dark. There might be nothing but the two of them. Edith might have no body at all, only an archipelago of nerves. Places made purely to take Tessa's touch.

Tessa straddled her knee. The silicone cock bobbing over her leg.

What do you think? Tessa could pull off a seductive tone but couldn't hide her uncertainty. *Do you want me to fuck you?*

Early on, Edith never had a real answer about what she wanted: she liked normal things. She didn't want to be hit, or choked, or pissed on. If she'd been less self-conscious, she would have said, I want to make love to you. I love you, Tess.

Yes, she said, and meant it. *Yes, Tessa, fuck me.*

It left her sore and throbbing. Wiping herself down in the bathroom after, Edith lost her sense of self. For a second, it was Tessa standing there, Tessa whose body she lived in.

(Stupid boy. Can't let your girlfriend fuck you without losing your masculinity.)

Then there was the pregnancy scare. By the time Edith asked, it

STILL LIFE 87

had been seven weeks since Tessa's last period. *I didn't want to mention*, Tessa said.

Should we be worried? The power of that *we*. Holding them. All their love and all their fear.

I've never been super regular. Fingers drawn across the hair on Edith's chest. *Maybe we should be better about condoms, yeah?*

Edith would have mistakenly called herself careful. What she lacked in control, she made up for in precise timing. So relentless and imperturbable was their desire for each other that all seemed riskless. Theirs was a story of odds overcome, not mistake and pain and blood.

Yeah, you're right.

Two more weeks passed. They didn't buy a pregnancy test; there was safety in not knowing. An impossible future: walks through the Common, hiking in the mountains, infant slung across her chest. Words without referent: my wife, my daughter. Who could dream such a thing?

Every time she reached for Tess's hand, every time they woke up pressed against each other, no matter that they kissed with the same fervor and professed their love every day—still that refrain: she wouldn't have to deal with this if she were with another woman.

And there were moments, out in the world, when Tessa was the first to drop her hand. That slight distance between them as they walked, no shoulder pressed to Edith's own. No arm draped across her shoulders. No kiss at parting. Edith knew the same refrain must run through Tessa's head.

Tessa wasn't pregnant. Edith had the idiot luck of countless men before her, and after. How horrible to find, then, that the worrying did not stop.

*

WHY DON'T you sign up for a community writing class? Tessa asked one night. She'd been at lesbian billiards late with Sapphic Somerville. *It'd be a good way to make friends.*

They're really expensive.

Joni, I love you, but how much do you spend on books each month?

A normal amount. The spare bedroom had become an ad hoc extension of Edith's library. Tessa called it the Piles, like a haunted fantasy locale. *You don't need to worry about me.*

Boston was not the worst place to become a writer. There were the bookstores, the esteemed faculty in the schools. Edith assumed she'd find community between the book clubs and readings and the packed shelves. She was still waiting to find it. She pecked away at her little stories: a man dated death, a horde of insects invaded a town. All her Puritan industry became shadow-flat words on the page and more empty hours in their apartment.

I don't worry, I only want you to be happy.

Thanks, Mom.

Hey, no psychosexuality at the dinner table.

Edith didn't lack friends. She and Charlie got a drink every couple weeks. And there was Celeste, a UMass grad student they'd met at trivia. Sometimes she and Celeste would go to a bookstore, an experience bogged down by Celeste talking about Early Modern theater and performance theory.

They were friends, but they weren't her people.

But Tessa had made a life for herself. Spring's thaw brought her out of their apartment cloister and into friends' embrace—all a little softer, a little paler than they'd been in the fall. For a while, Edith enjoyed the solitude Tessa's outings brought, but she'd gone on living as though it were winter.

One afternoon, she caught Tessa's eyes, magnified by her makeup mirror. She was getting ready for another meetup.

What if I came with you?

Tessa's eyes didn't leave the mirror. Highlighter, eyeliner, shadow. *You hate hiking.*

It's not real hiking. There's nothing larger than a hill around here.

I don't want you to get stuck having a bad time. You sulk—you know you do, Joni, don't try to deny it.

Only to signal I'm ready to go.

Believe me, you don't need to signal. It's very clear when you're done.

Tess frowned, scrubbed makeup from her eyes. She patted them dry, reapplied.

So that's a no, then.

What if we got dinner with Colleen and Agnes next week? Agnes was the painfully shy girl Colleen was dating. She flinched when you said her name.

You're always telling me to meet new people.

Yes, but these are my people.

You mean gay.

You can say dykes, Joni. I empower you.

Do they treat you differently now you're bisexual? Tessa smirked but didn't answer. Edith knew she still thought of herself as gay. *If you're too embarrassed to be seen by your cool gay friends with your* boyfriend *you can say—*

Hold on. Eyes severe with liquid liner. She called Edith by her name—her given name. A child in trouble. *Don't try. How many times have you met my friends.*

You always call me your partner.

You want to be demoted? Slampiece? Piece of trim? What's your preferred euphemism?

Just say "boyfriend," Tess. Give it a try. If you burst into flames, I'll throw myself on the fire to put it out.

Dear boy of mine, I love you. My friends love you. But this isn't your place.

Yeah, yeah.

Tessa's eyes caught Edith's, and Edith did not hold her gaze. Each knew the rhythm of relationships. The glorious Golden Age could only last so long. But hadn't Edith dreamed this might be history's first exception?

Now you're sulking, Tessa said. *Where do you want to go?*

That night, their fight more or less forgotten, Edith told Tessa, *I think I'm gonna apply to grad school. There are a lot of good writing programs around here.* The applications were due in a couple of months; she wasn't sure she meant it.

But Tessa, being a considerate partner, and already wondering if there was a logical endpoint to their love, said, *That's great, Joni.*

T HE RAIN WAITED TO RETURN UNTIL EDITH WAS AT Adam and Michael's. The rush and roar filled the evening air as she stepped inside, and Adam looked up from the couch, startled.

She told you, he said. *You wanna talk about it?*

Edith crumpled onto the couch beside him. Adam set aside his computer and put his arms around her. She wished she were smaller. The boy-smell of his shirt, the soft hair of his arms. It was good to be enveloped.

Do you still have feelings for her?

Not like that.

But?

I feel so stupid. Edith shook her head. *Why the fuck did I leave, Adam?*

If you stayed, you'd always wonder what would've happened if you'd gone.

That's a bad reason.

Doors close, Edie. That's part of getting older. Do you want some tea?

Don't get up.

Okay. Each pressed harder against the other. Old bones scraping inside them. Edith wished Val were here, were anywhere besides buried in the dry Texas ground. The breezy affect when she answered the phone. The way she'd say No fucking way when Edith told her that Tessa was with a guy. They'd crack jokes about him being another closeted trans girl. It would lose its importance. Their col-

lective history would be sieved for relevant anecdotes and they'd talk
until one of them saw the sun rise, and then they'd leave it all behind.

If she answered her fucking phone, of course.

Adam said, *You know how shitbag transphobes always talk
about transition being "irreversible damage"?*

We're the transgender craze seducing their daughters.

*I mean obviously I want to go Judith-and-Holofernes on them
but I think they're essentially right about it being irreversible. Even
detransitioning only layers a new life over the old. You carry traces
of every earlier self. It's not a bad thing, though. It's life.*

You only say that 'cause you pass.

Maybe. If you could be cis, would you?

Of course not.

They stayed wrapped together. There'd been too few of these
moments in their friendship. How much closer they'd come in the
years they lived a thousand miles apart.

*If that doesn't work for you, how's this: remember the girl I dated
at the end of college? Emily?* Edith did. She'd almost taken the girl's
name when picking a new one. *I thought I was going to marry her. I
had this whole image of our life together, living in Park Slope with a
Westie and matching jobs at CUNY. We'd be the cool dyke professors who'd have all our gay students over for dinner and light gossip.*

Why did you break up? I'm not sure I ever knew.

Why else? Something was wrong. Edith had left a dark stain on
Adam's clothes. Sparse tears and the rain she'd carried in. *We mostly
make the choices we need to. I don't care if that sounds stupid,
because it's the truth.* He squeezed her, hard, and stood. *I'm making
tea either way, are you sure you won't have some?*

Edith closed her eyes and curled into the warm place Adam left
behind. This couch that was her temporary home. *Sure*, she said.
That'd be nice.

M ANY THINGS STAYED GOOD IN THEIR SEVENTEEN months of dating.

There were weekday evenings up late, marathoning monster movies and romcoms, curled on the couch with every part of their bodies close as could be. Too much popcorn on the stove.

You know, Edith said, *I feel bad for Robot Dracula. He never asked to be a robot or a dracula.*

That's fair, but he did disembowel a math teacher.

They'd find each other's eyes across crowded parties. Pass a smile like a kind of secret. There were all the keys to the world they cut together—inside jokes, fragmentary phrases. They'd had those as friends but now each took on more weight. Their loss would be greater.

At Tessa's birthday dinner, Meghan accosted them about the Joan/Joni thing. *It's so weird.* Edith and Tessa laughed and offered no answer. It would sound thin and silly if they explained: Joan Mitchell, Joni Mitchell, Joan Baez. It wasn't anything if you hadn't been there. Some things needed to belong to just the two of you.

There were all the pains and pleasures of being a person. Edith figured out, more or less, how to ask for what she wanted in bed and, more or less, how to take it. They talked through their fights without raised voices or dramatics.

Do you think, Tessa asked, *we might not listen to Prince during sex? He's awfully corny, isn't he?*

But something did not work. A resistance to public affection. A reliance on *partner*. Tessa kept going to gay social spaces.

I mean, you're not really a dyke.

Oh my god, you sound like Meghan.

That shut her up. But she wasn't imagining Tessa's new distance during sex. Less eager and less responsive.

Hey, she said, *isn't being uptight and distracted my thing?*

Sorry, Joni, I'm only tired.

Edith didn't miss sex much when they weren't having it. Tessa was so beautiful and warm and lovely that it was enough for Edith to kiss her, to thread her fingers through her lover's hair. Its absence wouldn't matter if not for fear of what it meant.

Valerie had camped out for a month at a queer co-op in Cleveland. She was working as a night watchwoman at the art museum, waking around the time Edith got off work. Edith walked home, enjoying the crisp New England air as they chatted.

I can't get past it, she told Val. *Like, really? I'm the guy you give up being gay for.*

I'm politically neutral in this. You know you're being too hard on yourself, right?

You're the one who told me not to pursue her.

What do you want, babe? I was wrong. The hissing and spitting of Valerie's coffee machine in the background. *I mean you did date a whole mess of lesbians in college.*

I only dated one, the other two were just sex.

Wow, really?

This is what I'm saying!

You know, babe, sometimes I wonder. Valerie yawned. Her housemate's dog whined for food. *How about I come visit? Moss, Lexi, and Barn are looking for a new housemate anyway.*

One of your housemates is named Barn?

It was supposed to be "Bran" but the clerk's office messed up. Turned out he liked it better that way.

Valerie had stayed away since Edith and Tess got together. It was probably weird for her, the shift in dynamic. Having her there would be wonderful. A neutral observer.

All right. See you in four to six business weeks.

Edith had submitted all her grad school applications by the time Valerie visited. Places dotted across New England and the mid-Atlantic—only a train ride or Megabus between them and Boston. Almost at random, in the final week of December, she picked the school in Alabama as a sort of safety. Nowhere was safe, though, not really.

The three of them celebrated Edith's accomplishment. She blushed when the girls toasted her. *I might not get in anywhere.*

You'll get in, Tessa said.

I can't believe you want to do more school.

Don't worry, once I have a master's I'll be twice as annoying.

They feasted on buttered rolls and squash soup. There was a zucchini salad and meringues and a book-shaped marzipan Val had brought. *You can get away with being annoying when you're famous,* she said.

I'm not going to be famous. She blushed harder.

Sure you are. Tessa reached for her hand. *Look at that face.*

Morning found Edith shoveling the sidewalk while Tessa slept. Valerie joined her in the ankle-deep snow.

How's the old room treating you?

I'm going to trip over all your books and break my neck.

Well, it'll make a great story at your funeral.

Edith loved the snow-packed city. The freedom to stay home. The world shut down and quiet. A reminder of her and Tess's first days.

If you kick the shovel, you'll break up that pack ice.

You're welcome to take a turn. Nothing from Val but a wide grin. She scooped up twin fistfuls of snow and packed a snowball. *What are you using all those farm muscles for?*

Mostly winning Lesbian Fight Club.

Edith's shoveling did not slow. *You are not in a lesbian fight club.*

Well, not anymore.

"Then Lesbian Alexander wept, for there were no lesbians left to conquer." Silver powder shone as it fell. *I feel like I have no idea what you've been up to.*

You've been busy.

I hope that's not it. Edith never wanted to be someone so absorbed by love that she ignored everything else. She was a man of few passions, but friendship was among them. *Is that all we're gonna get? Three years of school together, the time before and the time after only a shadow?*

Oh you're so fucking silly. I'm here now. Valerie insisted the untold things were not worth telling. Her own boyhood might as well have been a movie she'd seen once, late at night and broken by commercials. The cross-shaped scar was like her Texas accent—rarely apparent, quickly dismissed. *Poor boy,* she said, *all swept up in the romance of a lifetime. Then the cracks begin to show and you need Auntie Valerie to come shore them up.*

Now Edith did stop. She tried to lean on the shovel and the shovel leaned away. *Are you actually mad at me? I can't tell.*

I don't get mad, least of all at you, babe.

So?

The snowball became icy in her hands. A beautiful, almost translucent world. *Do you remember that eighties dress that Tessa wore to every party junior year?*

I thought it was from the fifties.

It only looked like it was. We all used to dress in the thirty-year cycle of nostalgia.

I remember she wore it to pieces. The hem got tattered and a tailor took it in. But the cloth—red and patterned in magnolia blossoms—became threadbare. She didn't remember whose idea it had been to throw the dress into the year-end bonfires. People threw in things besides the intended notebooks and exams: photos, love letters, posters for films they'd come to loathe. Tessa, Valerie, and Edith had cut the dress into thirds; the threadless flowers bloomed with flame and all that remained after was the image of light.

Exactly. Clothes don't do you any good hanging in your closet. But wearing them is how they degrade.

She's been more careful since, to be fair. The shovel scraped asphalt. A long tear in the city's silence. *I never see her wear out clothes anymore.*

Val, happy at last with her snowball, tossed it at the upper windows to wake up Tessa.

She never found another dress she liked so much.

That night, Valerie showed them pictures from her travels. Here was a library where she'd worked digitizing books. Here was a view from the top of a water tower, two smiling out-of-focus people caught in the camera flash. Here was a bowling alley engulfed in flames. Silhouetted figures watched while great sprays of water arced through the air. *The guy who owned it wanted someone to burn it down,* she said. *He was going to be out of town as an alibi.*

Did you do it?

No, it burned down on its own. A grin. *He didn't have an alibi, so no insurance.*

In bed, waiting for sleep to come, Tessa turned over. *Do you think her stories are true?*

Why wouldn't they be?

A million reasons. To make her life seem less sad. To justify the way she lives. To spark envy.

Do you envy her?

I *don't.* Tessa rolled toward the bedroom door. The thinnest light came through its cracks: a nightlight so they wouldn't stumble in the winter dark. *Do you think she really makes money doing all those things? Can you see her in a library?*

Feel like we're going in circles here, Joan.

Tessa yawned; Edith felt very awake. *She'd be good at sex work, I think.*

What does that mean? Because she's trans?

She's good at giving people what they think they want. Tessa's eyes stayed shut tight. *Wouldn't you pay money to sleep with her?*

Edith cornered Valerie on the day she left. She was packing while Tessa loaded the car. *So, what do you think?*

Neatly folded sweater skirts, turtlenecks, socks balled into their pairs. Her coat spread across the bed like an expiring angel. There really were too many books in the spare room—Edith couldn't close the door. The room had never felt like hers, even at the start.

The folding went on.

Val?

I can't tell you anything you don't already know.

That's not very inspiring.

It's not meant to be. Valerie zipped her suitcase closed. Half her worldly possessions in a beaten Samsonite. She crossed over mountains of books to hug Edith. *Whatever happens you'll be okay. I love you.*

Love you too. Why had she thought Val would help?

What's Winnicott say? "The breakdown you fear is the breakdown that's already happened"?

Oh good, so it's all uphill from here.

All downhill, *babe. That's the easy way.*

Later, Edith would think about how Valerie's first visit had inaugurated her relationship with Tessa. How less than a week passed before Tessa, her dinner untouched, said, *I think we need to talk about the future.* She would think about Winnicott, whom she'd never read, and how just because a breakdown has happened doesn't mean it's passed. But for those six days, she'd try to enjoy herself. Bake brownies, make lumpen snowmen. Bring Tessa morning lattes from Peet's. Sit up late reading shoulder to shoulder. Wishing she might never get into grad school and these days might never end. Close, closer, closing.

EVEN IN THE MAGICAL SPACE OF MUSICAL THEATER, Sondheim's characters are never made happy by the things they want. They are obsessives in pursuit of revenge, or art, or money, or a child.

Into the Woods exists in a world of overlapping fairy tales: Jack's beanstalk, Cinderella's slipper, Rapunzel's tower. Red's collision with grandmother and wolf. It's Sondheim's additions to these—a childless baker and his wife—that draw the stories together. They collect a totem from each so they might undo a witch's curse and have a child.

From the start, the baker's wife longs for more than the simple domesticity she's been given. When she runs into Cinderella fleeing from her prince's ball, the baker's wife grills her about the prince: Is he handsome, charming, clever, passionate? Is he everything Cinderella ever wanted?

"How can you know what you want till you get what you want," Cinderella asks, "and you see if you like it?"

This proves predictably fateful. By show's end, half the ensemble will be dead. Cinderella's prince reveals himself to be a cad, lusting after an unseen Sleeping Beauty and seducing the baker's wife in the woods.

Still. The final line of the first act is "And happy ever after." The curtain falls and rises again, proving this untrue. In the second act, this final line is repeated, but before the lights go, Cinderella's voice rings out, defining all the show's joys and tragedies: "I wish—"

Wishing is dangerous, wishing is unstoppable. It doesn't matter whether or not it's better to get what you wish for; you go on wishing.

EDITH SPENT the first part of the next morning at Peet's Coffee, jumping from scene to scene of *The Odyssey*. She wasn't sure she'd ever read it straight through, only absorbed its story in this fractured way. What was the book of *The Odyssey* anyway? One of the poem's endless variations. If there is no true version of a thing, then there can be no false ones.

The clientele at Peet's was either eighteen or sixty. There was the roar and hiss of the espresso machine, there were teens scrolling through TikTok. Edith would rather dwell on any other life. Any conversation but her and Tessa's. She'd rather lose herself in climbing or in a bookstore or find a guy on Grindr to fuck her until she forgot the boundaries between sexualities.

We don't get to choose what we think about.

For instance: their growing awkwardness, changing behind closed doors.

For instance: Tessa saying, *I don't think we should do this anymore.* And when Edith asked why, Tessa said, *Don't ask me that. Do you* think we should?

For instance: Edith saying, *No, you're right.*

What did it mean that Tessa was dating a man? More than dating—living with him. What did it mean about their breakup, and the path Edith had taken to transitioning, and what might have come if she'd never gone.

You make decisions and you live out their consequences. It takes years for an insight to arrive. Every choice made with incomplete information—was that fair?

Adam's voice: *That's life.*

It's a good thing Zoloft kept her from wanting to kill herself.

HEARTBREAK, LIKE JOY, MAKES SPACE FOR CLICHÉ; you run out of clever ways to say things.

Something hasn't been working for a while now.

We'll talk about it, we'll work it out.

Work what out? It's not a math problem you can logic your way through.

They slept in the same bed, they had sex, they professed their love every single day. But it was all flawed. It wasn't only that Tessa was gay. There was Edith's inability to make a life for herself here. The pressure of their pre-romantic history.

What do you want, you wanna call it quits?

I don't want that but that is what's going to happen.

We're not living in a fucking Greek tragedy, Teresa. We get to make choices. No one's making us not get married.

You'll go off to grad school and that'll be the end. It's clean that way.

And what if I don't get in? What then?

I don't know! Tessa was crying. Edith was crying.

One by one, letters had come rejecting her from writing programs. Edith spent eight hours a day refreshing her email. She answered every spam call in case it was the call of congratulations.

Even Meghan, when Edith ran into her at CVS, could not be brought to gloat. *Tessa is really hurting,* she said. *She didn't eat anything at lunch the other day.* Edith tried to hide the box of condoms she was buying, afraid Meghan would snark her for it. *I hope you'll do the right thing, my guy.*

An insane thing to say!! Edith was always trying to do the right thing. If Meghan knew of a magic fortune-telling machine that could print—ideally on a small, portable scrap of paper—what the right thing was, Edith would happily be pointed toward it! But Meghan was already gone and Edith was left in CVS with her box of condoms, feeling very much like someone who had already been broken up with.

Edith was waitlisted at the Alabama school. She went walking on her lunch break, pacing until the universe provided.

Tessa was more angry than upset. *You can't sit around waiting for me to fix your life!*

I'm not asking you to!

One of us has to, Joni. Where would you be without me? She meant it literally; it would've been easier to answer metaphorically.

You're right.

About what?

About all of it. No one was crying now. Eventually you had to stop.

Good things kept going. They read on the couch with their legs entwined. They played Magnetic Fields songs on Tessa's guitar. They made French toast on the weekends and made out at rooftop parties.

They were walking home one night when the news came: she was off the waitlist. She was going to Alabama.

Oh shit. Edith held her phone at arm's length. *There it is.*

Tess exploded with congratulations. Hugged her, kissed her, kissed her again. Sincere in her pride, her love for Edith and her hopes for the future. But it would be a separate future. That had been decided.

CHARLIE'S APARTMENT WAS CLOUD-COLORED CUR-
tains, snake plants in the windows. Photos tacked to the wall:
him and Polly in Iceland, in Croatia, in Greece. There were the things
she had not imagined, too. Space rewritten, fantasy forgotten: two
alphabetized bookshelves stretching to the ceiling; the Rauschenberg
print over the TV. Papers strewn around the room: printed sheets
and legal pads and loose leaves with tattered spines. The calico cat,
Ari, lazing in a deep window.

Edith! Charlie hugged her. He was wearing a sleeveless shirt.
Sorry about the heat, we don't control the furnace. Polly, Edith.

It's so good to meet you. Polly was shorter than she looked in
photos, her dark hair pinned up. *I've heard great things.*

So you've been lying to her?

*Don't worry, I'm well ready to talk shit when you're gone. You
still owe me fifty dollars from when we saw Vampire Weekend.*

In the kitchen was sourdough, smoked salmon, cucumbers. A
cream-colored spread. *I've gotten really into sandwiches since working at home,* Charlie said as he sliced the bread. *The humble sandwich is a tool of infinite flexibility.*

Edith, how has your time in Boston been? Polly asked. *Has it been
strange being back?*

It has and it hasn't. Had anyone else asked her that? *Everything
seems the same but I know it can't be—so I'm left trying to figure out
what's changed. It's like a spot-the-differences puzzle with only one
image. I guess I've changed a lot.*

Charlie said, *Maybe not as much as you think.* Edith must have made a face, because he hastened to add: *You look super different, I mean. But you're very clearly still you.*

The sandwich was delicious. The sauce—an aioli? Edith had never mastered what an aioli was—added a softness to the salmon, a creaminess beneath its delicate smoke.

What would life be, loving a boy who made you food like this every day.

Polly finished eating first, her plate immaculately clean. She gulped down her seltzer and, as if she'd been racing to this question, said, *What was Charlie like in college?*

I'm sure you've heard plenty of it from him.

He doesn't talk about it much.

You know about the dancing?

Oh, Charlie said, *already with the character assassination.*

Polly side-eyed her husband. *I know a version of it.* Charlie, cross-faded, picking some pretty girl out of a party's crowd to coerce her into swing dancing. *I still can't believe you know how to swing dance.*

I don't. Charlie looked very seriously at his sandwich. *That's what made it so weird.*

He was really good. Swinging people through his legs, kicking in perfect time. Everyone was impressed.

Aw, don't be embarrassed, love. She took his hand. A tiny intimacy, a familiarity with his body like the familiarity with her own.

I always told him, look man, some people have seizures and wake up speaking dead languages. At least yours is useful.

Did you have any hidden talents, Edith?

All my talents are hidden.

No, you did, you had the thing about hanging out of windows.

Oh god.

Charlie rubbed sweat from his palms. *See, Edith was always trying to get people to dare her to dangle out of upper-story windows.*

One time!

Three, at least. I have photos to prove it somewhere.

It had only ever been a game of chicken. An empty threat, a way to force her friends to prove they cared for her.

Ari sniffed their empty plates for salmon. Edith asked questions about their life together. They'd met on a group tour of Iceland. *Just the two of us and fifteen retirees*, Charlie said. After everyone was asleep, they'd gotten drunk on brennivín and snuck into a hot spring.

Polly grinned. *Charlie* insisted *we'd see the aurora.* Was it possible to be charmed by memories of the person you'd been so recently? Did marriage change you the way movement, graduate school, transition did? *"Odin will bless our union!"*

No swing dancing, though, thank god.

It was an improbable love, one that could only be god-given, aurora or no. The sort of story that belonged between scenes of a Nora Ephron movie. Were there dozens—hundreds—of people out there living like this?

Well, we paid for it quickly. Polly scratched Ari behind the ears. *Or Charlie did.*

We couldn't find our clothes. Charlie ran around the Icelandic night, teeth chattering so hard he thought they'd shatter. In the end, he'd run back to the hotel and claimed a reindeer skin to wrap around them both.

He let me stay in the water. A perfect gentleman.

She lied about seeing the aurora when I came back. "It was so incredible! You missed it!"

I did not!

Don't believe her, Edith.

The stories that made up a relationship. The rehearsed moves, the little tics. Was Edith charmed? By heterosexuality? That didn't seem right.

She'd thought more than once that Charlie could be trans. People in college thought he was gay, or at least bi, because he dressed well and did theater and sometimes wore fishnets at parties. People would've found his transitioning less surprising than Edith's. He'd never find out now.

Edith's life could've looked like this—if she'd never left, if she'd never become a girl. She, too, would have the money to go on package tours to expansive Nordic paradises. She would have a beautiful house and a beautiful wife and not care how she'd gotten there.

Had it been worth it? Any of it?

They asked questions about life in Texas. They talked about books she and Polly had read and the dating shows everyone watched. (*The moment they do a gay* Bachelorette, Edith said, *I will murder someone to be on it.*) Ari took all the petting Edith could give.

She forgot to ask Polly about her book. Didn't think to sign it until she was on her way to Adam's class. Would have doubted the pair owned it at all, except she'd found it immediately on entering their apartment, at the top of the second shelf.

ADAM'S CLASS was full of upperclassmen English majors. Edith recognized the blue-haired girl from her reading, the one with the Bible question. Some had printed a scanned excerpt of her book.

I figured to start you could talk a little about how you ended up being a writer. Adam wore a tweed jacket that fit him perfectly. He'd greeted each student by name. Would Edith ever be as suited to anything as Adam was to the classroom? *I've known Edith a long time,* he told the class, *and the whole time she had her eye on the writing life.*

Yeah, but being a writer is the least remarkable thing about me. Laughter from the kids. *I grew up in a house with two English teachers and a dozen packed bookshelves. My father used to read aloud from the boring parts of Moby-Dick to help me fall asleep.*

*It would be way more interesting if I'd become a particle physicist,
or a plumber, or tried to kill a president. But instead I'm a girl who
writes.* Edith had had a version of this conversation so many times,
it was easy to slip into autopilot. *At this point, I think it'd literally
kill me to stop. I mean, how many of you want to be writers?* All but
two students raised their hands. *Why?*

A boy kept his hand raised. *It feels like the egg riddle from*
The Hobbit. *"A box without hinges, key, or lid" with golden
treasure inside.*

Yeah, Edith said. *Egg treasure, sure.*

People offered other answers. Variations on a theme of art
and truth.

*Yeah, see, for me I have to write to fix myself. Everything in my
head is this big sloshing mass of liquid all the time. Writing freezes
it. Makes it less disruptive to carry around, if harder to see through.
You learn something and you give something up.*

Here she was, surrounded by bright young fantasies of the future.
In an hour she'd go back into the grayness of the day; in six hours or
a week or a year none of them would remember her. This was what
she had instead of love. Idioms and axioms. Knowledge she rou-
tinely found and lost by putting together sentences. She knew that if
you'd asked her at twenty-four to give up love for writing, she would
have reluctantly agreed. Children are fucking idiots.

The blue-haired girl raised her hand. *So what did writing* Someday *teach you?* Hers was the only copy in the room.

That I'm afraid of endings. No laughter this time. Edith met
the students' eyes one by one. More of them were trans than she'd
first noticed. Kids who'd been on hormones since high school. Kids
who'd maybe get to feel normal. *Not the endings of books. It's very
easy to be cynical, though, about everything.* At least she was getting
away from her stock answers. *You guys, many of you, are going to
graduate with a thesis about Eliot or H. D. or whoever and never*

look at it again. You'll get tech jobs designing UX, whatever that is, or doing tax law for the Koch family. Mostly our ambition outstrips our talent. We don't get to be geniuses if we get to do anything at all. We give up a normal life and drag twenty-five boxes of books from apartment to apartment and we never read Foucault. And you know who's really happy? People content to sit at home watching network sitcoms and getting food out five nights a week.

That's what you learned by writing a book? the girl asked. *That you'd be better off if you hadn't?*

What I learned writing a book is the same thing I learned becoming a girl: you still have to wake up every day and be the person you are. And now you don't have the promise of being fixed by some future choice you've been waiting to make. One hand turning over and over in the air as though in the final act of a failed magic trick. The other dead on the table's anonymous plastic. *So you keep on searching for new things, or waiting for the old things to work in ways they never have, and then one day you're twenty-nine years old and your ex-girlfriend is calling you to tell you that your other ex-girlfriend—if she counts, if she ever loved you in a way that matters—has died.*

Okay, Edith, Adam said, just short of reassuring. *Let's try to stay on topic.*

Sorry, sorry. Maybe if she had a comically large drink from Dunkin' Donuts, she'd have something to do with her mouth besides talk. *It's just that, you're absolutely never going to know if you've done the right thing or not. Maybe some people are lucky enough to not worry about it but maybe that's naïveté. Do you guys know the Greek concept of kairos?*

They all sat up straighter, happy to have a solvable problem.

A decisive moment for action, a boy said. *The turning point in the still world.*

A place where things might have gone another way if you decided differently.

Yeah, Edith said. *And if you write, then you can at least pretend that you know when those moments arrive. You can map out a plot and make sense of the world, take godhood over the lives of some innocent creatures. You can be a psychopath about it and no one, not even the fiction editor at the* New Yorker, *can stop you.*

I don't want to tell you that this is the best your lives are ever going to be, she went on. *If I thought I'd reached the best part of my life by now I'd straight up walk into traffic. But most of you— most of you—will not have the sort of love that songs are written about, and you will not do anything that lasts. You will live a small, still life in a small, still city and someday soon a combination of apocalyptic firestorm and plague will probably kill everyone you love.* They were all watching her. Some may even have been smiling. Edith felt depleted, out of breath. *It turns out that idea really scares me. Makes me want to believe in something else. And I guess that's what I learned, blue-haired girl, in writing this book. That wanting to believe isn't actually enough. Everyone but you is living a rom- com life. Your exes will all find people less fucked up than you to love and you'll go home and keep writing because it's all you know how to do.*

My name is Thea, said the blue-haired girl.

Sorry Thea, I'm not usually this honest.

It wasn't honesty at all. All of these kids had a better handle on their shit than Edith ever had. Or no—she'd had a handle on her shit when she was their age too. She knew exactly what kind of life she would have, the sort of woman she'd marry, the sort of man she'd be. A perfect, glistening middle-class existence stretching out toward the horizon line. The spell of heterosexuality, where every kairotic moment advertised itself in blinking neon. But if she were one of these kids she'd have transitioned early, and Tessa would still love her, and Valerie wouldn't be dead. Coffee would taste better and the War on Terror would have wrapped up.

Like I said, I'm scared of endings. I'm scared of what will happen when this class is through. I'm scared of how the fuck you live in the world when it keeps on getting worse. I don't know how to deal with the death of someone important to me, and, you know, I might as well get used to it. It had been too late, by the time Val died, to fictionalize it in *Someday*, to process it through her trans astronauts. Instead she had an ending tinged with hope, now ringing false. *Her name was Valerie*, Edith said, after a stretch of silence. *I hope no one you love ever dies.*

Okay. Adam had withdrawn. Edith had the absurd desire to hide her face in his lap. *Let's maybe read from the excerpt, shall we?*

When class ended, Thea asked Edith to sign her book. *You know, your writing has a lot more hope in it than you give off.*

I'm glad. To Thea, she wrote. I promise I'm not always like this. *The book is smarter than I am.*

You believe better things are possible.

Sure I do, Edith lied.

Adam and Edith walked back to his office. She couldn't believe she hadn't cried, still wasn't crying. There was only the lingering, manic energy.

Guess they're unlikely to forget that anytime soon, Adam said.

I'm sorry, Adam.

You don't have to apologize, they loved it. A writer having a breakdown before their eyes. They've all read Foucault, you know.

Oh good, that'll save them.

They passed through the cold, from one building to another. How novel, having class in a real city. There was so much else you could be doing.

What's the matter with you, Edith?

Your guess is as good as mine.

I mean it. Why aren't you talking to me?

Are you mad at me?

And fucking talk to Tessa too, while you're at it.

Who said anything about Tessa.

Oh my god, Edith.

Look, you brought me here. You should've known what you were in for.

It was the only way to get you to fucking visit! It's been six years, Edie, and we all love you. Only you would turn being loved into a crisis. Edith could think of at least one other person who would, but of course she was dead. *You've been here for days, you've had time alone with me and time alone with Tessa and time with all of us together when any of us might have talked through whatever bullshit you were feeling and instead you just, fucking whatever, self-isolate in your own private Texas of the mind. Moping and mourning and feeling sorry that the world has to bear the weight of your soul.*

I'm sorry.

Don't be sorry, goddammit. Adam swatted at her. *Mope if you gotta but be honest when you're moping. I'm going to worry about you so much more now.*

You don't need to worry.

You're doing it again! I can see you doing it right now. They'd reached his office door. Adam blocked the way forward. *You need to call Tessa,* he said. *I'll see you at home.*

And what was she supposed to say? Hey, sorry I'm having sort of a crisis re: your sexuality and my personal history, could you explain yourself to me?

Okay, Edith said, *you're right. About all of it.*

I love you, you asshole. Nothing has to be like this.

Yeah.

Adam turned to unlock his door. Tweed coat across his shoulders. So handsome and serious. They'd known each other for such a long time.

Adam?

Yeah?

Are you mad at me?

Jesus Christ, Edith.

Both laughed.

Sorry I'm like this, she said. *I love you too.*

THERE WAS SOMETHING PERFECT IN THIS GRADUAL ending. No question now of when the end would come. Edith said, *Like* Before Sunrise, *only very slow.*

They made plans: things to watch, places to go, more than could ever be done in the remaining months. They watched every David Lynch movie in a long weekend, dozed in the glow of Laura Dern's face. They had sex on top of their building. A hundred lives going on in the dark below, and the nearly invisible stars above, and the two of them, pressed together between, hoping they wouldn't cry.

Edith registered for classes. She found a place to live in Tuscaloosa. She called her parents about the move and her mother said, *Not exactly closer to home, is it?* It was all make-believe. No one could uproot their life like this. No one could abandon everything they knew. No decision had been made.

Sorry about all this, babe. The call of buzz saws in the back. Valerie was working in a theater scene shop in Oregon. *You're doing the right thing.*

Says who?

Breaking up is never the wrong thing. And at least this way you can stay friends.

Could they? They'd had so many conversations about the future on their couch that Edith was beginning to have a Pavlovian response to it, tearing up every time she sat down.

We need a clean break, Tessa said. *You've been such a big part of my life.*

I still want to be.

But we can't pretend like nothing's happening. There'd be some period of not talking. Neither knew how long they might need.

I don't understand why you guys can't stay together, Charlie said. They were eating dumplings downtown.

It's not that simple, Chuck.

Why not? He ate his dumpling like a corndog, speared on a chopstick. *Because of the gay thing? That's not a real issue.*

Edith fumbled hers to her mouth. Charlie's methods were effective but embarrassing. *How can that possibly not be an issue.*

It's an excuse, dude. You're both so scared about what'll happen between you that it's easier to call it quits. If it were a straightforward problem of sexuality, you'd never have gotten together in the first place.

Only one of us is an expert in dating lesbians.

Hands up in defense. *Only saying. If it were me, I wouldn't go.*

Love always looks so good from the outside.

I wouldn't, Charlie insisted. *It wouldn't be worth it, not to me.*

Back home she found Tessa in bed, reading Rebecca Solnit. Edith pressed her face to Tessa's hip through the sheets. Tessa's hand on her shoulder. *How was Charlie?*

Good. Exhausting.

You always hang around people with such strong opinions.

It saves me the trouble of having my own.

Ridiculous, you're full of opinions. She massaged a knot in Edith's neck. *Love you, Joni.*

Love you, Joan.

What if she asked? What if she stayed? What then. What if they broke up in six months anyway, and she had to move out. Left with exactly one friend, and no writing community, and a job she didn't care about.

You say something? Tessa's free hand still massaging the neck of the boy she loved.

No. Only sounds of comfort. *Keep doing that, please.*

———

EDITH WAS surprised to find she owned very little. She sold all the books she could bear to part with, studied pairs of khaki shorts and band T-shirts she never wore. There was a problem with her body she thought she might starve her way out of.

Tessa bought the minivan from Colleen for five hundred dollars. It had carried Colleen's family to national parks and baseball games. The summer she turned sixteen, she and her girlfriend used it to follow My Chemical Romance. Tessa gave it to Edith as a parting gift. *It's rickety, but it'll get you there.* Edith waited for the hand of god to intervene. A breakdown before she left the city. The van ran smoothly, humming where it met the street.

Charlie helped move the desk out. *Would've saved a bunch of time if we'd left it in storage*, he said. *Did you ever write at it?*

Some! It had mostly been a place to stack books. The faint ring-shaped scar of a months-ago mug of tea.

Make strong friends down south. That's my advice. If Edith wanted to bail on grad school a second time no one would come get her. No one believed she would, though. There was a sense of fate about it all. The click of sword drawn from stone. A lover freed from railroad tracks moments before a train plowed into them.

Come visit me sometime, Edith said.

I will. He wouldn't. Something bigger was being left behind.

They hugged. *I love you dude*, Charlie said.

Love you too.

On her final night with Tessa they ate Chinese from paper containers. Tessa's chopsticks nimbly coaxed noodles to her mouth. They didn't watch anything. Didn't play music. It didn't seem like the end of anything. Something would intervene. A messenger would arrive, bearing a stay of execution. First one week, then two.

I'm done crying, Tessa said. *It's not really a sad thing, is it? You're going off to do what you've always wanted.*

Yeah. I mean it can be that and still be sad.

But we'll stay close. I don't want a life without you in it.

Me neither.

They traded cartons. The television's dark returned the room in ghostly silhouettes.

Will you promise me something?

Meet at this spot in exactly a year?

You really do want this to be Before Sunrise. *No, dear Joni, what I want is this: so long as we're speaking, if either of us gets married, I want us to invite one another.*

Sure. No hesitation. She couldn't conceive of leaving tomorrow, let alone marriage. *Why, you have someone in mind?*

They finished eating, cuddled on the couch fully clothed. Their time left in each other's arms was measured now in hours. *Tessa, no one deserves to have a good life more than you.*

We all deserve a good life.

I mean it. I hope—god, she could barely finish—*I hope that when I'm gone you—you—*

Quiet now. Only her head on Edith's chest. Heartbeats bounding through them. *You've been everything I needed you to be.*

A lie—it had to be—but a kind one. Only, what if Tessa didn't want things to end? What if she was waiting for Edith to sit up and say, No, actually, she wasn't ready to move on. That if she wanted a good life, that would be a life with Tessa. Maybe—

It was too late for that. The next day would find them on the hill outside their apartment, saying *We can't stand here forever.* For now, the sun was down. Might it never rise.

I T WOULD BE EASY TO FIND TESSA'S NEW HOME. SHE'D told Edith herself that it was across the street from the old four-plex. The slope that tested her lungs as she walked up it, the scrape of cold air. Edith had seen no reason to come back to this part of the city and found, now, that this was the right impulse. There was no sweep of nostalgia, no memories freed from cobwebs. It was nothing compared to the warm mouth of the T station, the backstreets of froyo shops and poetry bookstores. The dead sweep of campus trees. Anything held more secrets than all the street before her. If not for the fourplex's familiar seafoam façade, she'd think she was in the wrong place.

Maybe if she went into the old apartment. As a child, her father had taken her to his childhood home in Michigan; the woman who lived there had let them come in. People did things like that. They commiserated about doors that still stuck in the humidity, the lack of counter space, the shower's puny water pressure. So little had changed since her father's childhood. What was six years? A graduate degree, a tumultuous romance, the death of your closest friend. You became a girl and so what? Time kept passing. There was so much, too much, life left.

Edith didn't cross to the house that Tess and Devin shared. Up the hill a little farther and then no more, watching the windows for motion or light. She pulled her glove off with her teeth. Tessa picked up on the last ring.

Edith.

Sorry about yesterday.

No small talk, huh?

Is it a bad time?

It's okay. No sign of movement. Edith could stand here till dark, a shivering sentinel to a life that could never have been hers. Tessa and Devin spooning curry over rice. Watching an absurd action movie. Her legs draped across his. Keeping each other warm. The easy closeness that comes with love.

It was stupid. It doesn't matter, Tessa, I'm happy for you.

Of course it matters. We don't get upset about stuff that doesn't matter.

I don't think that's true.

It is, though, Joni. What else would it mean to matter? There was the sound of a sink running, a cloth pulled across a counter. She could picture the sky-blue waffle weave. She could picture the bowl of oranges on the table. A box of pasta, ready for the pot.

I do mean it, though. I'm happy for you and Devin.

Thank you. A breath. *You would really like him, I think.*

I mean—

Another time.

Right. Inside there'd be a tank, but all the old fish would have died. They wouldn't even be a memory to the new fish. Edith's ungloved hand was going numb. *I'm headed home tomorrow.*

I'm sure Texas misses you.

Yeah. What did that mean? *I don't want to bother you.* A lie. All she wanted was to bother Tessa, once a day every day, until both stopped breathing.

Look, Edith, one more thing.

Yes, Lieutenant Columbo?

I shouldn't have left this for so late in the trip. There isn't a normal way to tell you this.

There was no fear or disruption in Edith's voice, not a tremor beyond the cold in her hands and throat. *Oh man, you're marrying him.*

Yeah.

A single concession: she sat on the curb. Concrete leaching all the warmth from her ass.

That's great, Tessa.

You sound like you mean it.

I do. Whatever she felt later, she understood this had nothing to do with her. Someone she cared about, someone she loved, was getting the ending her story deserved. *You should have all the happiness imaginable, Joan.*

So should you, you know.

Sure. Edith bit her nails. A little hurt, a little blood rolling in the nailbed. *Jesus Christ, Tess, you're going to have a husband.*

I know. Tessa laughed. *It's fucking ridiculous.*

I would've left it too late to bring up, too.

No, Joni, you would've just sent me a postcard from your honeymoon.

Well, never fear, now I'll be rubbing your face in it. If ever it happens.

When it happens.

Sure. Boy it'd be funny if she died out here, now. Maybe they'd put up a statue to her, or an eternal flame. The Grave of the Lonely Trans Girl. *Well look, I should probably fuck off.*

Hang on a second, Joni.

Yeah?

It really was good to see you this weekend.

You too, Joan. It wasn't about nostalgia, or counterfactuals. It was because Tessa was one of the best people she'd ever known. *Congratulations again.*

You mean it less this time, I can hear it.

No.

We'll get used to this, Edith. This, like everything else. Now Edith was crying. *Don't stay away for six years again, okay?*

I won't. Steady as she could. *I promise.*

SHE LISTENED to *Into the Woods* as she stowed the sofa bed, packed her clothes, washed her face. "Oh if life were made of moments . . ."

How good would it be to never leave? But to stay would mean a real life here. Traffic and delays on the T and incomprehensible rent. This weekend wasn't life, only a moment in the woods.

Adam drove her to the airport.

It's been so good to be here, she said, trying not to cry. *To be around friends.*

You have friends in Texas, I know you do.

It's not the same.

I know.

You know someone for ten years, twelve. You see all the ways they changed. You go on being friends.

Adam took her hand. *You're literally not allowed to stay away this long again.*

I already promised Tessa.

Good.

They'd talked briefly about Tessa's impending nuptials. She and Devin didn't even have a ring, or a venue, only the vague promise of next summer. A whole cycle of seasons between then and now. Edith was fine. She and Adam and Michael had spent the final four hours of the night squeezed onto the couch, watching MTV's *Room Raiders.*

They pulled into Logan Airport. Adam hugged her, told her he loved her. There was no drama, no sense of denouement. People did this every day.

She let herself cry in the security line. The intersecting fairy-tale lives of *Into the Woods* on repeat in her headphones. Her backpack knocked a McDonald's bag from its place atop the trash can and photographic slides spilled out across the tile. She stopped crying long enough to gather them up. They were photos of places with no people: a log cabin, a clearing in the woods, a lake. Edith didn't wonder that someone had felt the need to leave these behind, that this ballast had been too much to carry. Later, she wished she'd taken one with her. Instead, she replaced them all in the bag, replaced the bag atop the trash. Someone had been unable to bring themselves to throw away these trace memories. Let yet another person be their custodian. She had crying to do. She was leaving.

EDITH HADN'T DRIVEN FAR. TWO HUNDRED MILES, maybe three. The old speakers rattled with a Drake album. It was nice to be in the flow of a long drive, weaving between cars. A system that only worked so long as everyone did their part. The wend of bodies, metal, plastic. The arterial American highway system.

She wasn't thinking of her friends, or the life ahead of her. Only driving. A rote series of steps like washing your hair. And it came unbidden, in the second person.

Ah shit—what if you're a girl?

TESSA'S CALL CAME ON A SEPTEMBER AFTERNOON, seventeen months before Edith would return to Boston. There was silence on the other end.

Tess? Everything okay?

There were no tears, no hitching breathy sobs. Only a long, slow sigh. The gentle whisper of dying leaves. A cigarette's crackle.

Tessa.

It's Val, Edith.

Valerie's phone made it through the crash immaculate; her sister found Tessa's number in her texts. Edith asked how it had happened, and Tessa said she didn't know. Edith asked where, and Tessa didn't know. She might as well have asked: What were her final words. What music was on the stereo. When the light went out of her, could she feel it go? Or did she sleep through it like a child at New Year's.

Edith found that she actually was asking these questions. They were broken by a stutter and a fist in her throat.

I was just getting used—she said. Used to what? The idea that Val wouldn't be around? *It's so fucking stupid.*

It's so, so stupid. Tessa's voice was thin.

Who dies in a fucking car crash.

There would be no correct questions. No amount of sense-making would unkill her.

When she stopped crying long enough to see, Edith priced flights to Boston. *I think I might come up there*, she said. *I don't know what else to do.*

Come, Tessa said. *I don't either.*

As if that would make her any more certain how to move, how to live, how to come back from this loss. As if she could decide anything so easily.

It was gauche to reminisce about better days. It was impossible to talk about the present or future. They sat there, listening to each other breathe. Like falling asleep in the same bed.

FOR WEEKS, EDITH DID NOTHING BUT WATCH *GOSSIP Girl*. Rich teens got drunk and broke each other's hearts. Some days they were a little less rich, or a little more. Every episode ended in a party. Having lost the beat of her life, this reliable pattern would have to do. Treats followed her every time she stood to get black coffee or snack cakes from the kitchen. In sleep, she clenched her teeth till the plastic cap flexed, the still-raw stump of her tooth aching her awake. She sat in the bath until the water went cold and listened to Sondheim. She did not read. She did not write. At night, she ran the dishwasher half-full because it sounded like northeastern rain. In seven months, her lease would end. She had seven months to decide what came next.

Eventually she went to the dentist, and a permanent porcelain crown was fixed to her mouth. *We had to add fluoridation damage*, the dentist said, *so that it would match all the other teeth*. His fingers in her mouth, she could not say, Why bother? Why should it look real?

SEB GOT her out of her apartment. *Buy me dinner*, they said. *Tell me of your adventures to the wild north.*

The air was feverish with hints of spring. They went to Patrizi's, a food truck attached to a bar in the center of town. The bar had live bluegrass on Wednesdays; there was a theater space where she'd seen a puppet show about the Radium Girls. She and Seb sat at a picnic table with noodles piled onto paper plates.

We shouldn't patronize this place, Seb said. *They fired that trans busser because she was trying to unionize.*

This was your idea.

Sure but, if anyone asks, we didn't come here. They popped a ball of noodles into their mouth. *So. Beantown. Details.*

What's to tell? It was good seeing people.

If you don't give me something I'm gonna start spreading wild rumors. You got into a fistfight with Ben Affleck in a Dunkin' Donuts. You took a shit on the JFK House lawn. Another twisted knot of noodles sucked from their fork. Seb could unhinge their jaw. *Seeing your ex was good? Marriage revelations aside?*

(When she'd told Seb Tessa's news, they'd let out a long whistle and said, *You dodged a bullet. No one who marries a cis boy can be trusted.*)

I don't want to talk about it. Edith could barely get her noodles to stay on her fork. *I ran into this straight guy I lived with in college, actually.*

Oh yeah? He cute?

He's married. All her feelings sounded ridiculous to her. *I had a really nice time chatting with him and his wife, weirdly.*

What's weird about that? Their waiter brought them a stack of garlic bread, and they spent some pleasant minutes tearing it to pieces. *You're in your Frances Ha era.*

Don't say that, I'm too old. Frances Ha was too old for her Frances Ha era.

You'll never get anywhere going in circles like that. You want that last piece?

All you, bud. After two slices, Edith felt full to bursting. *I think Boston was the last place I was happy.*

Go back to stay, then. That's an easy one.

My life is here, Seb. Who'll buy you pasta if I leave.

You want to stay here forever? You want to die in Texas? Seb had lived in Texas longer than Edith and only had another year in them, tops. They were trying to emigrate to Argentina—easier said than done when your only credentials were a queer studies Ph.D. and a dozen bookstore jobs.

I figure we have fifteen years before the water runs out and I get gunned down by cannibal transphobes, no matter where I live, Edith said. *You can't go back to the last place you liked and expect to find the same life waiting for you.*

T WOULDN'T BE FAIR TO CALL GRAD SCHOOL A TOTAL disaster. There was a brief period when it seemed like the world she'd dreamed of had opened to her. People treated her like a writer and talked intelligently about books, music, film. People knew who Thomas Bernhard and Ishmael Reed were. Her only responsibilities were to read and write and say clever things. What else could paradise consist of?

The new friendships soon soured. People backbit, gossiped, didn't read each other's work or tore it apart. She left every party feeling worse. Self-exile was easier than becoming someone's target. She slept with a quiet poet for six weeks until one night the poet said, *I think I love you*, and Edith laughed, *You don't know me.*

She didn't think about being trans. She shaved off her beard and adopted a gender-neutral nickname. But she wasn't trans. She figured that sometime when Val called she'd bring it up, half-joking, and Val would confirm for her. It'd be nice to have that door closed.

Her last conversation with Tessa was at a gas station on the Tennessee border. *A border is as good a place as any*, Tessa said. Edith crouched by the ice machine, sweating through her black skinny jeans. *I love you, Joni. I'll see you around.*

Valerie checked in every couple weeks. *How are you, babe? Having the time of your life?*

Another day swaddled in god's creation.

Val had fallen in love with a trans tattoo artist in Boulder. She'd been living there for two months—the longest she'd stayed put anywhere since college.

If she tattoos her name on your biceps, make sure she throws in a free cover-up if y'all break up.

In the south for three months and you're already y'alling. They wouldn't break up anytime soon, Valerie insisted. *It's the real deal.*

Edith hoped so. She'd never known Val to be in a serious relationship. They were all getting older, though. What people wanted changed.

A few weeks later, Edith was reading in her living room when Valerie called. *What's your address? I want to send you something.* Edith told her. The apartment faced a wall of trees and never got enough sunlight.

I don't need anything.

I'm sure you barely have room to move for all the books. How's school?

I'm writing discussion questions about Sappho. A guide through the incomplete. Someone's going to get mad at me, a straight dude taking charge of the discussion.

You might be my only straight friend. Are you really straight?

I don't have the bandwidth to consider if I'm not.

Yeah, that's for sure how identity works.

Static rush of wind through the phone. *Where are you driving? Getting supplies for your love nest?*

Not exactly. A car door slammed. The gravel crunch of footsteps. *Is this whole house yours?*

What house?

Yours, dummy.

Edith was surprised by her own anxiety. *It's a fourplex,* she said quietly.

Well, come downstairs.

Edith nearly fell as she rushed down the steps.

SEVEN MONTHS UNTIL HER LEASE EXPIRED, SEVEN months until her rent caught up to the untenable market standard. Seven months until she had promised the editor a complete book. Maybe she could sell her underwear online.

At the neighborhood coffee shop, she opened the file for *Black Pear Tree*. Boston was a reprieve, but now it was time to work.

V. said: The truth is, when you find the last person you'll ever love, you'll thank god for every failed relationship. Every move that led you here, every life you did not live, because this is the one that means something. This is the one that's solid as the lid of a coffin or the glass observation deck of some tall building.

I knew that she meant well. She did not want either of us to be stuck here, hung up in the feverish Alabama dark. But what I wanted to say was, Shut the fuck up, V. What I wanted to say was, Let me make a life with you.

And, later:

I was very clear about what I needed and you were very clear you didn't want to give it to me.

V: You're the one who got in too deep. I got in the exact amount of deep I could take.

Edith and the editor had only ever spoken by email. She was a conjecture of keystrokes, her emails all questions and desire for explanations. When Edith googled her, the images that came up were grainy, as though taken at a great distance and cropped. She sometimes sent emails at four o'clock in the morning, and when Edith asked if everything was okay, she always said that her dog had woken her.

Maybe the trouble, Edith had written, *is that my life is super boring*. What she meant was that looking too closely at her life was like shining a laser pointer into her eyes.

Don't make me quote Flannery O'Connor at you, the editor responded. *Tell me what kind of book you're trying to make.*

Edith did her whole spiel: sad women in New York who were sexually obsessed with Albrecht Dürer. *That's spiritually the kind of novel I want anyway. The kind that white women with eating disorders publish with Semiotext(e).*

What's Dürer's role in it? I don't mean this rhetorically.

I don't know. These people were always reaching outside of themselves, churning through culture until apophenia found them and they could pretend their fictional analogues had been redeemed. *Maybe I need to read Proust. Anything to punch through all the messy brain stuff.*

Do what you have to. I trust you implicitly. Whatever kind of book you want, that's what I want to read.

This was too much freedom. Perhaps the editor didn't want to be an editor at all; perhaps she'd only arrived here after failing at being a lawyer, a confidence artist, a gasoline pumper on the Jersey Turnpike. In place of guidance and shaping, there was only formlessness.

Edith closed her email and the manuscript and pulled up old photos, ripped from Facebook before shuttering her account. She should have gotten a picture with Adam and Tess, a record of how they had and had not changed. Next time.

It didn't take much scrolling to reach photos of her life in Boston. Bare feet dangling some yards above the harbor. Sweatered and jacketed, snow dusting her beard like powdered sugar as she bit into a donut. Half-asleep on the T, her face resting against its ghost in the window. She'd felt so ambivalent about her looks back then. She didn't hate herself, but couldn't understood why anyone would find her attractive. Now, she'd sleep with that guy. He was cute, if a bit young for her. He'd probably put on the National while they made out.

He was so much better at being a guy than she was at being a girl. He knew how to style his hair. His clothes fit him. He was *one of the good ones*—a guy who didn't take up space and would walk his femme friends home at night. Now what was she? A depressed trans girl who slept exclusively with men because she didn't have to differentiate between being attracted to them and wanting to be them. What a joke.

If she'd really been good at being a man, of course, she wouldn't have stopped being one. But it was easy to look at these photos, all taken by Tessa, and dream.

IT WAS already hot at the protest. Edith sweated through her denim romper and flapped its collar ineffectually. A tall woman gave a speech about the importance of trans healthcare for teens. *Most people know they're trans by the time they're children*, she said.

Edith recognized three-quarters of the people in attendance. *We don't really know the whole trans community, do we?*

We know the ones who come to protests. A generous estimation. Seb was the one who went to protests; they had a fifty-percent success rate at getting Edith to join. The secret, they'd found, was to play on her white guilt. *Stop flapping.*

I feel gross. Why is this state so hot.

Why are you dressed like a Riverdale *character.* Edith had no comeback; she *had* bought the romper after seeing it on *Riverdale.* She scanned the crowd: septum piercings, hand tattoos, rough mullets.

It's like the T4T tab on Grindr out here.

Hush up, I'm trying to hear this.

The speaker was insisting on the importance of WPATH guidelines. *We know what these children need.*

They marched to the capital chanting slogans about burning down the state. There were signs explaining that trans rights were human rights, and there were girls with pink-white-blue knee socks. Cops watched the freak show pass by. This happened with their permission. After a few more chants the protest dispersed, and Seb and Edith walked through the streaming crowd to Seb's car.

Can we go to 7-Eleven or something? If I don't drink a Gatorade I'm gonna die.

Can't take you anywhere, Seb said.

But you do anyway, because I'm so cute.

You were, like, trying to cruise the crowd.

She was so transparent. *No, I was looking for the love of my life.*

They sat on the curb outside 7-Eleven drinking Windex-blue Gatorades.

Look, it's natural that you get thrown for a loop when your ex is getting married.

It's not only that. Everyone I know in Boston is in a serious relationship.

Up there, you freeze to death if you don't have another body around to keep you warm.

Yeah but does it have to be a cis dude? Because if Tessa's problem hadn't been Edith's dudehood, then what? Some essential flaw rendering her unlovable. Something she could not transition her way out of. *I am ready to be someone's wife.*

You've got—and I mean this from the bottom of my heart—to shut the fuck up. Seb took her hand in theirs; her fingers looked massive and deathly pale. *Look, you want a girlfriend? Go to Bookpeople, every month there's a new fresh-faced trans girl working the register.*

They're all twenty-three and studied photography and have snake tattoos. I'd have to learn what 100 gecs is. I'd have to watch anime.

Too high a price for intimacy, you're right. They held the sweating Gatorade bottle against their neck. *You have a snake tattoo.*

I wouldn't date me. What about you, how're things with Sara?

Seb's girlfriend was cis, and twenty-three, and had interned at the LGBTQ Research Center with them. They'd been the only two people of color working there. Edith pictured lots of steamy late nights digitizing lesbian zines from the nineties.

Things with Sara were fine. Seb never expressed strong feelings for her one way or another. A relationship like the lazy river around a swimming pool.

People don't want to bone down when it's hot out. That's in the Kinsey Report.

In exactly those words, I'm sure. Edith drained her Gatorade, surveyed the shimmering Texas sidewalks. *I don't care so much about being lonely. But I miss being in love.*

Do you know how fucking gay you sound?

Always nice to have a sympathetic ear.

Go get your shit wrecked, girl. You can't spend your whole life moping.

Wanna bet?

Seb squeezed her hand and tossed their empty bottle into the trash in a neat arc.

People run from the rain, Seb said, *but sit in bathtubs full of Cool Blue Gatorade.*

Thanks, Bukowski.

I'm always right about your love life. I have a Ph.D. in being gay. They took Edith's bottle from her. Another perfect shot.

Edith sighed, stood, and flapped her romper. At least it was cooling off. All this effort to look cute, and for what.

I T WAS MONTHS BEFORE THEY HAD SEX OR EVEN KISSED, but Valerie slept in Edith's bed that first night in Alabama. Val could make anything seem natural. Questioning it made you the weird one.

In the morning there was cereal and life updates. Coffee from the battered machine Valerie took everywhere. They sat on a small porch out back with their bowls of soggy Cheerios and watched birds mutter between trees.

So. The tattoo artist.

Val waved her off. *Tale as old as time. Girl meets girl. Girl wants to tattoo something on the other girl. Something small, like a bumblebee. Other girl feels daunted by the prospect of permanence. It becomes, as they say, a whole thing.*

A real fairy-tale ending. "*And it was a whole thing, forever after.*" Sips of coffee beat back the late-winter cool. *Sorry to hear that, Val.*

Don't be. I learned my lesson. Gaggles of hungover undergrads tramped through the yard. Val called out, *Helloooo boys!* and they all waved back. *I hardly recognize you without the beard*, she said. *And your nails.* Valerie studied the plum lacquer on her fingertips. *Grad school, though. You're surviving?*

I'm—okay.

Oh god, you hate it.

I'm doing good work.

You can always leave. More stragglers passed through the yard. Several of them wore clothes made of tablecloths, notebook paper, duct tape. *Weird that people still go to college*, Valerie said. *We were never that young.*

Not like they are. Edith taught a discussion section of American literature. She saw nothing of herself in their tired, disappointed child-faces.

Term papers in the library. Giving up sleep for dance practice. Giving up food. It was all the most important thing in the world.

Yeah, now we only give up sleep and food for the right reasons: because we're miserable.

Do you remember when you got kicked out of the library because that children's lit paper upset you so much? What was it about?

The paper had been about whether or not the narrator of Lois Lowry's *The Giver* died at the end. It was Tessa's. *I don't remember.*

After showering, Valerie insisted they go hiking. *The largest natural bridge in America is like an hour from here. I plan to stomp on it.*

Edith still had the minivan, but she drove Valerie's forest-green Subaru. The backseat was carpeted with fast-food bags and pairs of jeans. It smelled like a Dave & Buster's. Valerie kicked her legs up on the dashboard, queueing pop songs on her phone. No one mentioned Tessa.

Leaves in Alabama didn't change color but died suddenly. The knobby, ugly trees left Edith homesick. There was no sign marking the path to the natural bridge. You could walk by it every day and never notice. *Since when do you like hiking?*

I've always liked hiking. You've just never lived anywhere worth exploring.

The woods were still in a way that Tuscaloosa never was. On her back porch, any given night, Edith could hear Rae Sremmurd blasting from the undergrad bars on the Strip. Every other Saturday the streets filled with drunken revelers of all ages, decked out in crimson and houndstooth, eager to see bloodshed on the colossal football field. It was ugly out here in the woods. Life out here wasn't somehow more real than life in the city; but interjecting your humanity, the superficiality you carried everywhere with you, reminded you how little it mattered. Whatever you made of yourself would be buried like everything else.

On a treacherous slope of wet leaves, Valerie took her hand. *God it's empty out here. If you ever need to hide a body, this is the place to do it.*

Oh yeah? You gonna help me dig the hole?

For you, babe? Anything.

The natural bridge was unassuming. It was less the span of land than the ten feet of emptiness beneath it, weathered away on an inconceivable timeline. As promised, Valerie stomped on it. Jumped up and down. The bridge, uncaring, carried on.

Everything you dreamed? Edith watched from solid ground below. Why hadn't she asked Val to visit before? Here she was: a beacon of home, pirouetting in red Keds. She could survive any question, any answer, with Valerie nearby.

It's perfectly meaningless. Come up here. Edith stumbled up the damp hills. The bridge had a proper majesty once she was dangling her legs over its side. The earth's generosity holding you. And Valerie beside her, so light that even if the bridge crumbled beneath them, Edith knew she could not fall. *You know what I wanted to be when I was young?*

A dinosaur. A mailman. A big rock.

Not that young. I wanted to be Nick Carraway. Val rested her head on Edith's shoulder. The visible world ended a few yards away at the treeline. You could hide an entire life in there. *I wanted to be a person who was adjacent to the real story. Witness to it. I was tired of being the person things happened to.*

What changed?

I'm not sure anything did. At any moment, Valerie would brush the water from her palms and walk away from this subject forever.

It was the thing I liked best about dancing, you know. Being one per-former in a sea of them. What's extraordinary isn't when you stand out, it's how you all come together. Organic, almost. You could live in that if the music never stopped. Edith had heard versions of this before and dismissed it. Everything about Val's life seemed desper-ate for the extraordinary. But there was no twinkle in her eyes, no hint of ironic performance. There was only the trees, the vast noise of insects and leaves, the two of them nowhere near the center of the world. There was the water soaking through their jeans. Valerie had been a wonderful dancer. Her body turning in perfect time, each limb in the place it needed to be. Edith never missed a performance. *I want a place where I fit the puzzle. But somehow I never do for long.*

Edith didn't say, Stop moving around so much you asshole. Didn't say, Stay here with me. It wasn't a problem with solutions. There could only be new, deeper problems, complicating it until there came something like a state of grace.

And now there were their clammy hands, damp with leftover rain, entwined. In a perfect world, they would still be there: emp-tiness below, the sky threatening rain above, and the two of them between. Baffled but not alone.

I T HAD BEEN WEEKS SINCE SHE'D CLIMBED. EDITH HAD lost strength in her fingers and forearms, back muscles stiff and straining the moment she got on the wall. At first, climbing had been a way to make friends. Now it struck her as a socially acceptable form of self-harm. Her body dragged across the rough face of the wall. The calluses on each finger fell away, leaving tender, stinging pink. She fell, stood, and began to climb again.

Up and up, her arms straining. Hands dusted with other hands' chalk. Swinging, hip pivot, swap one foot for the other and if it slips, so what, it'll be an ab workout getting back in position. She reached the top and kicked off the wall. The soft floor caught her and she lay there, sweaty, sore, and gasping.

She'd told Seb the truth: it would be useless to move back to Boston. Hers was not an unhappiness you left at state borders. Still, it might be nice to live somewhere that didn't actively want her and all her friends to die.

Edith was pleased to see the Climbing Woman on a nearby wall, proof the world hadn't changed much in her absence. The Climbing Woman would pick a single spot, a single color, and climb it endlessly. If someone else wished to give it a shot, she made space for them, sipping from her tempered-glass water bottle. When they finished, she was on the wall again, pulling herself skyward with the same graceful movements. Edith thought she must have been a dancer, more comfortable in repetition than change. Seb thought she was crazy. *There's something in her life she lost control over. This is her compensating.*

That had to be what brought them all there. Only you could rely on yourself not to fall, to hold on, to reach far enough. You could measure progress, unlike in life; how high you rose, how your body ached.

She stood, climbed, fell, rested. The problem was, as you got better, your body became more resilient. Edith left her early days of climbing feeling steamrolled. She'd emerge, sweat-drenched, into the punishing Texas heat, hardly able to command her car home. Now, she had to push herself harder.

EDITH READ books to learn how to be a person. They were little Rube Goldberg machines that let you see where your worst and best choices might lead you. People often seemed to think that real life was more complicated than books, but, in fact, Edith found it was often precisely as simple. Life was a series of stimuli that most everyone responded to in the same ways. This was why there'd been such a panic in the nineteenth century about women reading—*Madame Bovary, Eugene Onegin.* Everyone knew it would make girls too powerful.

When she'd lived in Alabama, Valerie returned from the road with a dozen novels like the ones Edith had described to the editor. Visions and revisions of lives half-lived: *10:04* and *Motherhood* and *Outline.* In the throes of gender limbo, Edith found comfort in the autofictional frameworks—that you could give your life story a novelistic structure and come out knowing yourself better. She'd read to unlearn one sort of life and learn another. If you could learn number theory, or Italian, or the history of classical music by reading, surely you could learn how to be a person. How to be a girl.

Around the same time, she'd become obsessed with the diaries of women artists. Nin, Woolf, Sontag. At home she flipped through Katherine Mansfield's; she'd mostly bought it because they'd both had tuberculosis. There was so much boredom in these books, the dailiness that Woolf would later call "cotton wool." And Edith loved how boring they were, how they didn't teach her anything.

HEY BITCH. You get your back walls blown out yet? Seb's voice was distorted, distant. They were driving.

You can't say "bitch" anymore, Seb. You ceded your rights when you transitioned, it's misogyny now.

You're goddamn right it is.

Hi Edith! Sara's voice was bright and clear. That was being twenty-three. That was the girlhood Edith never got.

Sara, tell your joyfriend they're gonna get crucified by a bunch of women in pussyhats if they don't reform their ways.

Sara repeated this verbatim while Seb spat and fumed over the word *joyfriend.*

Where you guys headed?

Dallas. The Kabakovs exhibit. Seb had invited her, but Edith begged off. Treats curled up on her lap and protested when Edith petted her too roughly. She'd never been to Dallas. She'd never been anywhere in Texas, really. Held down by inertia and her fear of gas station bathrooms. *We'll be back by Saturday, though, are you coming to Bernard's party?*

Sure. It was useless to decline Seb's party invites. They'd drag her by the hair if they had to. Edith loved this about them.

Cyrus will be there.

I already said yes. Her dormant sexuality had been awakened while watching Cyrus pour cider into a docile femme's mouth. He'd pulled her up by the chin and kissed her while her partner watched.

The act's odd taboo undercut by everyone's polyamory. Edith regretted telling Seb any of this.

Does Edith have a crush on Cyrus? Sara asked, failing to whisper.

Everyone has a crush on Cyrus. Get in line, Edith.

Hanging up now.

Seb, she caught Sara saying, *I don't want to listen to Taylor Swift, I want to listen to Oingo Boingo.*

Edith didn't want to only get fucked; she wanted to get fucked and wake up next to a beautiful woman she loved every day for thirty-five years. Edith had barely dated at all for the last year—the prospect of knowing and being known was too much—but seeing people happy had a way of making you want, quite suddenly, what they had.

She redownloaded Tinder. She began with her real name, real enough information. The ironic detachment people expected from trans girls: *5'6", full idiot, calls all vampires draculas. cat mom not a catgirl. Judith seeking Holofernes.* But by the time she went to select photos, she couldn't bear them. She only looked girlish at a distance or in low light. It would be unclear, later, the chain of decisions that led her to select from the old photos Tessa had taken. A different person, a boy who knew how to fake it. She erased all the personal information.

She named the boy Harry—a name that had never been hers but that she'd always liked. Harry was twenty-six and five eleven. *I am like every other boy who went to a liberal arts college,* his bio read. *I am probably being crushed to death under a bookshelf. don't say you're "looking for adventure" if you aren't going to help me steal the Declaration of Independence.*

Edith had never used the apps as a boy. As a girl on Grindr, people were at least straightforward about wanting to fuck your throat. As Harry, she swiped right on every girl until she ran out of swipes for the day.

There was a shoebox at the back of her closet—rattling, light. The top folded back and there was the knife. Punisher logo dull with wear. Stolen from Valerie's bag the last time Edith saw her. Now she only looked at it. There were no photos of the two of them. The knife was all.

THE FIRST TIME VAL LEFT TUSCALOOSA, EDITH expected she'd stay gone. She had not said where she was going; probably she had no plan. There were restless nights picturing her in Boston, reporting Edith's state to Tessa. Edith would not be pitied. Their breakup had been the right thing—what Tessa and Edith needed to become the people they wanted to be. She was writing and reading. She was buying girl clothes online.

She thought of Val most while going to sleep and waking up. A warm body beside her in bed. Someone to share the morning with. An excuse to cook real food instead of boiling more pasta.

After only two months she came home to find Valerie smoking a cigarette on the front stoop. All Edith could think to say was, *You don't smoke.*

Empirically false. Val took a drag.

I've never seen you smoke.

You've never seen me do a lot of things, babe. Let me look at you. She stomped out the cigarette as she stood. Held Edith's shoulders. (The same pose of inspection that Tessa would, five years later, greet her with in Boston.) *What name are you using now?*

I'm sorry? What could be known by looking at her? People shaved their beards, people painted their nails and grew out their hair.

Straightforward question, I thought.

It's complicated.

Look, if you don't tell me, I'm going to have to make up a name for you. I mean I can't exactly call you— Call you Joni, she didn't say.

Judith. Edith bit her cheek. That wasn't right; it was all she had. *Can we go inside?*

Sure, Judy. The cigarette end smoldered as Val bounded up the stairs. *Love what you've done with the place.* Her sheets and pillows were spread across the couch. Three different mugs harbored desiccated tea bags. The coffee table was a mess of books, balled tissues, and unread *New Yorkers*. Cracker crumbs Hanseled and Greteled their way from kitchen to hall to bathroom. *I thought writers just became alcoholics.*

All the tissues and half the *New Yorkers* went into the trash. After a moment's thought, Edith tossed the mugs in too. *I wasn't expecting company.*

I was scoping out abandoned houses in Detroit a few months back. There's a bunch of people living off salvaged copper. Some of those houses, people have been in and out of for years. They write their names on the walls, or leave behind a balled-up thong. You'd be right at home.

Shut your eyes and keep talking. It'll be sparkling by the time you're done.

Valerie had come from New Mexico. *I wanted to see* The Lightning Field. *You need a reservation, so I wasted five or six days trying to flirt my way in. Finally got there and, wouldn't you know it, no lightning. And I don't think the guy I slept with really was the assistant director of the Dia foundation.* She'd been planning on going north from there to a co-op making nut butters in the shadow of the Rockies—but came to Edith instead. *I drove across west Texas for you. It's the closest I've been to home in, hoo boy, years.*

How was that?

Fine. I put on My Chemical Romance and drove ninety across the state. I screamed the whole way. I'm probably on a list now.

Oh, Val. You were already on so many lists.

Sweeping crumbs out of the wall-to-wall was a Herculean labor. Edith looked up and found Val's eyes open.

Who else knows, Judy?

Nobody. She swept more vigorously to no real effect. *Nothing to know.*

Valerie studied her face again. *Hormones?*

Not sure I want them.

Sure you do.

She gave up on the crumbs. The dustpan spilled back onto the carpet. *You knew. Before I left Boston, you knew.*

Judy—

You don't have to call me that.

—I think everyone is trans, it doesn't mean anything.

You could've said something.

Valerie laughed—stifled, at first, and then unrestrained. Breathy and wild. A new sort of disarray. *Good fucking god, girl.*

They cleaned together. Not unlike her body, Edith only noticed her surroundings when someone else was there to pay attention to them.

Still haven't hung up your posters?

I haven't decided how to arrange them.

Valerie rolled them out on the gray-brown carpet. She didn't think long before tacking them around the living room. Here went Egon Schiele's strained self-portrait, there went the Nan Goldin print of an empty bed. Here were Cézanne's apples—a housewarming gift Edith's mother had mailed her—so rich and red that you could feel the century-old juice swelling under their skin.

Why do you have a Radiohead poster?

I'm sorry, did Radiohead stop being good? Are we pretending we're too cool for that now?

Valerie refused to put it up. Even so, the apartment looked less like a ghoul's hovel.

Can you believe I'm nobody's wife? Look at how fucking domes-

tic I am. For pure aesthetics, Valerie had put on an apron. *If you put a few plants in here I bet you'd be fifty percent less miserable.*

Is this what you do now? A businessman going state to state to visit all your secret families.

How many people do you think I know?

Thousands. Edith's gesture left a splatter of takeout Thai on the carpet. She dutifully wiped it up.

Val slept in her bed again. Tuscaloosa was the darkest place she'd ever lived. When Val's hand found its way under Edith's shirt, three fingers circling the soft down of her back, Edith couldn't see her face. Couldn't see whatever need, or hope, or want was in her eyes.

Valerie.

Judith.

Some would call whatever's about to happen "ill-advised."

I'm a big girl. I can handle it. That Edith wasn't talking about her hardly mattered. Val's body hearth-warm under the covers. Never mind how long it lasted. *Everything, Judy. Anything.*

Edith kissed her so that she would not say that name—the wrong name—again.

BEING A GIRL HAD IMPROVED EDITH'S RELATIONSHIP to parties. She was a charming drunk—she made jokes and pulled stories from strangers like a magician's colorful string of scarves. The trouble was that she had no way of knowing how drunk anyone else was. Afterward, in her sick daylight sobriety, she judged every move as if only she had been messy and strange.

But it was an excuse to put on a slutty dress, put effort into her makeup. Sloppy drunkenness, all its carelessness and stupidity, was acceptable from a girl.

Bernard lived in a house on the east side, a grubby bungalow he shared with a rotating cast of other trans dudes and two ginger corgis named Gumball and Jonestown. When Edith and Seb arrived, everyone was in the backyard. "Heart of Glass" poured through the empty house. Out back, they were greeted by a chorus of their names and the two excited dogs. Seb rubbed both their bellies.

You guys are just in time, Bernard said. *We're going to watch Di do a backflip.*

Watch Di beef it, you mean, Cyrus said. His top surgery scars visible through his open shirt. You could trace them with your tongue.

Cy, don't say that, you'll jinx her.

I am unjinxable. Di was one of the few trans girls in this group. Her black cotton skirt flowed around her as she warmed up for the flip. Edith never understood why they weren't friends—why every trans girl she knew had too few tgirl friends. She assumed if she were hotter this problem would solve itself.

Can I get you guys drinks? Bernard was sweet, tall, stolid. He opened a Yeti cooler packed with White Claw.

No distractions, Di said. Edith thought watching anyone permanently injure themselves was probably more trauma than she could take on right now. The backyard was patchy grass, a doghouse with fresh white paint, a bike with weeds growing through it. There was a bucket of golf balls that partygoers chipped over the fence and into the woods beyond. There was a geologic index of Bernard's parties back there, moon-white Titleist balls stained with earth.

I cannot do this with everyone watching. Cyrus booed. Others sighed in defeat and relief. *Everyone close your eyes.* Edith laughed. *I'm serious.*

How will you know if one of us cheats? Seb asked.

I'll know.

They formed a line and held hands. Edith stood between Seb and Bernard. Her hand bound in the strength of Bernard's, his rough knuckles.

Ready when you are, Diana.

I see you peeking, Cyrus.

I am not!

I will hit you in the nose, Cyrus. It will sit sideways on your face and all the pretty girls will laugh when you try to kiss them.

My eyes are closed!

A twitch of desire moved through Edith's stomach. Not a butterfly, but the kick of a dead thing hooked to electrodes. Bernard ran his thumb across her fingers.

Listen closely, because I am only doing this once.

People sieved the silence for something that sounded like a backflip. Even the dogs stood at attention. Bernard's thumb swept back and forth. Edith didn't know when in the process of transition she had come to feel desire in the base of her sternum. She felt it most often watching Wong Kar-Wai movies: Tony Leung leaning into

Faye Wong; a pair of painted toes turning over in bed. It was like she was suspended on a meat hook. It would take a stronger pair of hands than her own to get her down.

There was a whoosh and thump. *Ta-da*. Di was red with exertion as if she'd been crying. Everyone clapped uncertainly. This invisible feat out of the way, the party began in earnest.

By her third White Claw, Edith had hit a comfortable rhythm. She chatted on the couch with Seb and identical twins who had done quite a lot of ketamine. She bummed a cigarette from Cyrus in the backyard; he was deep in conversation with a girl who'd looked more fem before her transition than Edith did now. Out front, they played a game they'd learned from watching *Funeral Parade of Roses*: you walk a chalk line and remove a piece of clothing whenever you fall off it. Edith chased Gumball and Jonestown until her ribs ached. She effused about *Sweeney Todd*, *Riverdale*, Chantal Akerman. Immoderate, immodest, alive. She made out with Cyrus, and Bernard, and one of the ketamine twins. It was fun. A reminder of desire. Bernard's hand on hers was a meaningless intimacy.

An all-star of cognitive dissonance, Edith still believed this when Bernard was fucking her on the floor of his bedroom. Her face buried in a pile of his clothes, each breath drawing the tang of his late-winter sweat. The silicone cock was abrasive—it had been a while, and Bernard was low on lube—but she half-turned to him, watched him labor and sweat, and insisted, *Harder*. She was a piece of paper, slowly torn along a perforated line. Edith guided one of Bernard's hands to her throat, one to her breast. On the other side of the door was Yes and laughter. She'd later identify the song as "Long Distance Runaround" but now she was free of thought. She puppeted Bernard, pressed his fingers into her throat. Not safely cutting blood flow but pushing on her windpipe. She dropped her hands for balance and Bernard's stayed put, crushing the lively, spiraling core of her.

He stumbled, dropped her to catch himself. *Are you okay?* he asked. *Yes.*

She throbbed in the places his cock and hands had been. More hooks in her.

I think I'm too drunk for this, Bernard said. *Do you want to cuddle?*

She wanted to be pulled apart.

Bernard handed her wet wipes, chattering about a Cary Grant film. The wipes mopped up the usual effluvia—lube, shit, blood. Sex was a test of the body's limits. What you could give, what you could take.

She slipped back into her dress and underwear, and they left his room one at a time. Nothing had changed in their absence.

EDITH WOKE THROUGHOUT THE NIGHT, STUDYING THE soft glow of Valerie's skin, certain she'd turn immaterial as dust in the light. She would sit up, say, *Time to stop being a pumpkin*, and drive her car into the ocean.

Val stayed for two weeks. Edith went to class and taught. Val walked dogs and handed out fliers for a new kickboxing gym. A couple of times she posted on one of the sketchy sites that replaced Backpage and found tenured professors who'd pay to fuck her. Edith's chief surprise was that this did not bother her. *Don't tell me if any of them are English faculty*, she said. Valerie came back to Edith's bed at night, half-drunk and slaphappy, murmuring, *Judy, Judy, Judy.* No one else called her by that name. If it was still wrong, it became blessedly less so in Valerie's mouth.

They played cards at home. They drank in the rooftop bar of Tuscaloosa's one decent hotel. Val returned from midday hikes covered in dirt and sweat and stripped in the middle of Edith's living room.

Could we have been doing this before? Edith scanned the back of Valerie's knees for ticks. She hadn't intended to voice this.

Everything happened the way it happened.

Wow, so profound, is that Siddhartha Gautama?

When do you imagine we might have "done this," Judy?

You mean because now I'm—whatever. Embarrassing that she couldn't say *trans.*

No.

Valerie was right. In college it would have been a mess. If they'd somehow made it work, there would have been social drama, tedious parties, thesis drafts. Manmade horrors that they, in this godforsaken football town, found themselves insulated from.

If they'd dated, if they'd broken up, where would Edith have landed? Whose lives would they be living now?

Before Valerie left, she gave Edith a three-day warning.

Gotta go north for a checkup.

But you'll be back.

Yes. Valerie kissed the corner of her mouth. *I'll be back in one month to the day.* And like a miracle, she was. She stepped from her car and tossed an orange pill bottle through the air. *Catch*, she said, and Edith did. The rattle of blue-green pills. *Valerie Green*, the bottle announced. *Estradiol. 2mg.*

A gift, she said, *for you.*

SEB AND EDITH WATCHED *GOSSIP GIRL* FROM OPPOSITE ends of her couch, their feet crossed in the middle. Popcorn spilled from a silver mixing bowl. Treats snoozed on Seb's lap, ears twitching.

I leave for six days and she decides she likes you better.

I'm the fun stepdad. I let her bite me for fifteen minutes without chastisement.

Oh so it's your fault she chewed through my sweater?

Popcorn?

In this episode, Dan Humphrey was inviting his friends to his book release party later that day; none of them even knew he had a book coming out.

This is the sort of shit you'd do.

No, I'd change my name and move to a different state.

Is that why you became a girl? They tossed a puff of popcorn and it stuck in Edith's hair.

Everyone on *Gossip Girl* was livid with Dan for fictionalizing them. Their lives were already a spectacle—reported by Page Six and its approximants—but it's different, seeing yourself refracted through the eye of someone who really knows you.

Do you feel jealous of these guys?

What, for my "lost boyhood" or whatever? Seb shifted their weight on the couch, shifted it again. At home but never comfortable. *Honestly, yeah, sometimes. But no one actually gets a life like that.*

I meant your acting career.

Oh. That. Seb grew up in California. They'd never trained as an actor, never done much beyond high school theater, but they'd been in the final round of casting for a network teen drama. Seb was half Honduran, half Filipino; *the exact right ambiguous shade of beige,* they'd said, *to play a plucky sidekick.* The network had chosen a different brown girl with a Juilliard degree. *You know, all the people from that show have podcasts now. Their income is just residuals and Stamps.com ads.*

That's luxury, baby.

And I'd probably be a huge asshole.

Good thing you're such a humble tenderqueer instead.

Thing is, Seb said, *you can end up as pretty much anyone. Either of us might have joined a cult or gotten Ayn Rand–pilled at a vulnerable age or—whatever, ended up as congressional pages who only fucked as a form of social climbing.*

You don't really believe that, do you?

Why the fuck not? You think you can measure the distance to your unlived lives in inches? They ornamented Treats with stray popcorn. *I'm cool, I'm smart. I don't hate myself most of the time. The world sucks but that's not my fault. What about you?*

Oh yeah, it's for sure my fault the world sucks. Seb rolled their eyes. *Do I feel envy for them? Yeah, also sometimes.* It was impossible to watch all the beautiful thin girls live their beautiful lives— trainwreck lives, but never unglamorous, or sexless, or loveless—and not wish she were one of them.

You think it's fucked up that Dan wrote a book about all his friends?

Why, you worried you'll alienate everyone who loves you?

Only a question, Seb.

A little bit. But mostly because he obviously hates them.

———

WRITING ABOUT your life was something that other people did—
people who had more things keeping them alive than fifty milligrams
of sertraline and a delicate fistful of friendships.

There had been lots of chatter the last few years about what it
meant to write about other people. What lives were up for grabs.
Every time some revelatory article came out (*I was the inspiration
for such-and-such!!!*) Edith thought, shouldn't you keep that to
yourself? Didn't it expose the petty disappointments of your life to
a level of scrutiny that no one should allow? Or was there so strong
a need to set the record straight that it didn't matter if you brought
down more ridicule, more ire. You took the wheel, even if it meant
crashing the car.

There'd been Tessa's play. The distress Valerie felt at seeing her
words repeated, twisted just gently enough that they fell into the
uncanny valley between reality and fable.

Maybe it should be a book like Wittgenstein's Mistress, she
wrote to the editor. *You know, a woman alone(?) at the end(?) of
the world(?).*

And she's sexually obsessed with Albrecht Dürer?

I feel like you're really hung up on this Dürer thing.

Not to say sexually obsessed.

Edith could never tell if the editor was joking or not.

*Aren't there enough books about friendship and love and
death and marriage?* she wrote. *Don't we need more books about
people languishing?*

*And what will they languish over if not friendship and love and
death and marriage?* Don't say Albrecht Dürer, Edith told herself.
Do not say Albrecht Dürer.

When she was a kid, Edith told herself an endless story using her
toys as props. A white Lucky Cat from Epcot became a powerful
sage, a force of light; a black rubber rat its natural antagonist. She

declared the cat's disciple, a mustached LEGO figure, part of the French Foreign Legion. The story was an endless series of reversals and soap-opera betrayals. Items from around her room, a marble or a watch-back, co-opted into magical totems. New LEGO worlds built for everyone to occupy. She had loved her characters, the good turning evil and the evil, good. But she'd kept the story secret. She didn't know if her parents noticed the way the room rearranged itself, if they heard her whispering dialogue to herself in the hot part of summer afternoons. She didn't think so.

It wasn't just that writing about her real life would expose her— all her slights and joys—to friends and strangers, her child-voice now audible through that summer door. It was that she was still too angry. She couldn't love her V. and her own nameless analog like she loved her trans astronauts and her persecuted Christians and Lucky Cat and the rat and the LEGO man she'd called Frenchy. She loved Val, but it wasn't enough, or it was the wrong kind of love. And without that, she could never tell the story right.

But there didn't seem to be another option. There wasn't another way to the other side of this hurt.

WHENEVER SHE finished writing her SEO articles about leather care and bathing with a new tattoo, Edith went walking. She called friends without notice, gambling on their willingness to chat.

She called Adam after reading his article on *Into the Woods*. Having not read Lee Edelman, Edith didn't really follow his line of argument.

There's a reason one of us didn't become an academic.

The point basically, he said, *is that all the musical's conflicts are driven by people's attachment to the children's future. It takes the framework of fairy-tale-as-guidance—lessons on the world's dangers—and morphs it into a set of parent–child relationships.*

Uh-huh.

It's interesting, right? A gay man writing a whole musical about the anxiety of reproduction.

This did not strike Edith as contradictory. *Into the Woods* was so clearly, for her, a musical about how bad we are at wanting. Wanting too much (a new and exciting lover), wanting the wrong thing (marriage, riches, a child, revenge). All the characters trapped between fairy-tale logic and life's relentless march. She was ashamed to tell Adam how strongly she identified with them.

How're things up there? she asked him. *Have there been a lot of protests?* A document had leaked revealing that abortion rights were in jeopardy. The sudden and unrelenting dismay surprised Edith; she thought they'd all known months ago that this was coming.

Oh yeah, it's like 2017 again. People in the streets every weekend. I think everyone's vaguely smug about it.

Right, it's us Texans who are to blame.

No one really thinks that.

"If only we'd killed RBG in the Obama years," everyone here is saying. "It would have been so easy to replace her necklace thing with the shotgun collar from Saw 3."

Adam laughed. *Edith, you're going to be put on a list.*

Well it's not like I can kill her now!

Don't blame the old woman. Everything was going to get worse eventually. Edith gave a pinecone a good, hard kick. It skittered into the road and was smashed by a pickup truck. *God, you know what one of the medievalists said the other day? She said that maybe now the Republicans have killed Roe, they'll lose steam. Like, no, Cynthia, I'm sorry, but they're already coming for trans people.*

Edith described the Texan protests. Everyone walked and chanted and yelled at the cops. One or two white men broke off from the group and got arrested. *It feels so safe. I hate it.*

What else are you going to do? You're not going to redacted a police station.

Our NSA handlers know what you mean even if you say "redacted," bud. She looked for another pinecone to invest with her ire. *What's the point, though? We could be in the streets every day and nothing would change.* Edith had gone to Occupy Wall Street during her first year of college; it had left her a pessimist.

It feels worse doing nothing. You should talk to Tessa about this, I'm sure she has something smart to say.

Yeah.

Have you guys been talking?

He knew they hadn't. *We send each other cake recipes that neither of us has time to make.*

You should talk. There's been enough years of silence.

There were only two options if they spoke: to discuss Tessa's engagement or to pointedly avoid it. Cake recipes were easier.

Still, the next time she went for a walk, Edith tried calling. Tessa didn't answer—a relief.

In her early days of transition, Edith had hated feeling in-between. Hated the scrutiny with which even well-meaning people tried to read her. She didn't want to transition, only to have transitioned. To emerge from her room the next morning a girl with clear skin and a respectable cup size. Waiting in this space where Tessa was getting, but not yet, married—where Edith was waiting to be in love again— was a bit like that. If only they could skip it. If they could be fifty-five years old and vacationing in the Berkshires with their spouses, making light of old times.

Sorry, Tess texted her. *Have lunch in fifteen, call you back then?*

Sure. Her easy reprieve, lost. Fifteen minutes to steel herself.

At least Tessa wouldn't invite her to the wedding. To be friends with your ex was one thing but to have them present for the quote-unquote *happiest day of your* (ever more hetero-passing) *life?* An impossibility.

Edith swiped through faces on Tinder as Harry. It was easy to match with an anonymous stranger, talk for a while, and abandon the conversations before anyone was the wiser. She'd become more discerning with her double's love life, only swiping right on girls she could imagine Harry happy with.

A girl asked what Harry was reading.

Norwegian Wood, Edith lied. *Have you read it?*

Another wanted to know what sort of things he wrote.

Right now I'm working on a long fable about a war between angels and insects.

Someone asked where he'd moved here from.

Iowa. Not the cities.

The girl's sister went to Grinnell, she actually knew Iowa pretty well. Edith blocked her.

The woman was hard to recognize in her set of static photos. She had the same facial expression in each: not quite smiling as she toasted with a glass of white wine, walked a fluffy white dog and looked over her shoulder. It was only because her final photo showed her—where else—on the climbing wall that Edith placed her as the Climbing Woman. In motion and rising. Her name was Natalie; she was thirty-five and an art librarian. Before Edith could pick which way to swipe, a call came through.

Hello?

Edith. Her mother's voice was sharp and tired. *Do you have time for me in your schedule?*

This was how her mother began every conversation lately.

I'm actually— She checked; no calls from Tessa. *I have a minute.*

In the aftermath of her father's illness, Edith had been better about calling. Though he'd been fine, there'd been the lingering guilt, the what-ifs. As life took her farther from the crisis, she'd reverted to her old ways.

I was watching The Philadelphia Story *on TCM,* her mother said. *You know, you don't get names like that anymore. C. K. Dexter Haven. Macaulay Connor. Tracy Lord. That's the sort of name you could plant an oak tree on.*

Is that the one with Tom Hanks? Edith baited.

After that, her mother went on, *they were showing* His Girl Friday, *have you seen that? All about writers.*

They're journalists, Mother.

What you do is a kind of journalism, isn't it?

What I do isn't a kind of anything, it's pure, unadulterated emptiness.

That Cary Grant, her mother said. *I would watch him read a pickle jar. He's the most beautiful man to ever walk the Earth.*

How's Dad doing? Edith missed half the answer, checking her phone again. Tessa said something had come up, talk another time? Edith sighed.

—on account of the squirrel problem. It's nothing to laugh at, having squirrels in your attic. They can do a lot of damage.

Edith was lucky, in many ways, with her parents. They taught English and the occasional film elective at a high school. (Not, thank god, the one Edith had gone to.) They'd given her a love of British modernism and Ella Fitzgerald. They weren't transphobic, just clueless. But she couldn't bring herself to be closer to them. She sat out holidays, only saw family when one of her seventeen cis, straight cousins got married. A crowd and a flood of booze to take the edge off.

There had been a time she'd hoped for more. As she aged and came into herself, as she learned better how to be a person in the world, she'd hoped they would find new names for an old love. They would be close the way Tessa was to her parents. Supporting each other through the tilting world.

Her mother was back to movies. She'd gone to a Billy Wilder retrospective in Richmond, she was going on about Jack Lemmon.

You know, Edith cut in, *I went on a date with a boy the other day who* loves *Cary Grant.*

Oh! Rarely did Edith share information about her romantic life. *Did he—does he know—*

I'm trans? Yes, Mother, obviously. It would take more strength than was available to her to explain that Bernard was trans too.

Lovely, dear. What does he do for work?

Bernard worked downtown as a living statue of La Llorona. *He's a performer.*

What, like an exotic dancer?

How's Dad?

He's fiddling with his drones.

Edith didn't ask if her father wanted to speak to her. She'd once timed the silence between them, that dull antiquated phone hum, at eight and a half minutes.

All set for a career with the military, then.

They wouldn't have him. One of his toys got tangled with a meteorological balloon. He got a citation. Edith was still thinking about Bernard. He'd come to hers and carried Treats around like a baby. The sex had been disappointing—gentle and rhythmic and full of check-ins. They'd ended the night watching compilations of commercials from their childhood.

Edith had once gone out with a boy who had her birth name. She kept this a secret from him, took pleasure in saying it at opportune moments. Calling across a crowded restaurant, or a soft expiration in his ear at a sentence's end. He'd also been too gentle. She wanted to scream at these boys. They'd been trained to be careful and loving rather than rampant and destructive. She found them pathetic. If they broke some part of her, she'd be gladly broken.

They have publications, her mother said. *Trade journals. Drone Weekly. Aerial Photography Enthusiasts' Club. Every week we get these things.*

It's good to have hobbies.

I think it's awfully weird. Her mother picked at the ragged ends of her fingernails. A sound like a leaky faucet's drip. *Looking at the world from so far away.*

WHEN EDITH walked or drove through the city, she rarely thought of Valerie. There was only the occasional whiff: the leftist bookstore on North Loop, the café porch overlooking the lake, the gas station where *Texas Chainsaw* had been filmed. The city had never really been Val's; Edith had picked it, and Edith had stayed here.

It was when she went anywhere else that she missed her dead friend. The flat ugly openness surrounding the city. The racks of deathless snack cakes crowding gas stations. Every pothole-pitted stretch, every fresh yellow line. The way power lines cut up the sky when there were no buildings to be seen. These things that had come to her through the phone, in all those months when Valerie was away. A day, and a day, and a day, and a day.

EDITH STOPPED TAKING THE ESTRADIOL AFTER VAL-
erie left Alabama. When Val returned with more, she was indignant to find the first bottle half-full. *It didn't do anything*, Edith said.

It's fucking slow, you nincompoop.

The truth was, Edith didn't know what she wanted. She thought
she could keep Val close through this medical blackmail. Somehow,
this didn't work.

But things were changing. Valerie was more likely now to call
from the road. She'd have Edith describe the full plots of movies
she'd seen; sometimes Valerie would take a few hours to stop at
a theater and watch herself, seeing how they measured up against
Edith's narrative. *I like it better when you tell it*, she said.

In turn, Valerie sent back stories of a sort of life Edith
couldn't imagine.

*You get so used to the people around you being trans that you
forget not everyone is*, Val said. A friend of hers had slept with a
woman—twice—and still didn't realize the woman was cis. *Whatever surgeon she thought had made a self-lubricating cunt, I want
their number.*

Valerie recited Wallace Stevens poems into the phone to help Edith
fall asleep. "Thirteen Ways" or "The Emperor of Ice-Cream." *"Let
the boys / Bring flowers in last month's newspapers. Let be be finale
of seem."* Soon Edith had them memorized, and they'd trade lines
back and forth. *It's Stevens by way of the Beastie Boys*, she joked.

There was a deeper investment in knowing for Valerie. She went into the world seeking tidbits, bowerbirdish, to bring back to Edith. While she scudded through the emptiness of northern Pennsylvania, she asked, *Did you know that annoying girl in your novel class had an abortion?*

I do, why do you?

I googled her.

Val, don't do that, it's weird.

It's not weird. She wrote a piece about it for her undergrad newspaper.

Valerie.

It's there for anyone to find, not my fault if I go looking.

She brought back battered books and squabbles with trail maintenance coworkers. Men at bars who tried to talk to her about *Franny and Zooey. How do I explain to a cis man that me reading this book and him reading this book are not the same.* Edith didn't know when she found time to read Sheila Heti or Elif Batuman or any of the other spine-cracked novels she'd leave behind; Valerie always seemed to be reading *Franny and Zooey.*

Isn't Salinger, I dunno, for teenagers?

No, actually, this is the best book ever written.

Valerie pulled Edith into her circle of non-men, pulled her into bed in the half-light. There were cuts on her leg she didn't try to hide. Faint stains on the handle of her knife. But when she was at Edith's, no new marks appeared. She took one of Edith's sweaters with her when she left. *It smells like you.*

As long as Val was around, Edith kept taking the blue-green pills. She turned back and forth before the mirror, hunting for any sign of change. *I remember those early days,* Val said. Eighteen. Living in the empty midwestern city, the college she'd leave for the east coast. *Every single thing that happens seems like it could be the hormones. You feel moody, or your sense of smell seems better, or you bruise more easily.* The hypersensitivity that convinced you the life you'd always been living was somehow new. *When the real changes come, there'll be no doubt.* But Edith didn't stay on them long enough to see.

She should have been happy for the guidance. The early days of Valerie's transition were under the surveillance of an older chaser called Frank, *some half-fag,* Val said, *grown tired of rimming the same ostentatious queens that sparsely dotted the fifty-mile radius around the college.* He had an adult kid living in California working for an online gambling startup. He gave her money, gave her clothes, taught her makeup. Frank had dated young trans girls before. *He'd sit on my chest and play with me,* she said. *Enumerating step by step how I'd change. The hair that would vanish, the way I'd shrink. The hard buds of my nipples.*

Sometimes he'd rent a hotel room and leave her handcuffed to the bed, straining. *I had to act like I'd been turned on all the hours,* she said, *aching while he was at the bar, probably failing to suck some other teenager's cock. It was so terribly boring.*

She didn't share these stories often. Edith knew they were true, but it was unbelievable. Valerie had never been so delicate. Had never been less beautifully *girl* than she was now. They weren't steps that Edith could follow.

But when Valerie was around, there were fewer questions of *who* and *what* and *how.* There was only the fact of their bodies in space. The next time she visited, Edith said, *What if you didn't go so soon?*

They were in bed. Val's skin cloud-soft. Both bodies raw and soaked in each other's sweat, spit, and come.

What do you mean?

That's not a real question.

Edith traced the cross-shaped scar with a fingertip. Valerie did not sit up. She didn't push Edith's hands away or withdraw into herself. There was light in her eyes. There was breath all the way at the base of her.

It is, actually, Val said, *or I wouldn't have asked it.*

Stay home with me.

Judy.

Three months. Two. You're here for weeks at a time, what's a few weeks more.

Val gnawed her lip and buried her face in Edith's neck. *Why do you think I leave?*

Their conversation in the woods had receded from fact. If Valerie really wanted to stop, she would. *You're scared of staying still.*

Oh, Judith.

Two months. Edith hated the strain in her voice. *It's awful here without you.* Valerie said nothing. *When's the last time you tried, you know? When's the last time you let yourself—*

Okay.

Okay? Was it that easy? She kissed Valerie's eyelids, her cheekbones, her chin.

Okay. Okay! Tickled as Edith moved down her neck. *Two months. It could be fun.*

I T WAS MAY, AND HER BOOK WAS GOING NOWHERE.

Give up, then, Seb said. Edith was visiting them at work. The bookstore's packed shelves offered little consolation. *Write something else. You already planned out your next four books or whatever.*

Yeah but I need to do it fast.

'Cause of your fucking deadline? A customer looked up from their Anna Moschovakis book. From the back, Seb's boss called, *Language, Seb.* More quietly, Seb continued: *You know that's fake, right. Ask the editor for more time.*

You have to set boundaries somewhere. Even if her rent went up, she could scrape by for another six months or so. Even if she sold the book, she wouldn't have enough to afford rent in Boston. She shouldn't go back, maybe ever. The September deadline was a test.

Of what, Seb asked, *how stubborn you are?*

To see if any of it was worth it.

Do you hear yourself? Do you hear her? Seb demanded of the eavesdropping customer. The customer returned to reading *Eleanor*. *What's "worth it" mean? Are you happy?*

I don't know how to answer that.

Is writing a book going to make you happy?

Not writing a book is going to make me miserable.

She'd been trying to write about the things she loved. The world bounded by her skull. She had to make something so small she might easily fill it with life. Its skin swollen with light and color like one of Cézanne's apples.

How about you? Working on any articles?

No. Seb busied themself, scanning new books into the register. *Sara and I have been playing music together.*

Oh my god, you guys started a band?

We're not a band, we make ambient drone.

You guys are so cute, you're like Mates of State.

We are not like Mates of State, I'm going to exile you from the store.

Their boss called out, *No exiling people, Seb.*

Seb gave her a book before she left the store. A woman's face on the cover filtered poison-green.

You've never read Annie Ernaux, right?

Edith flipped through, absorbing little. *I started* The Years *once.*

This one's a diary, you'll love it. All the sad and yearning girlies do.

THIS CHARACTER of V., the editor wrote. *I'm not sure I understand what she wants.*

Right, I sort of feel like that's the underlying enigma of the whole thing.

Is it? I thought it was the narrator's feelings toward her.

That too.

Which I'm not really getting on the page either. I fear you're not really being honest with yourself.

I thought whatever I wanted to write was okay with you.

Is this really what you want?

Edith wrote paragraphs about homecoming in *The Odyssey*. The analysis of *Into the Woods* she'd been mulling over for weeks. She tried to remember why she'd quit therapy.

It's a matter of being stuck, she wrote, *of needing your story to move on so that your life can improve, but the wave eventually crests. The good is undone by the bad. In fact, the good brings the bad. That's the real genie-logic of wanting.*

I keep seeing the problems with what I'm doing and trying to point them out, Edith said. *Lampshading flaws so that no one can call me on them. But mostly it means that I keep undermining any credibility I have.*

That's it exactly, the editor said. *Your first book did that, too. Undermining itself. Do you have any idea why you do that?*

THE BEST image Edith found of a false homecoming was in *Gossip Girl.* By the end of season four, it's revealed that Charlie—who we've believed to be the estranged cousin of wealthy, glamorous Serena—is in fact an actress named Ivy Dickens, hired by Serena's aunt to impersonate her daughter and get access to a family trust.

I'm sorry, Bernard said, *say that again? That's like two layers of abstraction too deep for my poor man-brain.*

Ivy leaves New York at the end of the fourth season, but comes back in the fifth, abandoning her chef boyfriend Will Gorski in L.A. She slips back into the character of Charlie, bluffing her way through every social situation. It's the performance of a lifetime—not broken when Serena's aunt tries to out her, nor when Will Gorski falls in love with Serena.

Wait, so where is Serena's real cousin? Dead?

No, she's at Juilliard.

So why—

There is only one "why" in Gossip Girl: *money and power.*

That's two.

It was Edith and Bernard's first time hanging out in daylight hours. She nestled under his arm, Treats curled on her lap.

Ivy's life mirrored what it was like to go back to Boston. She returned to New York and had to pretend to be someone else again. A person you were once so good at pretending to be. Edith didn't know why she daydreamed of moving back; she'd be performing all the time.

On screen, people got ready for a party. Edith checked Tinder for messages from the Climbing Woman. Natalie. The last thing Edith/Harry asked was if she'd been to the Twombly gallery in Houston. Nothing yet. She settled in deeper beside Bernard.

Ivy abandons the ruse. She knows the real Charlie from a play they did together. This is revealed after she's spent three months taking care of the real Charlie's grandmother—out of sincere compassion. But, the terms of *Gossip Girl* being what they are, everyone assumes she's doing it for money.

Can I ask you a question?

I'll draw you a family tree, it's not as complicated as it sounds.

Why do you keep checking your phone?

My brain is broken and if I don't I'll literally die.

No, I mean you look at it like a bit of fuzz you're worried might be a bug.

She sort of wanted to know what would happen if she told the truth. Maybe what she needed was to burn part of her life to the ground, a forest fire making way for new growth.

It's fine if you're seeing someone else, obviously.

Oh yeah, you think I'm in high demand? For some reason she thought that would sound flirty.

I'm only saying.

Look at the beautiful girls. Look at the palatial homes and the flowing golden clothes. Here's a Deborah Eisenberg cameo. Here's St. Vincent playing a private party. No choice Edith made could have given her such a beautiful and charmed girlhood.

Besides money and power, *Gossip Girl* is about storytelling. By creating the Gossip Girl blog, Dan makes himself a character in the lives of the Upper East Side elites, naturalizes his place among them. He's already rich, though, and hot; his father is a washed-up rockstar who marries Serena's billionaire mother. The only time he fails to fit the Upper East Siders' narrative frame is when he pretends he does not want what they have. That he's any different from them.

Ivy is an outsider with no happy ending. She doesn't get the luxurious childhood other characters do. You can only write your way into stories that you already belong in.

V AL ASKED EDITH TO CALL HER SLURS DURING SEX.
What kind of slurs?

Any of them. "Tranny," "faggot," "trap," "brick."

Uhmmm—

You can just, like, call me a bitch or a whore. Tell me my mouth is only good for one thing.

Before she agreed to stay, sex with Val had been meandering and slow. There was little concern for orgasm, hardness, penetration. (But the first time Edith felt Val's cock inside her there was a cool burst of light behind her eyes and she could not imagine stopping.) Mostly it was a matter of talking and touching. She might hit Val. (*Harder than that. Harder, you fucking pussy.*) Valerie might tie Edith to the bed and watch her strain. It was all very tame. A TV idea of kink.

Edith understood that whatever the violence of these words, it was definitely less than getting hit in the face. She understood the appeal of degradation.

Tranny.

Like you mean it, Judy.

You stupid bitch. She straddled Val's hips and took her small, hard cock in hand. *You can barely fuck me half the time.*

Wrong tack.

You little slut. You stupid bricked-up faggot. Everyone knows you're a man in a dress.

Don't stop.

You—you stupid bitch. There was the man yelling in Central

Square. There was genuine anger. There was her own fear of who she could not become. *You dumb brick.* She could feel Val's cock softening and she tugged more fiercely at it. *Your hips are narrow and your tits look fake.* They did not. These were middle-school insults.

She tugged for a few minutes more. She offered to slap Valerie but Val guided her hands away. *What if we touch ourselves for a bit?* Valerie asked so gently Edith was sure one of them would cry. *Would that be okay?*

VALERIE TAUGHT her to swing dance and two-step. They spun across the apartment to Ella Fitzgerald singing Harold Arlen. They went to a club in Birmingham in shimmering dresses and no one needed to know their names. Edith chewed tabs of estradiol, blue-green paste coating her tongue like Fun Dip. On rainy days they took one of Val's dog-walking clients through the arboretum's misty hills; they tossed sticks into the pond for the dorky pit bull to snap up.

Then there was the knife. Val pulled it from a secret pocket in her bag. It snicked open. The ridiculous vigilante skull visible between her fingers. *Will you cut me?* she asked. If it were a real question, the knife would still be closed.

When Val was young, Frank the Chaser had liked putting needles through the thinnest parts of her skin. He'd liked coming on her tits and face. When he fucked her, she lost room in her brain for language; there was only a great sweeping hunger. She said the pain kept her in her body. She said she loved him. He gave her the money to go east. He taught her how to safely be choked. So what if he hit her when they fought sometimes. So what if he smashed her vintage highball glasses into confetti—he was the one who'd bought them. They'd made a game of it after, shattering every dish in his apartment and buying a new set the next day. What did any of it matter? What did it mean that she gave Edith the same love as she'd given him?

Is that what you want, Edith wanted to ask. Do you want me to be awful. Would that make you stay?

There was a clean honesty in the meeting of blade and flesh. Without thinking, Edith made a half-inch nick in the flat white plane of Valerie's back. She made a second, longer cut. She could carve her whole, wrong name—exorcise it from both their tongues. It was easy, in the end, and they both came. The scars on Val's thighs and stomach were invisible in the dark. Only later, when the blood had all been cleaned, did Edith worry.

THEY HOUSE-SAT for a professor, played with her cat. They cooked elaborate meals and read by dawnlight in the backyard. Edith sleepwalked through her classes, eager to return to these moments of real life.

The scabs on Valerie's back healed slowly; Edith refused to make more.

You'll understand when you've transitioned longer, Val said. *There comes a time when this is what you need.*

Don't condescend to me, Valerie.

Oh yeah? Val straddled Edith, teased the head of her hardening cock. *You don't like it when I treat you like some stupid girl fag?*

There it was, for the first and fleeting time—that hook of desire. It wouldn't return for a long time.

Shut your mouth.

Why don't you make me.

They didn't fight. There was only the morning when she woke and Valerie was not beside her, and she knew that two months had passed. It was impossible that it had been so long, so brief.

Her face in the pillow, seeking any scent of Val's. She knew they'd see each other soon, and she knew this wasn't enough.

E DITH STAYED IN SIGHT OF NATALIE AT THE GYM. SHE'D always liked watching her climb, her ropy body straining to grab the colored blocks.

It was funny that she'd thought of Boston as a finite place where the past would always return to you. Texas may sprawl, but you could run into the same strangers day after day. Maybe because of the sprawl—people weren't all packed into the lower part of the sky.

Here's what Natalie had told Harry about herself: she had a dog named Bruegel. She had gone to school in Illinois. She was allergic to bell pepper. Everything else was books, movies, art.

I saw Hirst's shark in Boston a couple months ago, it's incredible in person.

Ugh, Natalie said. *Hirst is a nineteen-year-old's artist. There's nothing behind the spectacle.*

Like Milan Kundera.

No, I quite like Kundera.

Kundera will write a beautiful and true sentence and follow it with something like "Women are all sluts who need a good dicking down."

Natalie was dauntless. Were Edith playing herself in this little techno-drama, she wouldn't have the gall to push back. She wondered how far she might go before the conversation broke.

More than that, she found herself telling the truth. Natalie often asked what she was listening to. They'd swap Spotify links without the imposition of a review; good and bad didn't matter, it was only a way to hear the other's world.

That day, Edith sent a short song called "Raytracer." *A friend of mine used to play it a lot*, she said. *She'd crisscross the country in her car and leave it on repeat for an hour or more.* Natalie sent Ella Fitzgerald's famous live performance of "Mack the Knife." Edith had heard it a dozen times before, but only now noticed that Fitzgerald forgets the song's lyrics. She begins to improvise without ever losing her rhythm. Never pausing or scrambling for the right words. Edith wanted to talk with Natalie about this. About her father driving her to school with Cole Porter songs on the radio. He'd shake his head whenever a lesser talent than Fitzgerald performed "My Funny Valentine" or "Stormy Weather." Edith wanted to say she still caught herself singing on rainy days: *Don't know why there's no sun up in the sky.* I lost the tune to the life I'd hoped for, she wanted to say. A life in which I was someone's girlfriend, someone's wife. In which I knew this year what next year would look like, and the year after. A real life.

But there were rules. Instead they talked about *The Double Life of Véronique* until one of them stopped responding, and they both came to the climbing gym, where they could go on not speaking in person.

VALERIE CAME BACK TO TUSCALOOSA WITH FOUR cuts along the inside of her thigh. She cooked noodles in Edith's cluttered kitchen where there was nothing for them but butter, salt, pepper. Her sputtering coffeemaker, dragged across America, made twelve cups of half-caf. There were two months of stories to tell: an eighteen-wheeler pushing her off the road, mediating drama in the aftermath of an orgy. They cuddled on the couch, half-comatose with carbs, and Edith read her pieces of what she'd been working on.

That's beautiful, Val said. *You're beautiful. I missed you, Judy.*

I missed you too.

So irritating. Life could always be this way if only Val could be a normal person. But then her lips found Edith's, her teeth found the skin of her neck, her hands traced the topography of her ribs. It was easy to forget.

Afterward, they lay in bed, Val's head on Edith's flat chest. The afternoon air was hot and bright and disguised nothing.

You know, you don't have to miss me. The ugly walls and dusty carpet were not a compelling recommendation to visit. *You can be here whenever you want.*

A small nip at the back of Edith's jaw. *I sort of like missing you.*

Well. That makes one of us.

You could get out of here for the summer, Valerie said. *It's not like you have class or anything.*

Oh yeah, just run away. That'll help.

It's gotten you this far, Judy.

What're you talking about? I don't run.

Mmm, my mistake.

For two months her apartment had grown wretched. Two months talking Adam through his own gender shit and two months of keeping hers to herself. Two months without eating real food, without seeing daylight unless she had to. Two months of missing Val. The neatness of their bodies together, their hands the same size. Maybe she was unlovable. Maybe there was one mistake she kept making.

It'd be so much easier for you, wouldn't it, Edith said. *If I just came with you.*

We're not trying to solve my life here. I have that on lock.

Which is why you're technically homeless.

Shut your mouth, Judy, before I shut it for you.

I'm serious, Val. She hadn't meant to be. *I want to fucking die when you're not here. I want to fucking walk into the river and let it sweep me away.*

How very Virginia Woolf of you.

Can you give me a real response, please?

This is a real response. Valerie's hands picked at the long scabs on her legs. Edith watched them bleed. The old cross-shaped scar. She never learned if it was something Valerie had given herself, or something she'd wanted, or if it was only meant to harm. *I was here for two months, I was gone for two months. There's balance to that.*

It's not enough.

You get as much of me as anyone gets.

Is that supposed to be a comfort? That I'm no lower in your esteem?

I'm sorry, would you prefer the alternative?

Edith sat up and Val's head fell to the pillow. *Don't tell me you're fucking happy when you're not here.*

Who do we know who's happy, Judy? Edith's hands followed Val's. She pressed a finger to the bright new blood. *I've decided happiness is something other people get.*

Don't say that.

I don't think there's a place for me. The best I can do is get a bit at a time—a little here, a little there. Valerie grabbed her hand. *I was having a nice time, you know.*

You said you wanted a place you could stop, a place you fit. How is this not it?

What do you want me to say? Do you want me to lie to you? She tugged Edith's hand. *You call this happiness?* There was blood in her fingers' whorls. A map to the heart of them both.

Edith yanked her hand away. *You make me happy. You make me not want to die. I thought that was clear.*

Okay, Judy.

Stop calling me that.

How were they still lying down? It should all be so much more Edward Albee than this. They should clomp the breadth of the apartment in their anger, knocking over the furniture and staining the carpet with spit and wine.

Valerie stayed a week. It was a good week—one of the best. They played Magnetic Fields songs on repeat and played game after game of gin rummy and when the brief Alabama summer rains tore the sky, they sat cozy and dry on the porch, watching the earth churned to mud. Listening, as if to music. The fight had not meant anything. Not by itself.

Valerie left without warning and did not return for a year.

A FTER THE BAKER'S WIFE DIES IN ACT TWO OF *INTO the Woods*, the baker flees from his child, his friends, and the giant trying to murder them all. He finds the ghost of his absentee father in the woods and insists he's done with all the fairy-tale trappings of his life: no more riddles, curses, quests. His father says, sure, why not run away? But "where did you have in mind? . . . Unless there's a 'where,' you'll only be wandering blind. Just more questions, different kind." It isn't enough to leave. If you aren't running toward a new, specific life, you will always be haunted by the life you leave behind.

In Act One, before their lives sour, Cinderella flees her prince. Knowing she would, he's spread the palace steps with pitch, trapping her midflight. She might give in to the trap and let him catch her. But the prince doesn't know her, only her ensorcelled performance, the fantasy version of her. She's left with an impossible choice: go home and stay safely herself, or give in to the fairy tale. Let the prince find out if he loves her more than the idea of her. Her choice is no choice at all: she leaves behind her shoe, giving the prince control over the story's familiar end.

There's no chance the prince won't pursue Cinderella's clue. She acts as though he might find it in the pitch, shrug his shoulders, and go home to marry some richer woman. And there's no way the baker can leave this story. The whole world is only his house and the woods. It isn't that he doesn't know what he's running toward, it's that the story has nowhere else to go. It's the appearance of flight they want, knowing the real thing is beyond them.

This is the way the story's told. This is who we are.

*

BERNARD AND Edith agreed they were better as friends. She figured this meant they'd still fuck now and then but at least she didn't have to worry about long-term satisfaction. It was only a way of blowing away dust.

They watched *Minority Report* on his couch, Edith's head on his lap. Tim Blake Nelson put Tom Cruise into a horrifying carceral limbo. *God*, Bernard said, *no one gives me gender envy like Tim Blake Nelson.*

Really?

Don't say it like that. Bernie played with her hair.

No he's great. He's the perfect amount of fucked-up looking.

Only dudes get to be that ugly and still be hot.

Why was she trying to be friends? Edith didn't want to stay in Texas. She'd lived here for years without building a life—pulled away by Val's magnetic draw. Why start now?

Do you think you'll leave, she asked, *if things get worse?* The two of them had gone to a protest the week before. The court had blocked a law qualifying trans healthcare as child abuse, but they all assumed it'd return like a horror movie slasher: gnarlier, harder to kill.

Not really. I grew up here, not like it's anything I'm not used to.

Yeah but like. If they start taking away hormone access or whatever.

Trans people survive all the time without doctors' support. We'll survive. His hand trailed down to her ribs. *All we can do is take care of each other and live the best lives we can.*

Wouldn't you rather do that in a state that didn't hate you?

And which state would that be? Edith's body strained toward his fingers. She always got like this the day after her shot. Unwise, feral.

But Bernard, resting his palm on her rib cage, only said, *Have you been eating enough?*

T WAS EDITH'S FINAL YEAR OF GRAD SCHOOL, AND HER astronauts were finding their way home. The Roman Christians were facing death but would live on as martyrs. Here were lives she could control. She was done with classes and hadn't seen another writer in months.

Adam sent her a picture of his face, his upper lip faintly shadowed. He'd been on T for six months. *How's your gender stuff?* he asked. *You still feel good about being called Edith?*

She did. The surprise of the name gave her vertigo. The rightness of it.

It's, like, impossible to get on HRT in Alabama, though.

I wish I could mail you some. Or you could drive up here.

She didn't tell Adam about the bottles of blue-green pills she'd poured out in a final, inconsequential ritual. A winter's dream of drawing Val back. *I'll be out of here soon*, she said.

But not back to what she'd left behind. All the cigarettes shared on cold New England sidewalks. The press of Tessa's body. An endlessly iterated joke, laughing until her cheeks ached. The miles covered in Val's car—to Birmingham, to the movies, to get ice cream cones at Trader Joe's. Wherever she went next, she'd go alone.

At night she dreamed of empty industrial landscapes. Someone walked beside her and did not speak. Silent ex-girlfriends lounged in pools of clear blue water. One night, she was pushing a hospital gurney through the blighted world, a body hidden beneath its sheets. Not dead, she knew, and not asleep.

Adam told her he wished he could give up sleep to get more work done.

Not me, Edith said. *There's nothing that feels better than sleeping.*

S EB HUNG OUT WHILE EDITH GOT READY FOR THE CON-
cert. *I don't understand why you're going to this show.*

*I can do things alone, Seb. I'm an adult woman. I hear they're let-
ting us drive now.*

No, I mean, *have you listened to anything besides* Into the Woods
in like four months? She hadn't. *That's probably why you're so
depressed. All that sublimated homosexuality.*

It doesn't make me depressed, I'm working through stuff.

"Working through" implies you'll find the other side.

Edith's eyeliner smeared across her brow bone. How many times
had she done this? She was so inconsistent.

What are you up to tonight? Not too late to join.

I'm supposed to hang out with Sara. She'd gotten back the day
before from visiting family in Pakistan.

Band practice?

Not a band. Seb watched her struggle in her makeup mirror. *Here,
lemme do that.* They drew two cat's eyes with a practiced hand,
steadied by years of misapplied femininity. *I dunno, man, I feel like
she's gonna be so tired, and just want to like cuddle and talk, and it's
gonna be so boring. Sometimes I feel like everyone we know could
afford to be a little less gay.*

The show was crowded with straight couples. The band's
alcoholic-beat-poet aesthetics must draw them out. Edith searched
for any sign of queerness—a mullet, a denim jumpsuit.

Have you seen them before? asked a man nearby. Edith said she hadn't. The man introduced himself as Ken. *Like their last album*, he explained. *My husband and I caught them on that tour*. Edith thanked whatever god watched over fags. She'd lose this if she passed better, disappear into the sea of girlfriends. A porcelain tooth, a forged Rothko.

Ken's husband, Ryan, returned from the bar with two cans of beer. The men were taller than her, with salt-and-pepper hair, and identical black blazers. *This is Edith*, Ken said, and they all chatted amiably about local music. Ryan had missed a William Basinski show that Edith had been at. *Oh I'm so mad I missed it!* Ryan said.

It was great. Something very unreal about hearing his music in a room full of strangers.

Rub it in, why don't you. Ken pressed her arm. Edith searched for a playful response, but the lights dimmed and the band took the stage.

Afterward, the three of them walked out together.

The singer definitely seemed hungover, Ryan said.

Still a lot of energy.

I wish that were me, Edith said. *When I'm hungover I only want to eat popcorn and die.*

Ken and Ryan laughed, and Ken brushed his fingers against hers.

Edith, I think we're going to grab a drink at Cheer Ups, you want to join?

Edith could tell they had money. She'd probably get a free drink and make out with at least one of them in the all-gender bathroom. Maybe they had coke.

Sure, that sounds fun.

Ryan had run publicity for a label that put out half the seminal Midwest emo records. *I spent like half my junior year of college crying in the shower to those albums*, Edith said. *The sad trans girls of America owe you so much.*

They both laughed again. It was such a victory, making strangers laugh.

And they were cute. Edith didn't have the standard tgirl daddy issues, but there was something very alluring about older men. It was part of the package of girlhood. Every cis girl she'd known had had at least one fling with a man twice her age. Well, almost every cis girl.

What was Tessa doing tonight? It was a Wednesday after all. Edith could only ever conjure the same image: her ex-lover's legs thrown over her future husband's, something simmering on the stove.

The men asked her about her writing. *I write about girls who are sad for good reasons.*

What do you know about being sad? Ken asked.

What does she know, Ryan said. *Pretty young thing like you.* They searched her book on Amazon. *Oh wow, eleven reviews.*

The next book I write isn't going to have a plot. Only the motion of people through the world. Their emotional physics.

Emotional physics, Ryan said. *See, this is why she's a writer.*

Me, I'd never come up with that.

They drank more. They danced uncomfortably under the particolored gaze of Cheer Ups' sign. An obscure, neon symbology: a planet, a pentagram, a flame, a gem. Ryan told stories about the bands he'd worked with. *They're all creative writing teachers now*, he said. *I could try to hook you up.*

An empty offer, but it made her feel alluring and entertaining. A thing worth having.

God you're so young.

Not that young.

You're so young you don't know how young you are.

They shimmied and swayed and brushed against each other until they grew tired. She walked to their apartment, an arm linked through each of theirs. *I feel like Dorothy, off to see the wizard.*

Ken and Ryan laughed. Too hard. *That's right. I'm the Tin Man and Ryan's the Scarecrow.*

Their apartment was the sort of soulless new construction tech workers chose. There were no decorations on the wall, no color in the furniture. Edith had hoped for better.

Do you do a lot of this? Ken poured wine into glasses so thin they seemed rendered out of air.

What, cavorting with strange men?

Are you cavorting with us?

What word would you use?

They drank their wine. Edith was tired and sour-stomached, but she wanted to keep alive whatever temporary light there was in her. She wanted to be done talking. Ken rose and put on an American Football record. Ryan's hand found her knee and pressed it like an unripe peach and moved no farther up her leg. This was the issue with letting other people take control: you had to move at their stupid pace.

What's the sluttiest thing you've ever done? Ken asked. He did not move from the turntable. She looked from Ken to Ryan and back to Ken. Their almost clinical gaze.

Uhm. What the fuck kind of question was that? Were they in high school? But she had to play along with their fantasy or bail. *One time I fucked my friend's brother while my friend was sleeping in the same room. If that counts*, she added, with no real coyness.

Oh, that definitely counts. All their teeth were purple-red and gleaming. *Do you like us, Edith?*

You know I do.

Why don't you kiss Ryan?

Finally, she was getting somewhere. Ryan's tongue was none too aggressive. Edith grabbed the back of his head, pulling him into her. His fingers trailed up the faintly clammy skin of her leg. Ken fell to the couch beside her, kicking over her wineglass. No one moved to

mop the burgundy puddle. Ken was not so good a kisser as his husband. He was all plunging tongue and wet lips. But whatever. She
hadn't come here in search of goodness or charm or even pleasure.

What kind of underwear are you wearing? Ken tugged at the hem
of her dress, groping at her boyshorts. It didn't matter that Edith felt
sexless in them. If she said nothing, the men's fantasy would go on
filling the room.

Soon, Ryan was on his knees sucking her half-erect cock. Ken
watched, an eagle-eyed study of her arousal. *Show us how much you
like us*, he kept saying. His pants were around his ankles and he was
touching himself through his threadbare boxers. *Show us.*

Edith made noises of approval, echoes of pleasures past. It wasn't
unpleasant, having this warm and eager mouth on her. The vague
perversion of Ken's witness. But it was boring. It was a chore like
flossing. At least flossing left some blood in your mouth, some proof
that something had changed.

Look, Edith said, and thought better. No sensual sentence has
ever begun "look." *What can I do to make you guys feel good?* She
reached for Ken and he slapped her hand away.

*I want you to fuck my husband's throat, Edith. Can you do
that for me?*

There were five more minutes of disconcerting fellatio. When it
became clear that no, she could not fuck anyone's throat, the men
sighed, zipped themselves up. Edith had no desire to put her underwear back on; she'd have left it there, crumpled and grotesque,
except that Ken picked it off the floor, dusted it off, and threaded
her legs back through. Edith wanted to laugh—at this display, at the
entire thing. She wanted to find goodness in this moment.

The wine's probably going to leave a stain, Ryan said, picking one
of Edith's hairs from his lips.

I'm sorry you guys. But the men weren't paying attention. They
were already in the rhythms of domesticity, pulling towels and

Lemon Pledge from a bin in the closet. She could, specterlike, stand here unseen all night, learning what their life together was really like. Instead she left the way she'd learned to, unnoticed and without a word. No lies that it had been fun and maybe they'd see each other around. She left while traces of dawn were still a long time off—an hour that people in love, huddled together in their too-warm beds, probably never saw.

T EN DAYS BEFORE EDITH LEFT TUSCALOOSA FOR GOOD, she heard the fourplex's front door swing open. Footsteps on the stairs. The door opened and Val slouched in the frame, hair frizzed by humidity. *Hey Judy. You're looking well.* Edith wordlessly continued packing. She was excising the books she'd brought from Boston and still not read. *I knew I'd find you here.*

Barely.

Judy, will you look at me? I've been gone a while but—

It's Edith, now.

Okay, Edie, will you stop for a second? Edith threw a copy of *Mason & Dixon* across the room and it splayed atop the cardboard boxes. Valerie got a good look at her. The skin against her bones. *It suits you better. The name.*

Why are you here, Val?

I think that's obvious.

Edith tugged open the old desk's drawers. As long as she carried the desk with her, every bedroom would be a refiguration of her unused Boston room. She swept old library cards, notebooks, and bank statements into a shallow box.

Edie—

Run out of people to make you feel good? Run out of places to run to?

And where are you running to? She hated Valerie's impenetrable defenses. Edith could never hurt her the way she'd been hurt. *Back to your fabulous domestic New England life?*

Texas, actually.

Valerie's whole body stiffened.

When Adam had asked her about moving to Texas, Edith had been cagey. It was a place she might start over, she said, far from the various lives she'd lived before. She wouldn't need to worry about the painstaking process of reinvention. All this was true, and all this she said. But she also thought it might be a ward against Valerie. Might keep the girl out of her life long enough for her to forgive or, at the very least, forget.

You don't want to do that, Val said.

Valerie. The ruffle and smack of another book hitting the wall.

I'm sorry, you're right. Go with god and yeehaw.

Where the fuck have you been?

Ju—Edie. The bed squeaked as Val sat. No one but Edith had been in it for a year. *I've been the same places as always. All over and nowhere at all.*

And which of those are you now?

Now I'm here. Valerie pulled at the skin of her face. Not impenetrable. Something else. *Edie, I want to apologize for disappearing.* Apologize, then. *I want to, but I don't know what I'd really mean by it. I did what I had to.*

You abandoned me.

It isn't to do with you.

You could've called.

So could you.

As if she hadn't thought to. As if she hadn't picked up every spam call wondering if it was Valerie at a payphone in some godforsaken Mountain Time town. Heart jumping at the phone's ring only to see her mother's name shining from the screen's blank face. It was embarrassing.

Enough sorting. Edith stuffed stacks of books into boxes at random—these to take, these to give away. She saw the appeal of nomadism. The chance, every few months, to rid yourself of everything that didn't fit.

I'm sorry I hurt you, Valerie said. And, after a minute more of silence. *What are you going to do in Texas?*

I'm going to fucking have a real life.

For money, I mean.

Maybe I'll try what you do: landscaping, dog walking, and fucking strangers.

Oh, Edith. Valerie couldn't keep the pity from her voice.

Edith didn't offer Valerie so much as a glass of water; she didn't kick her out either. Valerie sat on her bed, only interrupting when Edith packed the copy of *10:04* Valerie had brought her years earlier. *Is that box kill or keep?*

Keep.

Good.

They sat in this angry silence, neither fighting nor letting go. A small silence following the year's large one. Valerie would always leave, but Edith knew well enough now that this sort of squabble would not be the thing that drove her off. Maybe, given world enough and time, she could decode Val's patterns, always knowing when she would go and when she would stay.

Days later, Val would set her terms. She'd follow Edith to Texas and, no matter the horrors held by the state's borders, would return there again and again as the years went on. *Can't things be nice most of the time, and you only miss me now and then?*

Even on that first night, Valerie slept beside Edith.

There are worse things than missing the person who loves you best.

I N ACT TWO, CINDERELLA'S PRINCE SEDUCES THE BAKER'S wife in the language of moments. If they could be killed by a giant any second, they should take advantage of their time together. "All we have are moments," he says, "memories for storing. One would be so boring." The baker's wife gives in; throughout the musical she's wished in secret for a royal romance. After they sleep together, when she asks if they'll meet again, the prince again uses the language of moments to leave her: "This was just a moment in the woods . . . leave the moment, just be glad for the moment that we had."

The baker's wife is left behind, shocked. She convinces herself that these brief bursts of pleasure are not meaningfully real. This wasn't her, only a moment's indiscretion. "If life were only moments," she sings, "then you'd never know you had one." She'll go home with a renewed appreciation for the stable, loving family she has. And then, on her way back to her old life, she's killed by the giant.

Edith didn't know whether her death was a kind of horror-movie morality (she cheats on her husband and must be punished) or further testament to how capricious wishing is (you may get what you want only to die immediately). She only knew that feeling, that dream of a life that vanishes the moment you walk in the direction of home.

She left Boston all those years ago as if someone would give chase. If she'd stayed behind, she might have never found her way to being a girl. She had to trade the life she could have had there—with Adam, and Charlie, and, after they finished mourning their relationship, with Tessa—to become the person she was. She still didn't know if that was a trade worth making.

This is the thing about wishing: it isn't enough to do it once. You must wish over and over and over again, or the unwished-for world catches up with you.

I'VE DECIDED sleeping with cis men is a mistake. Edith and Seb were at the art center near the river. Sara was there, staring at a painting of either gory balloon animals or something's entrails.

Wow that's so T4T of you, Seb said. *Very trans separatism.*

I'm sorry, are you coming to cis men's defense?

Cis men are simple. They do what it says on the tin.

You've never had one ineffectually suck you off for fifteen minutes.

I've had much worse than that, girl. Believe me.

The woman behind the front desk frowned at them. Transphobe, Edith thought.

The next painting: more entrails. The show was called *Icthyomancy*, after the practice of reading futures in the spilled guts of fish. The artist had painted the entrails photorealistically, marking the time and place they'd been spilled. The project supposedly had something to do with global capitalism.

You know, this guy had a big show in Marfa, Seb said. *Fifty separate people who went blacked out the whole thing after.*

What do you mean?

Like they went through the show with their wives or their friends but couldn't remember a thing about it afterward. They'd lost maybe an hour of time.

I don't think that's true.

You can read about it in Artforum. *It's a whole thing. People kept going back to see if it would happen to them. Some said it did but there's no proof.*

Sounds like mass hysteria, Sara said.

Sounds to me like they were bored to oblivion.

Everyone's a critic.

It doesn't matter, Edith said, *we're going to forget all this anyway.*

There was a certain awful power to the paintings. Like a portal into the abattoir beneath all life. Each had sold, which felt like a mistake. Each one hanging by itself, a lone scrap of gore removed from its siblings. Domesticated. Toothless.

Anyway, if you ask me—

I didn't, but go on.

—you need to get more intentional about who you fuck.

Sara tapped Seb's shoulder. *Guys, the receptionist is staring.*

I'm not a receptionist, said the receptionist. *Please keep your voices down.*

We're the only people here.

No, I'm here and I don't want to hear it.

Not really a good look, Seb shot back, *yelling at a couple of brown kids and a trans girl.* The receptionist did not rise to the bait. Seb turned back to Edith. *Anyway, you can't walk through life waiting for some beautiful girl to fall dick-first into your mouth.*

So, what, I'm supposed to go around trying to fall mouth-first onto—

Basically!

Look, Edith, Sara said, *this one was done in Boston!*

The Bostonian fish guts were a soft pink. There was no indication what they portended.

If I'm so bad at this, Seb, why don't you choose someone for me to date.

Okay, fine. Hey, receptionist! Their voice echoed through the empty hall. *Do you want to date my friend?*

Seb!

The receptionist stood. Edith thought she might actually say something more interesting than no. *You guys need to leave or I'm calling security.*

In the car, Edith asked how their band was going.

Not a band.

It's good! said Sara. *I have like ten pedals. My guitar sounds like an ocean.* They were going to play a show sometime later in the summer. *Maybe find an outdoor space to make bracing tones in.*

Edith said, *Love a bracing tone.*

My dream is to set speakers up around an art gallery or an empty school. You could have different notes coming through them all at intervals. So the real performance is how you move through space.

Sara, you're wasted in academia, you could've been a sound artist.

No, no, I only like the ideas.

Yeah, it's easy, said Seb, *when you don't have to put them into practice.*

They dropped Sara off at her apartment and Seb carried on with Edith.

So since when are you the fucking relationship expert.

What do you mean?

Don't you think you should be nicer to Sara?

I'm plenty nice. Seb slammed their horn as a car cut them off. *There's a lot you don't see.*

Oh yeah, like what?

Seb took a breath. *Pancakes.*

You make pancakes.

Every morning before she gets out of bed. They're her favorite.

You make her pancakes. Every morning.

Are we in a fucking church?

You really love her, don't you?

Oh, come on.

You're so fucking gay for her. You want to live in the back of a

*camper van with her and your five children and a pit bull they can
ride like a horse. You want—*

Edithhhh.

*—to go on a tour of notable bed-and-breakfasts and make a hun-
dred pancakes every morning and—*

Edith I will steer this car into oncoming traffic.

EDITH/HARRY'S LAST messages to Natalie were about the
neglect of Elaine de Kooning's work. Edith scrolled back through
the earlier threads: song recommendations, exhortations to go and
look at the moon, a long discussion of time in Richard Linklater's
films. If only there were a way to turn this into a real relationship. To
arm herself with this knowledge and insert herself into the Climbing
Woman's life. But even Harry seemed ill-equipped to share any real
intimacy with her. They hadn't exchanged phone numbers.

Hey, Edith tapped into the chat. *I think I've seen you at the climbing gym some, do you go often?*

Natalie's response came quickly. *I've seen you there too.*

For a brief moment, Edith thought Natalie had seen through her
subterfuge. But no—it was only that Harry looked like so many
other ordinary boys.

Why didn't you say hi?

You were with people. I wasn't sure of the protocol.

Natalie was one of those people who was incapable of small talk,
eager only to share the flashiest parts of herself. Edith could feel herself succumbing to the poorly reasoned calculus that kept her in relationships past their expiry: if only x were not true, if only we could
get back to y, then things could be perfect.

Still. It didn't hurt to wish a little.

Next time, Harry said, *say hi.*

AFTER WEEKS of trying, she and Tessa found a chance to talk. *It's getting warm up here*, Tessa said. *Everyone's so pale.*

I'm envious. When it gets warm here, all I think is, "Here we fucking go again."

Their conversation was a weaker version of those they'd had in Boston. Tessa's friends, a new show at the ICA, movies they'd both seen. Edith didn't have much to offer; as of late her life was a series of sexual errors.

How are things with Devin? A pause. *Not a trick question.*

They're good. And another. *What do you want to know?*

Whatever you want to tell. Edith sat on the curb and pulled a cigarette from behind her ear. *I didn't exactly give you a chance to before.*

I should've told you some other way.

Stop that. Tell me about the Devster.

Well for one he loves *being called the Devster.*

Whatever Tessa told her, she could twist into an insufficiency. He was a cis guy, for fuck's sake. Edith was less prepared for how much he would remind her of herself. Devin was a bassist, a poetry reader, and he loved Prince.

Oh my god you're stuck with another *guy who makes you listen to Prince?*

Tessa's laughter filled her up like smoke. *The misfortune is not lost on me.*

Devin loved small, disabled dogs, and had taken Tess to specialized shelters. Just to look, he said. He did data analysis for an environmental nonprofit. He was good at making pies. His mother taught philosophy at Hampshire College and his father had died of a heart attack.

Can I see a picture?

If you're sure.

He looked a little like she had. Skinny, tall, scruffy. Wire-rim glasses. He could have been whoever Natalie confused for Harry.

The picture was of Tessa and Devin together, arms thrown around each other. Crisp leaves, casualties of a real autumn, were strewn around their feet. All that was missing was a three-legged chihuahua mix.

They looked right. Happy.

When's the wedding?

A longer pause. Would they ever be able to talk about this without tiptoeing around it?

Next July. In Northampton.

It was so far off as to be functionally never. Edith could have joined a cult by then. She could be dead or married herself.

Most days she felt fine about Tessa getting married, which was to say, most days she forgot. It was not unlike Valerie's death in this way. In both cases, there was a life just out of frame, a love that might have saved her. In another world she would have gone to the wedding with Valerie, the two of them happy for Tessa and in confederacy against her. They'd dance drunkenly under the Northampton moon and whatever the morning may bring, the night would be theirs. But there was no chance she'd be invited to Tessa's wedding.

She imagined being that boy. Standing at aisle's end as Tessa approached in bridal whites. Knowing that a permanent thing was happening—no matter who died, or divorced, or betrayed the other, there was a commitment more permanent and real than any piece of paper or ring could connote. Everyone she loved, everyone who loved her, watching and wishing for her utmost happiness. Valerie would be there, of course. Charlie would be a groomsman. Her father would cry during the first toast.

Ridiculous.

She wanted to tell Tessa how happy she was for her. That it was a good life. She'd choke on the words if she tried.

Are you sure he's cis?

More laughter. *You think everyone is trans, Edith.*

T HE CALL CAME BEFORE EDITH COULD FINISH UNPACK-
ing. *Mom?* she asked, certain it was a pocket dial. At the other
end was a snuffling and snorting, a static of something besides words
scraping across the phone. Edith hung up.

What was that? Val asked. She examined the walls of the Texas
apartment, unrolled the Cézanne print across the coffee table. The
splotches of red and yellow and green.

Not sure.

What do you think of hanging this here? She held the print up to
the blank wall over the TV.

It's a little college, isn't it?

It's not like it's Klimt.

Put it wherever.

Are you okay?

Edith's phone rang again.

Mom I think your phone is—

Your father went into the hospital this morning.

What—

They don't know, she said. *You need to come here.*

Twenty minutes later, she and Valerie were on the road to Vir-
ginia. Heart's *Little Queen* on the stereo. They didn't need the GPS.
It should take around twenty hours if we minimize stops, Val said.
Close your eyes for a bit, okay?

I don't want to. A duffel she'd packed in Alabama lay on the backseat like a sleeping dog. *What's going to happen, Val?*

We're going to drive to Virginia. You're going to see your parents. Everything will be fine.

It had been years since she'd seen them. She didn't know if she was legibly their son anymore. If she'd be forced into conversations she'd hoped to put off indefinitely. Or if it would all be swallowed by her father dying.

Valerie and Tessa had seen her parents plenty in college. They never quite seemed to believe Valerie had once been a boy. Edith wasn't sure if her friends and parents got along because of an honest connection or because her mother and father always took them to an oyster bar. Neither Tessa nor Val had to deal with them in any real way.

Somewhere before the edge of Texas, she fell asleep. It was raining when she woke, hail pebbling the car. *I can take over whenever.*

Are you joking? Val chewed a rat-sized wad of gum. *Do you know the farthest I've driven in a day?*

Don't tell me, it'll make me worry.

Val cranked the stereo louder. "Raytracer" filled the car.

You know, around a month ago, I was driving across Kansas on Highway 70. People say there's nothing to look at in Kansas but that's not true. Val liberated another piece of gum from the package by the gearshift. *Anyway, it's getting late, I'm getting hungry, I pull off at a Subway for a sandwich. And the woman behind the counter, she asks me where I'm going, and I tell her. I ask for more cucumber and not too much oil. It's not until she tells me about her son who's studying engineering that I realize: I've had this conversation before. Like déjà vu but I can pinpoint it. A date, a time. I almost tell her, but what would the point be?*

People like to be remembered.

People like to be memorable. No one wants to remember how many times they've made you a sandwich. Valerie plunged through the elemental murk, eyes scanning the rain for movement and light.

So I'm eating my sandwich, and I know what's going to happen next. I'm going to get back on the highway going ninety miles an hour like everyone else. I'm going to get stopped by a cop who's going to spend too much time scrutinizing my license, ask what I'm doing so far from Massachusetts. He'll ask if I have anything illegal in the car, and I will think of the Punisher, wrapped up in socks in my bag, and not remember the Kansan policy on switchblades, even though I looked it up last time.

Last time?

All of it happened before. It was like I'd stepped back in the stream of the past.

"Listen: Valerie Pilgrim has come unstuck in time."

I could see it perfectly—every move, every word. And then I began to worry.

That it wouldn't happen?

That it would.

And did it?

The wad of gum sat unmoving in her cheek. Lip bit with the expectation of a lie, a dodge. Instead: *Yeah. It did.*

On the stereo, "Raytracer" again. The storm was softening. Cars with Morse-code hazard lights idled on the roadside. Blurred faces lit by phones. Sealed off from every ill the world could throw, and by so thin a membrane.

Edith wanted to ask if that was why Valerie had come back. She was afraid of either answer. *Where were you going?*

Friends' out in Boulder. Barn and them.

You keep in touch with Barn?

Not like I do with you.

They reached Virginia an hour before dawn. Edith scrounged in the back porch planters for the spare key. The two of them tiptoed to the guest room, her mother's snores audible above.

Edith fell into bed and kicked off her shoes. Valerie stripped—

shorts, socks, shirt. She studied her reflection in the tarnished mirror. The jut of her hips, the sateen camisole. *I didn't even drive,* Edith said. *How are you still standing.*

Is your mom going to be unhappy I came?

My mom loves you.

It's different now, isn't it?

Edith's mom didn't know they were, whatever—dating/lovers/ friends who fucked. That wasn't what Valerie meant.

Valerie and her double. The soft swells of hips and breasts. The press of her rib cage. Edith hadn't had time to go to the gender clinic in Texas. It was ridiculous, wasn't it? Wanting. Trying.

She crossed in sock feet and wrapped Val in her arms and did not look her own reflection in the eye. Edith kissed her girlish shoulder. *I'm happy you came.*

I'd do anything for you, Edie. She kissed the knob of Edith's wrist. *Anything I can.*

Edith was too tired to list the things this must exclude. *You can't call me that here.*

Obviously, Val said. Meaning, of course I could. Meaning, wouldn't that make it easier. But it wouldn't be hard to revert to the old name. Edith looked the same as she always had.

In the morning, Edith found her mother making a stack of peanut butter sandwiches.

I didn't think you were here, her mother said. *No one in your room.*

Here I am. Valerie, too.

And Tessa?

Tessa and I broke up, Mom. Val and I are dating now.

Always used to be the three of you. We used to joke you'd end up married to them both.

How's Dad doing, Mom?

The Warrens are having a birthday party for their son. Up the street.

We'll probably head to the hospital as soon as—

They've rented a donkey ride. All the children in the neighborhood are invited.

Mother—

They're taking care of it. Spread spread spread. There was a second jar of peanut butter, a second loaf. *Being there won't change anything.*

Still.

Pick up a knife, she said. *Help me.*

TELL YOURSELF ANY STORY YOU WANT. WHATEVER happens, it won't be that.

Edith still had all the books Valerie had brought her in Alabama. Chris Kraus, Rachel Cusk, Elif Batuman. Books that worked through life's problems with familiar tools. They made you believe it was possible, if not easy, to arrive somewhere.

Do you think making art is immoral? she asked Seb.

They looked up from their copy of *The Transsexual Empire* and said, *Yeah.*

Because you're mining the world for, like, information instead of living in it?

You can't make art without cutting yourself off from other people. You have to distance yourself, alienate yourself from the world, to capture it. From somewhere in the midst of Edith's piles, they pulled out Sigrid Nunez. *"If reading really does increase empathy,"* they quoted from memory, *"it appears that writing also takes some away." It's inhumane.*

She reread Akwaeke Emezi, Anelise Chen, Kate Zambreno.

At her request, Seb read the abandoned draft of *Black Pear Tree.*

I don't see why you're so worried. No one could reasonably be mad at this.

Being written about, Edith pointed out, had a tendency to escape limits like "reasonable." *No one wants to be misapprehended.*

Okay, but being written around isn't so hot either. What do you think all these jabronis got out of writing the books you're reading?

Somehow this question had never occurred to her. The revelations about their fictional stand-ins must have been outdated by the time the book reached shelves. They all kept living life. Making new mistakes, writing new books.

Seb scrolled the document. Edith had highlighted every instance of their name for ease of their appraisal. *Alternatively, why do you think you're writing this?*

Because not writing—

Will make you miserable, yeah. But like, why your own life all of a sudden? The short answer—because this was the sort of book she liked reading now—was incomplete. She felt she'd spent all her life *writing around* instead of *writing about*. She was still writing around.

Edith tried reading Annie Ernaux's diary but couldn't get into it. The romantic obsession was too familiar. You see your lover, you gather experiences with them. Those become fuel for the fire that burns in their absence. You worry you'll never see them again.

Maybe I should become a nun.

That's a good call, Seb said. *Nuns fuck.*

EDITH'S MOTHER WAS RIGHT. EDITH AND VAL WENT TO the hospital with a fistful of flowers and a book to read aloud only to be told to come back when her father wasn't sleeping.

What's the problem? Valerie asked.

Something gastrointestinal, a nurse said. *We'll know more soon.*

They left the flowers in the hospital, left the copy of *The Optimist's Daughter* in the cluttered backseat of Valerie's car, and drove around town.

Give me the grand tour, Valerie said, though she was driving. *I always wanted to visit.*

Why didn't you?

I guess wanting wasn't reason enough.

There were the intersections where she'd gotten into car accidents. Her high school on the hill. The bookstore she'd been going to since before she could read; one of her first memories was of a ceramic bowl at the checkout filled with foreign coins. The bowl was gone, but the two of them spent pleasant minutes inside, searching through used books.

I'm buying you this, Valerie said, pressing a familiar green spine into Edith's hands.

You already have. Edith had sold the copy of *Franny and Zooey.* Val's gift for her twenty-sixth birthday. Inscribed: To Judith, my little pilgrim. *Don't you own like four copies.*

I leave them here and there.

Stopped at a traffic light between the bookstore and her parents' home, Edith caught the man's eye. He was pudgy, balding, idling in the next lane. He didn't seem happy or sad to see her as he leaned out his window. *Hey*, he called out, *hey*— The jagged disorientation of being called her old name. Caught between Valerie, who knew her real name, and everyone else, who did not.

Hey, Travis.

What's up.

Oh you know. My dad's in the hospital. My mom is losing her mind. I bought nail polish remover at a gas station in Arkansas.

Cool. The light changed. Travis drove off. Valerie idled at the line until the car behind them honked.

Edith was embarrassed to feel tears.

Who was that?

He played drums in my high school band.

I didn't know you were in a band.

Sure you did. Val pulled off into the parking lot of a gun store. Edith had gone to school with the owner's son. *Do I really look the same?*

People see what they expect to.

But who expects to see me here?

It doesn't occur to them that anyone leaves.

Valerie asked for the name of a neutral place—anywhere—and Edith directed them to a park across town. There was a bench with a view of the river. A train trestle that bridged its banks. Every year, some dumb college kid died trying to cross.

When I was fifteen, Valerie said, *my friends and I used to drive to empty parking lots and set off fireworks in the stupidest ways we could think of. Mostly we threw bottle rockets, letting them go right before the fuse burned out. You had to trust physics to point it away from you. When it didn't, we'd scramble.*

Or we'd have Roman candle fights, she went on. She took Edith under her arm, never minding the Virginia heat. Two smooth-skinned girls, stuck together. *You'd think those sparks burned but mostly they bounced off like nothing. Some girl caught one in her mouth once, and it lit up her teeth and tongue like a haunted puppet show.*

She didn't wait for Edith to respond. She talked about the abandoned buildings she'd broken into, the spiral staircases that had rotted away. The friend who fell from a roof and wandered to a party next door, so that for thirty or forty minutes everyone wondered if he'd vanished into the sky. Boys and girls she'd kissed in the middle of the desert under a sky like a broken hourglass.

Why are you telling me this?

Val pulled her closer. *Because I haven't before.*

NATALIE STOPPED RESPONDING ON TINDER. EDITH saw her at the gym, scaling blocks the color of a washed-out night over and over again. Had she gotten bored with Harry?

The only person Edith told was Bernard. They were lying in his bed, fully clothed, another party winding down on the other side of the wall. *Cyrus if you do not stop playing that song I will circumcise you*, Di called across the house.

Do you think I'm like, deeply fucked up? Edith's hands were crossed at her throat. This was a compromise; she wanted to curl into a ball so tight that no sound, light, or touch could reach her.

Definitely not. In the living room, "Down with the Sickness" began again and Di shrieked. *That's not in the top five most fucked things people at this party have done.*

Maybe not fucked up as such. But pretending to be your pre-transition self to get attention from cis women? That's pretty bad, right?

Do you want me to tell you it's bad? Do you want me to tell you you're fucked up? Bernard uncrossed her hands. *Why don't you talk to her?*

Literally what would be the point. Did Edith feel affection for Natalie? Or did she just like having someone to talk to about the stupid bullshit she thought about?

It'd stop your moping.

But I love to mope.

Well, at least you're honest about it.

And if I solved my problems, what would you and I talk about? The weather??

I dunno, man, maybe then we could actually be fucking friends.

We were already fucking friends, Bernard, and we agreed we'd be better as the regular sort. She moved to cross her hands again and Bernard slapped them down. *Did you invite the ketamine twins? I'd like to try it.*

Oh good, more solutions.

I mean how would you feel if you tried to create the most palatable, cis, reasonable version of yourself to get people's attention and it didn't work? If you discovered that the problem was not that you'd made yourself an unlovable and monstrous tranny but that you were unlovable and monstrous purely on your own terms.

I think I'd feel pretty good about it.

I don't think you would, Bernie, because I feel quite terrible. He sat on the bed's edge. Now Edith rolled over, facing him, missing his warmth in the over-conditioned air. *I mean you learn your supposedly gay ex-girlfriend is head over goddamn heels for a cis boy named, of all things, Devin, and—*

Don't you ever get tired of pitying yourself?

Never have yet.

Change your goddamn life, Edith. Get a dog, get a hobby. Find something, someone, somewhere that'll make you happy.

Because it's that easy.

You want to be friends, that's fine. You have shit to work through, okay. But you have this—I don't know, this image of who you are that's so infuriating. You need to get your shit together. Snap out of this, whatever this is.

Don't be mad, Bernie.

I'm not. He sounded mad. In the kitchen, footsteps chasing footsteps. *I'm going to hide the knives,* he said. *Figure something out by the time I get back.*

Figure what out?

I don't care. Anything.

By the time he returned, she was curled up, asleep. They lay with their arms around each other all the hot, short night. In the morning it would be too late for anything new. Bernard would check in a few days later, hopeful that something in her mood had changed, and she wouldn't respond. Some people only made the world more tangled.

*H*OW DO YOU FEEL, DAD?

Help me up. He didn't look sick, was the thing. It was the hospital itself that seemed an illness—the beeping machines, the sterile sheets. The ugly faux-Impressionist flower paintings. Pages spilled as Valerie leapt from her chair. She grabbed Edith's father under one arm and Edith grabbed the other. *Good to see you, Mr. McAllister.*

Valerie! When did you get here. Between them, he weighed almost nothing. They helped him to the bathroom.

Val and Edith gathered the scattered leaves of Edith's astronaut book. *What do you think so far?* Edith hadn't shared it with anyone but her thesis committee.

I have to see how it ends. Pages came together without order. *He's going to be fine, by the way.*

What makes you say that?

Lifetime of observation. Last night she had told Edith about friends who died. Preventable deaths and freak accidents. They lay in the semi-dark living room under the same Cézanne print that hung in Edith's apartment. A still point.

They helped her father back to his bed and he asked Edith about school. *I'm done, Dad, I moved to Texas.*

Lots of guns down there. Stay away from shopping malls. He pressed his hands to his stomach and groaned. *And how are you, Valerie?*

Good, Mr. McAllister, I've been traveling.

You still dancing?

All the time. Edith didn't know if this was a metaphor, or if Valerie really was dancing in far-off places.

Where's Teresa? her dad asked. *How's she doing?*

Still in Boston, Valerie said.

Well tell her to come here. She reads Stoppard with all the voices.

She's busy, Dad.

Too busy for a sick old man? More groaning.

There was history to unpack. There were harder things waiting to be told. Seeing him here, hurting in his bed, Edith almost found the words. Dad, I'm a girl. I'm your daughter. I need you to know—

Tell me about your travels, Valerie.

She described the views from the Pacific Coast Highway. Her pilgrimage to see the Spiral Jetty. Attending a pagan christening ceremony of sorts. Condensed to a paragraph, her life became only these things—a series of picture postcards that could be fixed to the fridge, read every morning over orange juice and cereal.

Lovely, her father said, *all what's in the world.* Soon he was snoring, and the girls snuck out.

At the house, her mother pulled tablecloths from the hall closet and piled them on the floor. Had her parents always been this useless? So incapable of dealing with strife? Or did part of you break as you aged and realized this was it—it was only going to get harder from here.

Dad seems okay.

Do you smell that? Her mother sniffed dramatically. *Help me take these to the porch.*

Edith sighed, scooped up the patterned fabric. *The nurses say it's not his gallbladder, so they're going to have to do more tests.*

There's so much shit in this house. Non-evaluative. A statement of fact. *Live in a place half your life and suddenly your thirties are the dust in the corners.* Tablecloths flapped from the porch rails. A series of white sails bordered with florals. Stained with chocolate, coffee, wine, blood.

Mom, why don't you go see him? Val and I can take care of dinner.

Stay out of my kitchen.

Edith could only take so much of this before she erupted. Before she tried to force her mother to look at the possibility of life without her father. To look at her own face, see the girl she was becoming. If she could just do that, she thought, everything else might follow. The only question was time.

S OMEHOW IT WAS JUNE. EDITH'S LEASE WOULD END soon and she had nowhere to go next. No matter where you went, you brought your problems with you. You had to sort yourself out first.

Texas was becoming worse. There were new attempts to classify gender-affirming care as child abuse. Soon Medicaid would stop covering it. In Florida, children were being forcibly detransitioned. Alabama would follow. Eyes followed her in the women's room more than ever before. There had to be better places than this.

On the phone, she asked Adam, *What have you heard about the wedding?*

Tessa's wedding? Yes, obviously. *It's still ages away. I hear normal stuff, mostly. Cake tasting and dress shopping.*

God, doesn't that all sound sort of, I dunno. Straight?

I'm not going to talk shit with you about our dear friend, sweet Edith.

Aw, but how can you resist when I'm so cute. Had Tessa always wanted this sort of life? Or was Devin, and her love for him, strong enough to sway her? *I'm not sure I've heard you say one word about our so-called dear friend's so-called fiancé.*

You don't really want that. Or you shouldn't.

Of course I do! I can process information in such a normal way.

It seemed so easy once you were in love. A person who could follow you places, or help you find a new place to go. Some shoulder to sleep on when your flights were delayed. Some sharp eye to find the lost back of your earring. It embarrassed Edith how much she wanted this.

When are you and Michael gonna tie the knot? she asked.

Adam laughed. *"Tie the knot"? Are you someone's southern grandmother?*

I am the people's southern grandmother.

I don't think we're the marrying sort. It'll make it so much harder to have a string of torrid affairs in middle age.

Maybe Val had the right idea. Floating from place to place—live wherever, fuck whoever for however long, and carry on your merry way. Never mind that it had killed Val. Never mind what it would do to Edith.

When she didn't have anyone to call on her walks, she listened to Michael's podcast, *I Love "I Love the 80s."* Michael's voice had that NPR mellifluousness. It was like listening to a hypnotist.

It's so interesting to think, he said, *of the mythos that New Coke has taken on. No one from our generation knows what it tastes like, only its reputation. A reflection of a reflection. We might not hate it at all. It might be the best thing we've ever tasted.*

Someone had to put her life in order. She needed a paradigm to squeeze herself into. The clarity of hindsight; a decade reduced to ten hour-long episodes.

V ALERIE LEFT EDITH ALONE WITH HER MOTHER FOR A few hours of the night. All the tablecloths hung out in the warm and windless dark. A choir of tree frogs filled the air. Edith found a bottle of cooking sherry in the back of a cabinet—the only alcohol in the house. It had been her first illicit drink when she was thirteen, snuck in the middle of a sleepover. It had been the first drink she and her mother had shared, three years later, while her father was off working as an AP exam grader.

This bottle, grubby with dust and its label peeling, could be the same one.

It's good to have you home, love, her mother said.

Yeah, it's good to see you.

You could do it more often. Her mother clicked on the radio. Satie's slow furniture music. The sherry tasted terrible and both poured a second glass. *You and Valerie,* her mother said. *Is it serious?*

Ordinarily she'd lie. *I don't know.*

Would you have children with her?

Well she can't—no, Mother, I wouldn't.

Not very serious then. They took turns thumbing a loose corner of the sherry label. *You know, when your father and I met, he was engaged to a woman who already had a child. She'd gone through college with one foot in each world.* Insane, every time, to think of this anonymous other child, almost her father's step-daughter. From the time she first heard this story at fourteen, Edith had often imagined that she might meet that other kid out in the world. She had—if she's being honest—imagined falling in love with them a little. Or at least kissing them on a bridge above a river full of starlight.

We met at a picnic, her mother went on, *and I could see how he loved that little girl. How eager he was to share the world with her, and have her share it with him. And I knew—that was going to be my children's father.*

Child's, Edith said.

You were enough, weren't you. Though I always thought your father wanted a daughter. It was hard to believe her mother said this. It was surely only in the rewriting that this sentence came out—something Edith wanted or misunderstood, built from a jumble of half-heard phonemes. *He adored that first child. That first child. His and not.*

Drops splashed across the table as Edith refilled her glass. There were often moments like this. Brief points of conspiracy when she could talk about whatever she'd been putting off. The couch in Boston with Bing Crosby playing. The night-swathed Alabama bed. It was the emotive equivalent of a musical swell, a place where there seemed to be no choice in the matter, only a letting go.

Mom, she said. *Look.*

We were good to you, her mother said. *We did what we could. What we had to. And soon I guess we'll both be dead.* She turned the glass this way and that, catching light in the syrupy liquid. *Your father goes, I'll go soon after. There isn't any love in that, you have to understand. Only, at a certain point, that's what life is.*

Listen, Mother, I have to— But there was nothing left. Everything was slipping away like colored sand.

B EN LERNER'S *10:04* PRESENTS ITSELF AS AUTOFIC-
tion: the narrator is named Ben, he teaches at the same college
as Lerner, he goes to the same artists' residency. He shares Lerner's
thoughts and interests. Certain world-historical events coincide.

But it's resolutely a novel, full of invention. One of its primary
concerns is Ben's relationship with his best friend, Alex, as she tries
to get pregnant. Lerner's real wife, Ariana Mangual, appears only as
an absence: his brother asks "Where's Ari? Did she go to bed or is
she coming?" and Ben replies "She isn't in this story." A second mention of her, of Ari, comes as the book nears its end—pictured in the
back seat of a cab. To write about the person he loves most, Lerner
must write about other people entirely.

Identifying these sorts of moments is, I think, one of the pleasures
of the things we've opted to call autofiction. The reminder that it
isn't a self-same life. Neater than memoir, less sprawling and daily
than a diary. We're always telling ourselves stories about our lives;
they're only sometimes legible to others.

Kate Zambreno explains this somewhere in her book-length
study on Hervé Guibert, *To Write As If Already Dead*. I can't find
the quote right now, but in essence, it's this space between biography and autofiction that creates tension, that invests us with the
power to pick apart the fictionalized world. To understand something about life, and people, and writing.

It's only on rereading these books that Valerie had left her that
Edith began to understand this. That writing about life is antitheti-

cal to living and vice versa. That you must empty out certain parts, must fill those gaps with something else. A wedge between the story and how it's told. Whatever is fixed by the story's end will be undone by the next's beginning.

("I wish—")

D AYS WENT BY AND THE DOCTORS' TESTS WERE INCON-
clusive. Her father's gastrointestinal tract was shutting down.
Her mother was cleaning leaves from the gutters. Sprawled against
the Virginia sky at the top of her ladder, a seventy-year-old scarecrow waiting to beat back god's angels.

All Edith and Val could do was drive. There was a circuit of roads
called the Loop, backcountry with no speed limit. A place where
teens in cluttered hatchbacks raced, parked, hotboxed, and groped.

I wish I had a fucking cigarette, Edith said.

Trans girls aren't supposed to smoke.

No one is *supposed to smoke.*

Edith was comfortable behind the wheel of Valerie's car. It swung
into the gravel shoulder as she turned onto the next road in the Loop.
The air was cool with A/C and Orbit gum.

What if he dies and I never come out to him.

He's not going to die.

*It's so weird talking to them without talking about this. Like I
have nothing to say because my brain, a whole hundred percent of
the time, is trying to work out gender stuff.*

Is it weird being back here? As a girl, that is.

*Am I a girl, Val? I feel like a stupid boy who spends an hour a day
shaving his chest in the shower.*

Oh shut up.

Is it weird? I have no idea. It makes everything feel less possible.

In lieu of a cigarette, she chewed more gum. She was amassing quite a wad. *I mean how does anyone do this. You're carrying around a whole history inside you, and there are a million people who know you, and—what are you supposed to do, just cut out the whole first quarter century of your life?*

You mean like I did.

Yes. I mean—no, Valerie—

Edith you have no idea—

How lucky I am? Yeah, yeah. She bit a hangnail until blood showed. *Your parents are fucking creeps, horrible people, whatever.* No matter how much of her past they discussed, Valerie's parents were always shadow-players. Banished before the curtain rose.

Val squeezed the handle above the door. *Actually, I was going to say, how little this matters.*

Oh, are you going to go in at me about ""chosen family"" or whatever?

It's not about family at all. It's about the people you keep. What you do for them and what they do for you. Edith tried not to look at her as Valerie said, *You were always upset with me for leaving, but you know, I didn't have to come back.*

Yes, sorry, you deserve a medal for that.

Don't you wonder why I never keep in touch with people from home? Valerie never called Texas "home." *The kinds of fuck-ups I was friends with, there were kids called Knuckles or Candy or Nut. No one really cared if you asked to be called Val. If you wore a skirt and called yourself a girl.*

But that's not enough, Valerie went on. *Sometimes you leave a place and there's nothing pulling you back. Some days, who you were will be too much. It doesn't matter when you transition. It's fucking impossible to be a person without giving up certain parts of the past.*

I love you, is the thing. Even when you act like a fucking asshole,

I love you. And if you never have a real relationship with your parents, whatever. They're no realer than the people you or I went to high school with. I'm real. Adam's real. Fuck it, Tessa too. Give up on the rest. I love you, Edie. There was only the road, the steering wheel in her hands, the voice in her ear. And Edith said nothing. *I love you.* Edith said nothing.

E DITH CLIMBED UNTIL HER FINGERS ACHED, UNTIL SHE could feel her tendons' tug in each new grip, and then she fell to the ground, and then she looked for Natalie. There she was, on the same orange climb for almost a month now. It took her all the way to the top of the wall; she fell onto her back without fear.

Can I ask you a weird question? Natalie looked up at her. Edith felt she was looming; she knelt. Sweat beaded Natalie's upper lip.

Sure thing. Her voice was higher than Edith expected. Odd to have spoken so much and never heard it.

Why do you always climb the same problem?

How do you do it?

Edith climbed by wandering the gym, guessing what she might be capable of and trying, until she settled the question either way.

It never occurred to me to do it any other way, Natalie said. *That sounds exhausting.*

I guess that's sort of the hope.

They introduced themselves. Natalie fell naturally to chatting. Edith asked questions she knew the answers to: what Natalie did, how she spent her time, how long she'd been in Texas. Natalie asked what she was writing and Edith scrambled. What had she told Natalie? Which truths, which lies?

Mostly I'm writing about how the sun looks when it hits water.

Oh very cool, Natalie said. *I was driving down Lamar the other day at sunset, looking at all those new high-rises. And I thought about how the last things the light touches are the tallest things around. How, once upon a time, that would mean mountains, and maybe trees. But now we are, all the time, building things that claim the last of the falling sun.*

Right, Edith said. *Yeah.*

You know, you look extremely familiar. Have we seen each other around town?

I go to the movies a lot, Edith said, though she hadn't been since winter.

That's probably it.

Natalie stood, brushed chalk dust from her hands. *I'm going to get back to it.*

Right.

Would you like to get coffee sometime?

Oh! Was life really this easy to command? You wanted something, you went after it for five minutes, and you got it? *Yeah, absolutely.*

Great. They swapped numbers. Thank god she'd never asked for Harry's.

Natalie mounted the wall once more. Hands finding familiar holds as easily as one lover finds another in the dark.

IN THE END, VIRGINIA WAS A NONEVENT. EDITH AND VAL drove the Loop every day. Her mother distracted herself and her father got better. It was his gallbladder after all. There was a celebratory dinner of spaghetti and prosecco, with Martinelli's sparkling cider for her father.

All together again, Edith's parents fell into an easy rhythm. Her father loaded more spaghetti onto her and Valerie's plates. They reminisced: about Edith sneaking out to go to a Christian Hell House. (*I didn't care about Jesus, I just liked ghosts!*) The trip they'd taken to Niagara Falls where each of them, one by one, got food poisoning over the course of four days. (*Oh good god*, her father had said when it struck him. *I suppose it's my turn at last.*) When Edith and Valerie went with Tessa to Saratoga. (Edith: *You wouldn't stop singing "You're So Vain."* Valerie: *I wanted to bet on the horses! It was for luck!*) They were a family. The first step in a new pattern.

After dinner, her father fell asleep in a recliner watching *Columbo*. Her mother cleaned up and kept cleaning, scrubbing every baseboard in the house.

She and Valerie collected the clothes and books they'd strewn about the guest room. Only ten days since they'd arrived and already such disorder. Ten days since Valerie had studied her body in that mirror. Ten days since Edith, aching-eyed, had crossed the room to hide her face against the person she loved most.

Hey Val?

Hmm?

Sit with me a sec?

They perched on the edge of the bed, arms around each other. Two girls, frightened and confused but never quite alone. There was a thread-thin awareness that bound them even across vast distances.

Sorry about the other day.

It's fine, Edie.

It isn't. Look, I want you in my life however you come. If that means you need to go away sometimes, then go. I mean it, she said, before Valerie could interject. *There isn't some other version of you I could love better. There's only you, the same person you've always been. With all of your stupid foibles and flaws. That's the person I love. And I love you so fucking much, Val.*

Valerie smiled, only a little sadly. *I love your stupid foibles and flaws too, Edie.* She sensed a *but* coming; none did.

The next day, they drove back to Texas. Edith and Valerie took turns behind the wheel. They ate Zebra Cakes for lunch and laced their sticky fingers together. When Valerie wasn't driving, she played "You're So Vain" on repeat. She read aloud from *Franny and Zooey*, never looking at Edith for a reaction. No doubts about what she had.

Back in Texas, Edith woke alone for the first time in almost a month. Thinking of whatever had been left unsaid. The Cézanne print still sat on her coffee table with no clear place for it in the wall's vague plain. She tore it to pieces and put it with all the boxes waiting to be recycled.

S EB WAS SOBBING WHEN EDITH PICKED UP THE PHONE. *Can I come over?*

Yes, absolutely.

Edith had been staring at a blank Word document. Frightened of beginning.

By the time they arrived, Seb was dry-eyed. Edith wrapped them in her arms. There had to be a way to protect the people you loved from all the things you felt. What was the point in living otherwise? They lay down together on the too-small couch. Edith's narrow hips turned vertical and still half falling off.

Edith.

Yeah?

I hate this fucking couch.

Whenever I leave this place we can destroy it with hammers.

They lay with the sound of breath between them. Edith's slow, trying to bring Seb's down. Treats watched from the coffee table.

Sara broke up with me.

I figured.

She said I wasn't very nice to her.

You weren't, to be fair.

I know. They wrapped their fingers through Edith's hair. This was real. They were. *We were having band practice—*

Not a band.

—and something broke. I've never seen her angry before.

What do you need?

Another pause. The sky the limitless blue of every Texas summer. Edith wished for rain.

I really loved her, Edith.

I know you did.

What's wrong with me?

Nothing that isn't wrong with most of us.

That's not good enough, though. That's letting me off the hook. And you.

It was too easy to respond to someone's pain with pat solutions. Too easy to pretend that all things could be fixed. Every hurt heals in its own time, or it kills you.

Hurt people hurt people, she said.

Seb laughed, slapped her collarbone. *You fucking jerk. You fucking cross-stitch of a human being.* They burrowed into her. *What were you doing before I came?*

Trying to write about Tessa.

Oh good, at least we're both a fucking mess.

I feel really sanguine about it, actually.

I can tell when you're full of shit by your diction, you know.

I mean it. She felt remarkably unconcerned by the impending marriage. Still a year away. She was learning the impossibility of that life. Trying to learn what might come in its place.

Bernard's mad at you, by the way.

We're just airing grievances now, huh.

Maybe not mad per se but frustrated. What happened?

I wasn't very nice to him.

Edith pulled Seb closer. This was what she imagined it was like to have a twin brother—someone whose closeness never needed to be complicated.

Life is a series of near misses, isn't it.

They fell into a restless doze, Edith jerking awake each time her hips threatened to fall. They watched *Gossip Girl* while Seb browsed

Grindr. It was dark when they left to rendezvous with a stranger: *Time to get the sad fucked out of me!* There were no clouds in the night sky. Edith ran the half-empty dishwasher and put on *Chungking Express* and felt fine. She wanted to feel that hook.

Chungking Express tells two love stories about cops. The first cop, He Qiwu, spends most of his days buying canned pineapple and calling his ex-girlfriend's house. Each can of pineapple expires on May 1, his birthday and the one-month anniversary of their breakup. By collecting thirty of these, he thinks, he can bring her back.

The second cop—known only by his badge number, 663—becomes the object of romantic fascination for Faye, a woman working at the titular snack bar. Faye is an obsessive; she is often found blasting the Mamas and the Papas' "California Dreamin'" on the snack bar boombox, drowning out customer orders. When she's supposed to be paying the restaurant electric bill, Faye regularly breaks into 663's apartment and lingers among his things, close to him even in his absence.

On April 30th, the clock ticks past midnight; it's He Qiwu's birthday, with no news from his ex. He eats all thirty cans of now-expired pineapple and meets a stranger, a woman in a blonde wig, in a bar. As he fails to get to know her (he never learns, for instance, about her failing smuggling operation), she reflects silently that there's no way to know people when they keep changing: "A person may like pineapples today and something else tomorrow."

Eventually, 663 catches Faye in his apartment. They make a date to go to a bar called California, but she never shows. She's gone off to the real California, starting a new life as a flight attendant. She leaves a letter for 663—a hand-drawn boarding pass that gets rain-soaked past the point of legibility. Faye returns a year later to find that 663 has taken over the snack bar. He's kept the battered boarding pass tacked to a corkboard all this while, and invites Faye to draw him a new one. Anywhere she wants to go, he'll go too.

He Qiwu keeps the blonde woman company while she sleeps in a hotel room. He pulls her shoes off so that her feet don't swell. He leaves her to go running, dehydrating himself so that he has no liquid left for tears. When he finishes and, breathless, checks his messages to see if his ex has called, he instead finds only a message from the blonde woman wishing him a happy birthday.

The first time Edith watched *Chungking Express*, she thought it was mostly a movie about falling in love with the idea of someone. Faye idealizes 663 until he proposes a real date, and then she has to flee to preserve that idea; He Qiwu is obsessed with reconnecting with his ex, the magical thinking behind his many cans of pineapple. But on repeat viewing, it's about the way small gestures foster love. The birthday phone call from a stranger, the boarding pass kept for a wordless year. The gestures' importance is their smallness: anyone could do these things, but not just anyone would.

It's this sort of thing you need to fall in love. The little things, the quiet ones.

NATALIE WAS running late to coffee; Edith filled the space with fantasy. Not a relationship, but something new. Something to add activation energy to her life in Texas, to get her through another six months, a year. One person could upend your life: introduce you to new friends, new passions, make strange the city that had grown contemptibly familiar. There was inherent value in meeting strangers. At a minimum, she might have a second friend. Edith doodled spirals in the margins of Knut Hamsun's *Hunger*. Her fantasy was a lie. But in the moment of waiting, it was a lie she could keep telling.

Sorry again, I'm late! Natalie dropped her bag onto one chair and pulled up a third. She was wearing a midnight-blue romper. Edith had never seen her out of workout clothes.

No worries!

You know Hamsun was a Nazi, right?

Everyone knows that. Edith laughed despite herself. *I know one or two other things besides.*

I think you can get the same feelings elsewhere. Natalie pulled her phone from her bag, checked it, set it on the table. Her wallpaper was a Cézanne. A different painting of apples than Edith's discarded print.

She wanted to get back to the shared language of affinity. Talk about Ella Fitzgerald and Krzysztof Kieślowski. *Do you like Cézanne?*

Oh, he's my favorite.

I used to like him too.

Used to? Nothing got past her. *That won't do.* She tapped a query into her phone. *I'm going to send you something, and you're going to read it, and it's going to change your mind.* Edith's phone pinged. A PDF: "Merleau-Ponty—Cézanne's Doubt."

Natalie tapped her phone again. Who was the problem here? Were some conversations simply unsustainable outside text's methodic pace?

Is it okay if my boyfriend joins us?

I'm sorry?

He lives like a block and a half from here. I think you guys would get along.

Why, does he also hate Cézanne?

Not anymore.

How bad could it be? A third person would take the pressure off. Natalie relaxed the moment Edith agreed.

Tell me how your book's going, Natalie said. *Tell me about light and water.*

Edith scrambled. *I'd be more interested to hear about your work. You said you work in the art library?*

I do. Had Natalie told this to Edith, or only to Harry? *Mostly no*

*one comes in. Students trickle in around midterms and finals. But
otherwise it's me and the books and the archives.*

Do you spend a lot of time flipping through them?

Natalie nodded. *I think reproduction is maybe the most important
human technology. The way one object learns to preserve another
inside itself.*

Finally, motion. *I went to this really amazing exhibit in Boston
actually. All reproductions of different sorts.*

I heard about that. Natalie looked at Edith. Something in the
focus of her eyes. *You know, you seem awfully familiar.*

It's a small city, Edith said quickly. *Every skinny dark-haired
trans girl looks the same.*

She was saved by the arrival of Natalie's boyfriend.

He looked almost exactly like Edith had when she was a boy.

Hey, Nat. He bent and kissed her cheek, and Natalie flushed with
pleasure. *Nice to meet you.* His hand extended toward her. *I'm Dan.*

Edith.

I'm gonna run inside for some coffee, you want anything? Natalie
asked for a red-eye, and Dan vanished.

Have you guys met before? Natalie asked.

He looks familiar. Edith was picturing herself having sex with this
boy who looked so much like she used to.

He's at the gym quite often.

She had never seen him there. She must have invented him—the
force of her nostalgia and loneliness had Frankensteined him out of
the digital unconscious into this skinny, bearded clone.

You were saying. About reproduction.

*It's democratizing. And through that democratization, the work
enters the memories of more people. Instead of being treated like a
precious, irreplaceable commodity, it becomes as basic as a perfume
ad in a magazine, discarded in a gutter.*

Don't you think some things should be allowed to disappear?

Allowed has nothing to do with it. Everything disappears eventually. It's a question of what happens in the meantime.

Dan returned with their drinks. He was all smiles.

Thanks baby. Natalie and Dan held hands under the table. *How was pinball this morning?*

It was good, Dougie got a high score on the Sopranos machine.

Edith felt a vertigo so powerful she thought she'd throw up. *So how'd you two meet?*

Natalie and Dan looked at each other and giggled. *God it was really strange*, she said. Edith instantly knew the rest. *I had been chatting with this guy on an app, you know, and he said he'd seen me around the gym and I should say hi. And the thing is, he looked* just *like Daniel.*

It was eerie actually, Dan said. *She showed me his profile.*

Anyway so next time I saw Dan at the gym I walked over and said, "Hey, hot stuff." Joking, obviously. I mean I would never. What in her conversations with Natalie had ever intimated she'd do such a thing? It was all performance, online and off. *He took it in stride, though.*

Actually what I said was, "What's up my good bitch?" My friend Emily gave me such a hard time afterward.

I thought it was perfect! Exactly matching the bizarreness of the situation.

Pretty soon we worked out what had happened.

But Dan had recently gone through a messy breakup, so I asked him to coffee.

And it turns out we have all sorts of stuff in common!

There was such a powerful taste of bile.

What sorts of stuff?

We both really love The Sopranos, Natalie said.

It's funny, too, Dan added, *because I've mostly been going out with guys.*

And I've mostly only been going out with women.

But here we are, now.

In love.

Edith's coffee was cold. Drinking it felt like being slapped. She gulped it down.

That's amazing, she said. *Truly unbelievable.*

D AY BY DAY, ABSENCE BY ABSENCE, HER LIFE IN TEXAS accelerated. If it were a film, you could cut the empty parts and leave a montage of romantic moments.

For instance. They went to the animal shelter. *Aw, look how sweet he is*, Edith said, a little orange cat sitting on her foot.

She, actually.

Most orange cats are male, Val.

Right, but not this one.

For instance. In winter when the power flickered out, they piled into the bathroom with a flashlight and a bag of hand warmers. They cocooned themselves in the bathtub and blankets and watched British quiz shows Valerie had downloaded onto her phone. Treats sat on a towel beneath the sink, warm in her coat's permanent fire. When Edith woke in the total dark, there was the sound of three bodies breathing.

For instance. Edith asked Valerie if it didn't make her miserable, being back in Texas. *No, actually.* They were making origami boxes for Treats to play with. Valerie's folds predictably neat. *I think that when you control your life, you can go to a place and make it yours—yours as much as it's anyone else's. Now it's been your home, and will be your home. No matter who else lays claim to it.* The boxes skittered across the floor and Treats smashed every one.

For instance. Val helping her draw her first shot of estradiol.

The way it felt to walk by the river, hand in hand, on the first warm February day.

The way Val's hands found her nose and mouth while they fucked, and Edith danced toward the point of passing out. Safe in the knowledge Valerie would not let her come to harm. The way hormones softened her body, and in the moments before orgasm she felt cool threads drawing to a point inside her.

For instance.

But Edith's memory couldn't excise Val's absence from these things. Those blank spots of film littering the cutting-room floor.

For instance. She sent Val articles, scraps of stories, photos of Treats. Sometimes Val sent back a heart emoji, or an empty sentence. Sometimes she didn't respond at all.

For instance. Valerie called her from the road. *I finished reading your book.*

Oh! Edith sat up so quickly that the cat hid beneath the couch. *What did you think?*

You're a very talented writer, Edie.

But?

Well. It doesn't ring true.

Something was flowing out of her at a frankly unsustainable rate.

What do you mean, "ring true."

It's like you've put all these symbols into a world rather than people. They're like an orrery. You know, a model of the—

I know what an orrery is.

They're all fixed points, spinning around one another. But they aren't real.

For instance. Edith finished rereading *Franny and Zooey*. She still didn't get it—so far as she could tell, it was a manual on how to be annoying in a god-honoring way.

She read all the books Valerie had ever left with her. Those gently fictionalized lives. Those middle-aged straight people who were getting divorced and having children. What had Valerie hoped to communicate to her by leaving them? What lesson did Edith need to learn in order to love and be loved correctly?

She pictured Valerie leaving a half dozen other genres at her stops around the country. Barn would get the biographies of Golden Age Hollywood actresses. Tessa might get books on ecology. Valerie was a Greek oracle, bringing you the knowledge you needed but not the power to understand it.

She spent sleepless nights wondering who Valerie was with, what she told them. Whether they, too, had trouble accepting the terms of her love. Edith thought not. She picked apart every conversation, every subtle shift ripe for interpretation. She did her stupid SEO job and watched every episode of *Gossip Girl* twice. She fell asleep in the hour before dawn with Treats purring in her ear.

Instead of making new friends, she called Tessa. Edith told her about Treats. The end of grad school. All her Val-less existence. The rich new things in Texas that did not quite make up a life.

I go to the movies like three or four times a week. Wild at Heart, Evil Dead, Barry Lyndon, she said. *The wax museum is free on Wednesday nights.*

Edith put Tessa on speaker so that the apartment filled with her familiar ghost. Mild news and the faint crackle of cigarette paper. *I've been reading Rilke a lot,* Tessa said. *I used to hate him but now I think he might be a genius. Is this emotional growth?*

Edith laughed. *No, emotional growth feels much more annoying. Or so I hear.*

They talked about college. "Naïve Melody" on the record player. The snowball fight where Tessa's foot went black with frostbite. No shortage of things to share and share again.

When Edith came out to her, they both cried.

It was all the same as it had always been. It was all very different.

AT SOME POINT, SHE GOT VALERIE'S KNIFE FROM ITS hiding place. At some later point, she reinstalled Grindr. She read while chatting with men. Sending old nudes and faking interest. Feeding fantasies. Eventually she got a message from Cyrus. His display name was "Cum Murderer."

hey cutie, wyd?

Having no flirty way of saying "reading Büchner's play about the French Revolution," she said, *not much, sorta bored, wbu?*

think I can entertain you?

Edith had not bothered nurturing her crush on Cyrus since last winter. There was nothing to it beyond the usual desire to be desired and destroyed.

I think so.

Cyrus's apartment was littered with boxes, discarded T-shirts. He answered the door bare-chested and in sweatpants, eating a bowl of Frosted Mini-Wheats. *Aw, you got all dressed up,* he said. She was wearing her denim romper. *Lemme finish eating.* A black-and-white cat rubbed against her legs. *That's Butter.*

How long have you had a cat?

I don't remember.

Coming here was a mistake. None of her fumbling sexual encounters brought her peace. Did she really think she could slut her way to self-knowledge? It could only complicate their friendship.

But were they friends, or were they just both trans? She petted Butter, who purred immediately.

He called from the kitchen, *Do you want anything to drink?*
I'm good!

Cyrus returned with a Tecate in one hand and a floppy purple dildo in the other. It was dripping and warm from the dishwasher. He pressed against Edith, his mouth to hers. Arms crossed behind her. Those cold threads of pleasure—real pleasure, real want— moving through her.

The night fractured. Her romper half off while she tried to obscure the fresh cuts on her thigh. Edith crouched over him, hands on his shoulders and chest, her hair a curtain between their faces and the world. The purple cock split her open and she pushed harder against it. His hand on her throat. Blood on the sheets. Cyrus, above her, slapping her flushed face. In a moment of, she supposed, divine inspiration, he tried to fold her in half to see if she could suck herself off; her vertebrae creaked. He covered her face with spit. The air was gasps of copper and amyl nitrate. Their bodies were sweat and silicone and lube.

She thought nothing. She was pure want. She did not ache in bits and pieces; she ached all the way through. Just a girl getting fucked by a boy.

Cyrus left her shaking on his bed. In the brief pause, it felt like something she'd invented. He returned—purple cock swinging, fresh Tecate in hand.

Had enough?
Not yet.

That's what we like to hear. He finished his beer, crushed the can, and tossed it into the corner. *I think I might not let you come. How would you feel about that?*

Kicked out into the night after, she thought: I could live happily if there were someone to wreck me like that every day of my life. She drove home blasting Charli XCX and fell asleep with a stupid grin plastered across her face.

Two weeks later, Cyrus moved to Colorado Springs.

N O FIGHT PRECEDED IT. THERE WAS NEVER A BREAK-down to obsess over. There were more cuts on Val's legs; there were cuts on Edith's, too. There were nights one or the other lay awake and watched the darkness fade. There were the boys Edith fucked in Val's absence; they only confirmed that she would not find comfort elsewhere.

They were sitting by the river, right before the weather cooled. Edith had been complaining about her parents again—the long calls going nowhere, the impossibility of connection—when Val grabbed her hand and said, *You know, even if you didn't want to date, I'd still come stay. I'd still be here with you, as long as you'd have me.*

This isn't dating, what we do.

Val dropped her hand. *That's fair*, she said, though it wasn't.

Edith had no sense of the dailiness of Valerie's life when she left. The minutiae that filled her day the way medieval astrono-mers thought ether filled the darkness between stars. When was she bored? When did she sleep badly, or get harassed, or get too drunk and say the wrong thing? They didn't share a life so much as they sometimes shared space.

They didn't have sex that night, but lay with their legs threaded together. This easy intimacy might be enough. Edith could spend her life gathering comfort from Val and burning through it when she left. Finding strangers to fuck her and say she had nice legs. There were no bounds on what was possible between them.

Edith understood now that she never knew when Val would leave.

Whatever pattern she thought she'd discerned proved false. And so for the next week and a half, she took pleasure in cooking bibimbap and quiches together, watching the sunset in a James Turrell installation, playing laser games with Treats. And when she woke to find that familiar cold, that empty spot on the bed, she did her best not to worry. It was enough that Val was out there. That she'd be back eventually.

A UGUST. HER LEASE WOULD END IN THIRTY DAYS. SHE either had to bind herself to another year here (impossible) or pick another place to go (also impossible).

Grace came in the mail.

Tessa answered the phone on the first ring.

I got your address from Adam, she said, *I would've asked you but wasn't sure how—*

Well I can tell you what's a bad way of doing it.

Please say you'll come, Edie.

Teresa Pacheco & Devin Murphy. July 15. Northampton, MA.

I'll have to check my calendar.

Devin's got loads of trans friends. You've never been to a queer wedding, have you? Did this qualify? *Adam and Michael will be there. It really will be so much more fun if you come.* Tessa took a deep breath. *Though I respect your choice if you'd rather not.*

Even though we promised.

That final night on the couch. Tessa's heartbeat matching hers. And all the crises, and all the catastrophes since.

I'm not sure either of us said "promise."

I want to come, Edith said.

Then come.

Do you think it's that simple?

It doesn't matter, actually, if it's simple or not. Just do it! What's the worst that can happen.

I get super drunk and derail the wedding. Try to win you back with a last grand gesture of love.

Right, well. Don't do that.

Easy enough.

Edith finished the cigarette she'd been smoking and lit another. In the courtyard pool, men and women volleyed a beach ball between them. Sometimes Edith thought her lungs were only truly full while she smoked. *Okay.*

Okay?

One condition.

Name it.

I want to meet Devin first. See what's what.

Done.

And no Ed Sheeran.

That's two conditions, sweet Edie, but just for you I think we can manage.

It was only after their goodbyes that Edith studied the invite again. Northampton, MA. July 15. Their names, and hers, calligraphed in a friend's steady hand.

She smoked a third cigarette, and a fourth. She called Seb, who came over immediately.

I DON'T think you're supposed to smoke in here, Seb said.

Thanks, Mom. Edith had transferred her books to the floor in unsteady piles. Treats wove through the new obstacles, mewling all the while. Seb wrinkled their nose and opened a window.

So she invited you to her wedding, so what. Don't go.

Oh, obviously I'm going.

You know what I really admire about you, Edith. How level-headed you are.

Here, help me load these into a box. It was far too large a box. Neither of them would be able to lift it once full.

Yeah, it's your level-headedness and the way that you don't smoke indoors. Those are the two main things. Books fell like coins into the box. Overlapping, indifferent. Seb winced to see the corners of the Annie Ernaux book bent back. *What if we, like, sat down.*

Couch is all yours.

You're not leaving the state tonight. Chill a sec, dude.

Edith couldn't. She couldn't think about the simple happiness given to everyone but her. Adam and Tessa and Natalie and Charlie. Seb and Sara had worked out a way to be friends. Bernard and Cyrus seemed to be thriving without love. Only Ryan and Ken were unhappy as she was. These were the options: you were either lucky in love or you'd watch your husband suck a limp-dicked trans girl twenty years your junior. At least they'd gotten a wedding.

Seb said, *Do you* want *to get married?*

Don't we all?

Wrong answer, babe.

It was the *babe* that did it. Edith shrank. The books she held fell to the floor. She wanted a real life and all she'd gotten was the pale forgery of one. Worthless overnight. A fake girl living in a fake city, faking her way through a book about her fake ex-girlfriend who was—the only real thing—dead. All the real things were receding further from her: Tessa, Adam, Boston, happiness, love.

She wasn't crying, or shaking, or doing much of anything at all. *I'm fucking tired, Seb.*

Tell me about it, man. I wish I could tell you that it only gets easier.

I'd call bullshit.

Of course you would. Hey, look. They crouched beside her. *What do you want to do?*

Go to Northampton. This was the plan she'd formulated: she'd move back to the great state of Massachusetts. You had to live somewhere, but you could make leaving easy. (*You can go to a place and make it yours.*) Lean into your impulses and come out the other side—not redeemed, exactly, or free of them, but better than you had been.

Then fucking do it. They settled into a more comfortable position. They pulled the cigarette from her mouth and buried it in a mug of ashes. *Look, do you want to go outside and scream at the sky?*

There are people in the pool. Plus that's, like, extremely Garden State *of you.*

Bitch, Zach Braff does not have a monopoly on cathartic screaming.

What she wanted was another cigarette. What she wanted was someone who had always known her to tell her things would be okay.

I love you, Seb.

I love you too, duh.

She stood. Protests from Seb: *I just got comfortable!* She helped them up, and they packed. Thirty days until she'd leave. Eleven months until the wedding. All the moments between.

AMONG OTHER things, Maurice Merleau-Ponty's essay "Cézanne's Doubt" is about the inextricable relationship between an artist's life and work. Everything we do is either in accordance with, or reaction against, the terms of our life.

Cézanne was haunted by the good-enough, the imperfect. He could make beautiful art but, lacking god's omnipotence, could never perfectly translate the world to image. It had to be flattened, rendered into color and stroke. He kept trying to make art and nature one, to make the chaotic perfectly ordered, intelligible, clarified. "Everything comes to us from nature," he claimed. "We exist through it; nothing else is worth remembering." He went on failing and it's in his art's failure that we find its beauty.

This is not about the worth of suffering. It's about the way one sees the world, lives in it. The way living seeps into work and work into living—a "single adventure."

Cézanne could never untangle himself from the world, the "wretchedness of his empirical life and his unsuccessful attempts." He never stopped needing other people to confirm it was worth something. "We never get away from our life," Merleau-Ponty concludes. "We never see ideas or freedom face to face."

And Edith did take comfort from this. Although you might live your whole life doubting, the two options available to you are versions of the same thing. Go or stay, be or do, art or nature. Warp and weft, color and light, it's all part of the same life.

WHEN SHE tried to explain, later, why she was nearly shaking when she finished the Merleau-Ponty essay—first to Seb, and then in an email to the editor—she couldn't recapture the feeling. It was only when she was on the road some weeks later, and half-mistook her face for Valerie's reflected in the funhouse mirror of a gas station ice cream cooler, that she had some idea of it again.

It literally doesn't matter what I say/do/think, Edith wrote to the editor. *I think this is what the existentialists referred to as a "leap of faith" but I'm not sure, as I was a math major.* Edith said that she was moving, that, as was probably obvious by now, she would not have a book ready by September. *I have no idea what I'm going to do next*, she admitted, *but I guess I'll do it a word at a time.*

The email prompted an immediate response: *Out of Office for the Time Being.* The automated message contained only an apology for her absence—*Unforuntaely* [sic] *I find my need for this stronger than*

my desire to stay—and the promise the editor would return eventually, and a scrap of Rilke:

> Be ahead of all departure; learn to act
> as if, like the last winter, it was all over
> for among the winters, one is so exact
> That wintering it, your heart will last forever.

EDITH DIDN'T KNOW IF SHE AND TESSA WOULD EVER properly be friends. But Edith loved her, and loved Val. There were relationships richer and more complicated than friendship, or family, or romance.

When she tired of filling boxes, Edith went back to her blank Word document. She typed: *Katherine's tooth hurt all the way to Boston.* She packed up her life a box at a time. The desk was going to a thrift store. Half her clothes. Her bed and most of her bookshelves. The Punisher she kept; it stayed hidden in a ball of socks at the bottom of her suitcase. Here and there, she returned to her open computer to write another sentence, and another. Putting things away, pulling things back out. The distance between that life and this.

S HE COULDN'T SAY WHAT COMPELLED HER TO TAKE the knife the last time she saw Val.

There were a few more visits between that trip to the river and the phone call, on a too-sunny autumn morning, from Tess.

It would be a better story if they'd never seen each other again.

Sometimes when Val was there, she wished Tessa would visit too. The three of them cooking breakfast in the morning. Going to the movies, Val yelling about useless male characters. No one loves you like the people who knew you when you were young. Others might love you better, but they don't love you the same.

Maybe it was insurance against something, the knife. Not to bring Val back to her, but because she noticed the deeper creases under her friend's eyes. The way she bit the skin of her wrist to bruising. Valerie told her all sorts of things in those visits. Things she'd kept hidden. The predictable things, and new ones.

Do you ever get tired of moving so much? Edith asked in bed one morning. They hadn't had sex since the river, but it would be too great a violence to sleep apart.

I didn't used to. She starfished across the bed's breadth. Her arm a band of warmth across Edith's sore, nascent tits. *Now it's easier to picture.* There was no suggestion that she and Edith might try their hand at coupledom again. But it was nice to think of her staying someplace.

Can you picture me visiting you? Edith laughed. *It'd be like college again. All that grandma furniture.*

I'm older now. It'll have to be Louis Quatorze or nothing at all.

There was a second—between Tessa's slow sigh and learning it was a car accident—when Edith thought: is this my fault? That Val hadn't had a way to defend herself. That she hadn't been able—But it wasn't about any of them.

Stealing it was easy. Edith went into Val's bag to find a cigarette and slipped the folded blade into her hand. You could do anything in plain sight so long as you did it well.

Or maybe Valerie let her. They lay in Edith's bed, both waiting for sleep, and Val said, *You're always going to be in my life, Edie. Whether you like it or not, you can't get away from me.* She was there in the morning. They had leftover popcorn for breakfast, kernels like salty Styrofoam. It took no time for her to pack her clothes and coffeemaker and go.

Edith stood in the parking lot, barefoot and shivering slightly, watching the space Val's car left behind. Thinking about the knife, and the threads of awareness that bound them—all of them—that could not be cut.

E DITH ADDED AN HOUR TO HER DRIVE TO AVOID VIR-
ginia.

(*You don't know how little they matter.*)

Treats mewled in her crate on the passenger seat. Unhappy whenever she was not napping. At rest stops she clambered through the
car and Edith had to extract her, yowling, from under the seats.
We'll be home soon, baby, she said, and Treats bit her finger.

She called friends while she drove.

Bernard was happy to hear from her. *I'm glad you got out. Texas
wasn't your place.*

Glad to be rid of me? She was slightly manic from the drive.

If you don't visit I'll be so mad at you. He told her about the last
party he'd thrown: the dogs had gotten in his new hot tub; Di had
done a backflip before everyone's open eyes.

Do you hear from Cyrus much? Edith asked.

*Cyrus isn't the sort to call. We'll see each other around,
somewhere here.*

Adam was thrilled she'd be so close.

Not as close as Somerville.

*It's better this way. Strike out on your own, make a new life for
yourself. Date a Mount Holyoke professor.*

Ugh they're probably all TERFs. Edith gnawed a piece of beef
jerky. She pressed a cat treat through the bars of the crate. *Hey
Adam, don't tell Tess yet, okay?*

Sure thing. No hesitation. He either understood or did not need to.

When there was no one to call, she listened to "Raytracer" on repeat for an hour.

When there was no driving left in her, she stopped at the nearest La Quinta and watched Treats sniff every sterile corner.

(*All those roads connect. You wouldn't believe where they'll lead.*)

("How does it happen? How did you ever get to be here?")

There was lightness in motion. Every foot of earth behind you by the time you noticed it.

Ugh, there was some disgusting shit at the capital today, Seb said. *People getting clobbered by the cops. Promise you won't forget our struggles in your northern utopia.*

Ah yes, Massachusetts—a state famously free of police brutality.

It's gotta be good for you, though. Do you remember what it's like to not constantly worry about your home state's particular violence?

Bernard's voice: Which state would that be?

No, I don't.

Seb said they might follow her up there. *Do they have brown people in Massachusetts? It's there or Berlin, I hear there's a real scene there.*

Oh yeah, I hear that Magnus Hirschfeld guy is doing great work.

Shut up, you. They laughed. *Tell Treats I love and miss her.*

A landscape like the landscape of her youth. Trees bled autumn. She pissed in the woods to avoid rest stop bathrooms; she ate in her car to keep Treats company. She ignored her mother's calls. She let the music play on. She'd left no forwarding address. Everything goes on unimaginably. Everything ends all at once.

(*We mostly make the choices we need to. I don't care if that sounds stupid.*)

(*I knew that was all correct. That nothing needed to be any other way.*)

Maybe this was all you needed. Maybe you could keep moving until you found a life that stuck, or got tired of searching.

When there was no one to call she listened to the 1995 cast recording of *Company*. We don't need to get into what it made her think of.

Would she make it to Tessa and Devin's wedding? Even the phrase, that conjunction, put her on edge. A life that would never be hers.

("I wish—")

But she would go. Wasn't that the point of moving? So that, by the time July 15 came, she would be grounded, imperturbable as a sea-battered cliff?

Edith didn't want to be in love. She didn't want to be still. She wanted to drive toward the opposite coast and let Cyrus fuck her until she forgot that her wanting mattered. She wanted to get hurt, stay hurting. Resolution was for suckers. Resolution would have its time.

NORTHAMPTON WAS exactly as she'd envisioned. Old buildings pressed together, a clock-faced steeple needling the sky. Her building was a fourplex. The night was cold, and there was no sign of her neighbors. The last tenant had left a particleboard desk that swayed under the first box of books.

Tomorrow she'd get a bed. Bookshelves. She'd have to build a life from scratch. It was, as Seb pointed out, costlier than staying put.

But so what. There was no rush. All her deadlines were arbitrary.

She slept that night curled in a sleeping bag on the cold floor. Treats perched on her hip. Of course she'd go to the wedding. That was how you turned your life into a comedy. And until then, she'd work out everything that could be worked out. She'd fill her blank document with words about a life like hers, a life that might be better, that might teach her the language of her need. Adam and Michael would visit. Soon she'd have a real life.

Streetlight came through the apartment windows. She'd need curtains. Curled up deeper in the dark, face pressed to her pillow, she thought: curtains, curtains, curtains. Don't let another night pass like this.

Sometime soon she'd talk to Tessa. She wasn't sure what she'd say. Close, but not too close, to home. Edith might tell her she was living here before the wedding, but you never knew. Perhaps by then she would have moved on.

Acknowledgments

Thanks to my agent, Danielle Bukowski—you're still the only person I've ever trusted with a first draft. Thanks to my editor, Mo Crist, for understanding exactly what this book was trying to be. Thanks to everyone else at Norton: Gabrielle Nugent, Meredith Dowling, Sarahmay Wilkinson, Rebecca Munro, Janet McDonald. Thanks to Greg Ariail—god only knows how much of my work you've read over the years. To Emet North, thank you for always letting me be insane at you. To Charlie Sorrenson for all the hours of conversation. To Julie Krzanowski for a million texts about gender and Chilean literature. To all the trans and queer friends in Texas: my life here would have been empty without you. Thanks to Rox Sayde, Paul Van Koughnett, Hally Waters, Tez Figueroa, Fern Stevens, and the rest of the Gay Oedipus Players. To Sunshine Kreidner and Alec Bersoux and all the other Anti-Binary Homies—all the parties in this book belong to you. To Jess Gritton and the rest of the Sunday kolaches crew. Thanks to Ginger Bloomer and Gary Poole. To Rose McMackin, with "well, actually's" and land art. To Annar Verold and Claire Bowman and Stephen Krause and everyone else who worked at Malvern Books. Thanks to my teachers: Patricia Worsham, Matthew Schultz, David Means, Hua Hsu, Michael Martone, Kellie Wells. To everyone who has ever worked at Alienated Majesty, First Light Books, BookWoman, Ernest & Hadley, Brookline Booksmith, Harvard Bookstore, Porter Square Books, and Givens Books. Thanks to Cady Vishniac, the first stranger to ever believe in my work. Thank you to my cousins and brother and aunts and uncles. To David Steenberg, the least repressed member of the family. To my parents, who read to me every night growing up (not just the boring parts of *Moby-Dick*). Thank you to Erin Leahy for understanding, friendship, and dragging me to Boston in the first place. Thank you to Erik Baker, who taught me more or less everything I know about Alfred Hitchcock. To Kevin Norwood and to Rae Beaudoin, my first and best Texas friend. To Justin Saret, I'm still very sorry about the unicorn birthday party. To Andy Cawley, who's been there since I was a dirtbag teen. To Simone Scott, who's been there even longer. To my cat, Jojo, who is biting my leg as I type this. And thanks and love to Gabi—I wrote the last forty pages of this book to distract myself from my insane crush on you. Look at us now.